PENGUIN BOOKS

SPEAKING WITH THE ANGEL

SPEAKING WITH THE ANGEL

Edited, and with an introduction by

NICK HORNBY

PENGUIN BOOKS

PENGUIN BOOKS

Published by the Penguin Group
Penguin Books Ltd, 27 Wrights Lane, London w8 5TZ, England
Penguin Putnam Inc., 375 Hudson Street, New York, New York 10014, USA
Penguin Books Australia Ltd, Ringwood, Victoria, Australia
Penguin Books Canada Ltd, 10 Alcorn Avenue, Toronto, Ontario, Canada M4V 3B2
Penguin Books India (P) Ltd, 11 Community Centre,
Panchsheel Park, New Delhi – 110 017, India
Penguin Books (NZ) Ltd, Cnr Rosedale and Airborne Roads,
Albany, Auckland, New Zealand
Penguin Books (South Africa) (Pty) Ltd, 5 Watkins Street,
Denver Ext 4, Johannesburg 2094, South Africa

Penguin Books Ltd, Registered Offices: Harmondsworth, Middlesex, England

First published by Penguin Books 2000
4

Copyright © for this collection, Penguin Books, 2000
Copyright © Introduction, Nick Hornby 2000
Copyrights © for individual stories: 'PMQ', Robert Harris 2000; 'The Wonder Spot,
Melissa Bank 2000; 'Last Requests', Giles Smith 2000; 'Peter Shelley', Patrick Marber 2000'
'The Department of Nothing', Colin Firth 2000; 'I'm the Only One', Zadie Smith 2000;
'NippleJesus', Nick Hornby 2000; 'After I Was Thrown in the River and Before I Drowned',
Dave Eggers 2000; 'Luckybitch', Helen Fielding 2000; 'The Slave', Roddy Doyle 2000;
'Catholic Guilt (You Know You Love It)', Irvine Welsh 2000; 'Walking into the Wind',
John O'Farrell 2000.

Set in 10/13 pt Monotype Sabon
Typeset by Rowland Phototypesetting Ltd,
Bury St Edmunds, Suffolk
Printed in England by Clays Ltd, St Ives plc

For Danny Hornby

CONTENTS

ACKNOWLEDGEMENTS

Thanks to Tony Lacey, Joanna Prior, Emma Noel, Martin Bryant and all the staff at Penguin; Caroline Dawnay, Annabel Hardman, Nicki Kennedy, Jessica Buckman and the staff of ILA; Emma Thompson, Lorrie Moore and JK Rowling; Christine Asbury and everyone at TreeHouse.

INTRODUCTION

Soon after I had decided to ask some the writers I knew and admired to contribute to this book, I read an interview with Bono in the *Guardian*, in which he talked about the Jubilee 2000 campaign, aimed at reducing the Third World's debt to the West. 'It's bigger than anything I will ever have anything to do with again as long as I live,' he said. 'So if I can open doors simply because I'm a celebrity, then I'll use that for all it's worth.' So far, his efforts have helped to remove $100 billion from the tab.

The interview brought me up short. I'm not Bono, of course, and I suspect that it would be considerably harder for me to open the door of the Oval Office than it was for him, but even so . . . Third World Debt! $100 billion! TreeHouse, the charity to which you have just donated a pound (unless you've been sent a review copy, in which case you can send some money using the form at the back of this book), is a small – at the moment, a very small – school for severely autistic children, and one of its pupils is my son. Luckily, I don't have to justify myself to you, because all you've done is buy a book that you wanted to read, a book containing a dozen or so new stories by some of your favourite authors, and your donation was, I hope, incidental. But I certainly owe those authors an explanation, and so this introduction is aimed at them. You can read it if you like, but I don't mind if you skip it. You'll get your money's-worth anyway.

Perhaps I should begin by explaining that my son Danny won't benefit from *Speaking with the Angel*. (I've pinched the title, by the way, from Ron Sexsmith, whose first album contains a song of that name which seems to me to be heart-meltingly relevant.) Danny's fine, he's sorted – which is one of the reasons why I wanted to put this book together in the first place. He is, in many ways (and if one excludes the huge slice of ill-luck that befell him in the first place), a lucky little boy, and though I am in a financial position to ensure that his luck continues, I am not able to spread that luck around, not as much as I would like to. Danny's good fortune is located in his attendance at TreeHouse, and, at the moment, very few autistic children are able to do the same. Indeed, very few autistic children are able to attend any school designed to meet their needs: there is a catastrophic underprovision of places in Britain. A TES survey in 1996 found that there were three thousand specialist places for seventy-six thousand kids, twenty-six thousand of whom were classed as severely autistic.

If you are a parent, then, your choices are unattractive. You can drive yourself mad by chasing after one of those three thousand places – a twenty-five-to-one shot, and almost certain to involve a move from one part of the country to another; or you can stick your child in a school that hasn't got a clue how to deal with him (he's probably male, your autistic child, for reasons that still remain obscure); or you can keep him at home and wait, while the precious months and years slip by and you know that all the research points to the urgency of early intervention. Over the last few years, distraught parents have begun to realize that the only response to all this is to found their own school.

One could put a kind of let's-do-the-show-here spin on this, and make out that founding your own school is fun, and self-improving, and so on, but of course it's not any of these things, as you probably suspected. It's a Kafkaesque nightmare of blackly comical bureaucratic buck-passing, and frantic worry. The parents who set up TreeHouse have done so with minimal help from local authorities – even though some of these local authorities now recognize the school as the best and indeed only alternative for their autistic children – and with no public assistance. (England's hopeless and ill-advised bid for the 2006 World Cup was eligible for Lottery money, for example, whereas TreeHouse was not.) Danny's school is now firmly established, but it needs permanent premises, and it needs to grow; we have a waiting list, and a duty to educate as many kids as possible.

And how do you educate severely autistic children? How do you teach those who, for the most part, have no language, and no particular compulsion to acquire it, who are born without the need to explore the world, who would rather spin round and round in a circle, or do the same jigsaw over and over again, than play games with their peers, who won't make eye-contact, or copy, and who fight bitterly (and sometimes literally, with nails and teeth and small fists) for the right to remain sealed in their own world? The answer is that you teach them everything, and the absolute necessity of this first-principles approach makes all other forms of education, the approaches that involve reading and writing and all that, look quite frivolous. Danny has to be shown how to copy, how to look, how to make word-shapes with his mouth, how to play with toys, how to draw, how to have fun, how to live and be, effectively, and TreeHouse utilizes a system that makes these elementary skills possible. Danny's education began with him learning how to bang on a table when prompted to do so, a skill that took him weeks to master. (Table-banging is not a part of the national curriculum, and sometimes debates about what the rest of the nation's young should study can seem to me preposterously refined.) What's the point of that? The point of that is hidden in the phrase 'when prompted to do so': only when a way has been found to penetrate the autist's world can any progress be made, and now Danny listens. He can't understand everything he hears, but at least there is now a sense that for some parts of the day – and for most of the school day – he occupies the same world as his teachers and his peers.

And he loves his schoolwork. He loves being set small and achievable tasks – to begin with, tasks like touching his nose or sitting down, and then, as he became better attuned to what was required of him, more complicated commands – and he loves the praise (and the crisps and biscuits) that accompany his accomplishments. And my guess is that he is grateful for these assaults on his insularity. He doesn't want to live the life that he would choose if left to his own devices, with its endless repetitions and routines and patterns – he wants and needs someone to come along and stop him from watching *Postman Pat and the Tuba* for the one thousandth time, or from doing the same simple jigsaw puzzle fifteen times in an hour (these figures are approximate, of course, but they are not exaggerated). And his mother and father want someone to come along and stop that, too. All parents of autistic children know the terrible cycle of guilt and apathy that comes with the territory: our kids are capable of entertaining themselves for hours at a time if we let them (and sometimes we do, because we're tired, and maybe despondent), but we know that the entertainment of choice – spinning round and round, lining things up, watching the same videos over and over again – is not healthy or productive. But few of us have the energy to do what Danny's teachers do. We cannot create scores of different activities each and every day, all of them designed to equip our children to cope better with the lives they are living now, and will live in the future.

TreeHouse is unique: its children receive an education unlike anything else that is offered in the UK, which is why those of us involved with the school are so passionate, so evangelical about it. We want TreeHouse to become bigger, and we want other schools like TreeHouse to start sprouting up all over the country, and the only way that's going to happen is if some of us start shouting. I'm not much of a shouter by nature, but *Speaking with the Angel* is my way of at least raising my voice. I can see that what is being provided for the majority of these seventy-six thousand children is hopelessly inadequate, and I want to give other parents the same opportunities that Danny has had – or at least help to create a climate wherein these opportunities are regarded as important.

This probably sounds like a bland if laudable desire, and if so then I have failed properly to describe the difference a school like TreeHouse can make, so let me put it this way. Somewhere in London – somewhere everywhere, but TreeHouse is in London, so that is the place I'd like you to locate this vision – there is a child who slept for maybe five or six hours last night. (He sleeps five or six hours every night, in fact, which means that if he can be kept awake until, say, nine, then he will wake up at two or three.) He is upset and frustrated, so he screams, and his parents, who have maybe slept for three or four hours, feel a mixture of exhaustion and depression and panic – they live in a small flat, and the walls are thin, and they know that they are not the only ones who are disturbed on a nightly basis. It is six hours until one of them starts work (the other would like to work, but in the absence of any suitable school place for the child, it is not possible), by which time the child will have attempted to hurt himself by hitting himself hard and repeatedly on the head, and maybe thrown some food around, and refused to use the toilet and ended up soiling a carpet, and demanded in the only language he has at his disposal (one word, repeated with increasing force and volume) to go out to the park, even though it's pitch black outside . . . and then daylight comes, and because the local authorities don't as yet have a suitable school place for your child (although they're working on it, they promise, and even right now they are having meetings about possibly starting up a school which may well be open by the time your child is seven or eight or ten), then you're looking at another ten or twelve or fifteen hours of the same thing, alleviated only by the prospect of the child falling asleep – sleep he shouldn't really be having, because it will make things worse the next night, but it's your only time off in the whole day. And there's nowhere to go, and no one to complain to, and there's no money in the bank that can be used to buy some respite care, because you're down to one income anyway . . .

And of course, *of course*, there are other charities, and other problems, some of them worse than this, if such things can be quantified in that way, and other autistic organizations that would kill for the money that this book is going to raise. But I can't worry about any of that. All I can say is that this book will change a family's life for the better – a real, specific family, a family currently living the life described above, and if you want, you can write to me c/o Penguin Books and I'll write back with the name of that family. As a result of *Speaking with the Angel*, TreeHouse will be able to expand, which means that there will be a couple of extra places for children living precisely the kinds of lives outlined above. And because the teachers there know what they are doing, and have at their disposal ways to make these children happier, more expressive, more confident, less frustrated, then the awful worry and exhaustion of bringing up an autistic child will be made a lot easier for a few lucky parents. Oh, I know it's not much. But nothing's much, if you look at it like that, and all that any of us who care about autistic kids can do for the time being is to try to carve a few school places out of nowhere.

My son has a friend now, a little boy in his class called Toby, whom he loves, and enjoys seeing and spending time with. There are some autistic kids who get no particular pleasure out of seeing or being with their parents, so a friendship of this kind is remarkable, unexpected, a constant joy to those who witness it. And he's generally calmer, especially in social situations, and he's beginning to play with his toys, and he's finally learning how to use a toilet . . . None of this would have happened if he hadn't been able to attend this one, particular, special school. So, Robert, Melissa, Giles, Patrick, Colin, Zadie, Dave, Helen, Roddy, Irvine, John: thank you, and I hope this introduction helps you to understand just how much you have done. As for the rest of you: like I said, I'm hoping that you'll feel you've done nothing charitable whatsoever, so never mind all this. Turn the page and get on with the book.

PMQ

ROBERT HARRIS

PRIME MINISTER: With your permission Mr Speaker, I wish to make a statement to the House regarding certain incidents of a personal nature. Some of these incidents have, in the past few days, entered the public domain in a lurid and garbled form, and a number of my ministerial colleagues have urged me to take the first available opportunity to set the record straight. This, with the indulgence of the House, I now propose to do.

Incident at the Greenford Park Service Station

At approximately five o'clock last Friday afternoon I left No. 10 Downing Street as usual to travel to the Prime Minister's official country residence at Chequers for the weekend. The party consisted of two cars. The advance car contained myself, a duty secretary from the Downing Street staff, a driver, and a protection officer from the Metropolitan Police. The back-up vehicle contained three additional protection officers.

For several years it has been my practice to take advantage of long car journeys as an opportunity to work. Among the documents which had been prepared for my attention on this occasion was the weekly digest of press coverage compiled for me by my Chief Press Secretary.

I have arranged for a copy of this document, which carries no security restriction, to be placed in the Library of the House. Honourable Members who consult it will see that it conveys frankly, and with detailed quotation, the whole spectrum of press comment about myself as it had appeared in the previous week's newspapers. The comment was, as usual, robust; some might say robust in the extreme. However, I have always taken the view that a free press is an essential element of a free society, and that, if you are in public life, you must, as Kipling has it,

> '. . . bear to hear the truth you've spoken
> Twisted by knaves to make a trap for fools . . .'

The route taken to Chequers is frequently varied for security reasons, and it is not official policy to disclose it. Therefore I shall not do so now. Suffice it to say that the traffic heading west out of London on this particular evening was unusually heavy, even for a wet Friday evening in the pre-Christmas period, and that, after an hour of travelling, we had managed to proceed only as far along the A40 as the Greenford Roundabout, a distance of some seven miles.

It was at this point – that is, at approximately 6 p.m. – that I began to feel unwell. The principal symptom was one of acute nausea, brought on, no doubt, by the effort of trying to read in a car which was repeatedly stopping and starting. I needed fresh air. Unfortunately, for security reasons, the windows of my official car are not designed to open. I put aside the press digest and directed my protection officers to pull in to the next available service station, informing them that I needed to use the lavatory. This request was radioed to the back-up car and a few moments later we turned off the A40 on to the forecourt of what I now know to be the Greenford Park Service Station.

I must emphasize that the responsibility for what followed is mine, and mine alone. No blame should be attached to my protection officers, who behaved throughout in their usual exemplary and professional manner. Having checked that the gentleman's lavatory was unoccupied, and having secured the area immediately in front of it, it was on my express orders that they remained outside whilst I went inside, locking the door behind me. Nobody else was present.

Several newspapers have described what followed as a 'moment of madness'. It would be more accurate, Mr Speaker, to describe it as a series of small but logical steps, whose cumulative effect was to prove fateful. On entering the cubicle I noticed that behind the lavatory basin was a window. This window was slightly open. By standing on the lavatory seat, I discovered that it was possible to open the window fully. I was thus able to bring my face into contact with some much-needed air. Only then did it occur to me that the aperture was, in fact, just large enough for the insertion of my head and shoulders. As the air was having a beneficial effect, this prospect seemed appealing. Unfortunately I then made what was to prove a regrettable miscalculation with regard to my centre of gravity. Questions have been asked about the failure of my protection officers to hear the noise of my exit via the window, but I can assure the House that the roar of the nearby traffic on the wet road was more than sufficient to drown out any sound I may have made.

I left the lavatory in a head-first position and it was this, rather than any subsequent event – and contrary to reports in the media – that produced the slight bruising and abrasions still visible on my face and hands.

It may be that I was rendered temporarily unconscious by my descent. I cannot recall. If I was, it was certainly only for a few moments. Upon rising to my feet, I found myself in a small area, enclosed by walls on three sides. To my left was a gap leading to an automatic car-washing machine. Honourable members will understand that, given the time of year, it was now quite dark. I had also lost a contact lens. Finding the space in which I was standing claustrophobic, and feeling slightly groggy from the effects of my fall, I ventured out along the side of the car wash. As the various diagrams printed in the press have shown, I was now invisible from the forecourt, and it was this route which, as chance would have it, led me away from the garage and out on to a neighbouring street.

I have learned subsequently that my protection officers waited two or three minutes before first knocking on the lavatory door and then, on receiving no reply, breaking it down. By then, however, I was several hundred yards to the south. There was, I repeat, nothing they could have done, and no blame attaches to them in this regard.

Telephone Call to No. 10

At this stage of the evening, as I am sure the House will appreciate, I had no particular plan in mind. It may well be that I was slightly concussed. At any event, I was content simply to follow my footsteps where they led me, enjoying the refreshing sensation of the damp night air. Ferrymead Gardens took me to Millet Road which gave on to Beechwood Avenue and later Melrose Close – street names which, more eloquently than I can hope to do, describe the peaceful English suburb in which I found myself. I felt no sensation of danger; rather the reverse.

I am aware that my actions have since been described in the media as 'a gross dereliction of duty' (*Daily Telegraph*) and 'an unprecedented endangering of national security' (*The Times*). Yet, as the noble lord, Lord Jenkins, has pointed out (in today's *Evening Standard*), there is an historical precedent. On the night of 4 May 1915, Herbert Asquith walked from Mansfield Street, near Oxford Circus, to Downing Street, lost in thought about his feelings for Miss Venetia Stanley, who had just disclosed to him her intention of marrying one of his Cabinet colleagues. If one Prime Minister can walk the London streets unprotected during wartime, why cannot another do the same in peacetime? Does a Prime Minister not enjoy the same civil liberties as any other citizen of the United Kingdom? These are questions which the House may wish to ponder.

Of course, I was aware of the undoubted anxiety which I was by now causing to those who were concerned for my welfare. Accordingly, I took steps to reassure them. The duty log of the No. 10 switchboard records that at 6.27 p.m. a caller claiming to be the Prime Minister attempted to make a reverse charge call to the Downing Street Press Office from a public telephone box in

Greenford. The same caller tried again two minutes later. On this second occasion I was finally able to convince the switchboard operator of my identity, and my call was put through. The House will thus see that within approximately twenty minutes of my alleged disappearance, my office was aware that I was safe and well and acting of my own free will. So much for the so-called 'night of frantic worry' (*Daily Mail*) to which I am supposed to have subjected them.

My Chief Press Secretary, with characteristic presence of mind, took a careful note of our conversation, and I have arranged for a copy of his record also to be placed in the Library of the House. According to this note, I told him not to worry about me, and reassured him that in due course I would return to Downing Street of my own volition. He frankly disapproved of this plan. He believed my actions would quickly become public and provoke damaging speculation in the media. He urged me in strong terms to stay where I was, adding that he would arrange for my protection officers to pick me up: they were, he informed me, at that very moment patrolling the neighbourhood looking for me. The duty log shows that I terminated this conversation at 7.01 p.m.

It was raining quite steadily by now, the streets were quiet, and the realization was suddenly born upon me that unless I took swift and decisive action to vacate the area, I was likely to face the embarrassing situation of being apprehended by my own security officers. Irrational as it may seem with hindsight, I was seized with a powerful desire to postpone such an encounter, at least for a little while longer. But how was it to be avoided? A taxi, if one could be procured, was the obvious solution. But now I faced a further, and unanticipated, problem.

The House may be aware that the first thing a Prime Minister loses on taking office is his passport, which is removed from him by his Private Office to ease his official travel arrangements. The second thing to go is his ready money. Why, after all, does a Prime Minister need cash? How would he spend it if he had it? Where would he obtain it if he wanted it? The sudden realization that I had no money placed me in a quandary.

It was then that I noticed that the telephone call box in which I was sheltering stood adjacent to a small row of commercial premises. Among them was a branch of my own bank. I had retained my personal cheque card from my days as Leader of the Opposition, and it was the work of but a few moments to hurry across the pavement and insert it into the automatic telling machine (ATM). However, my relief quickly evaporated when I realized I had only a vague recollection of my personal identification number (PIN). On my third attempt to enter my PIN, the ATM informed me that it had retained my card.

My reason for giving the House these apparently minor details is to make it easier to comprehend the sequence of events which followed. I was wearing only a light business suit. I was thoroughly wet. I was cold. I was eager to be on my way. The only object on me, I realized, which had any monetary value, was an inscribed wristwatch, given to me during the last G8 summit by the President of the United States.

The sequence of events by which this wristwatch came to be in the possession of a fifteen-year-old schoolgirl has also excited considerable media speculation, most of it of an utterly fantastical nature. The facts are more prosaic.

'Miss B'

As luck would have it, no taxis were available to hire in that particular part of Greenford at that time of the evening, either for cash or barter. Venturing into the road, I therefore attempted to flag down a passing motorist. Perhaps not surprisingly, the spectacle of a man bearing a striking resemblance to the Prime Minister, bleeding slightly from a grazed forehead, looming out of the darkness on a rainy Friday night with his suit jacket held over his head, caused him to panic. Far from slowing down, he accelerated away, a pattern of behaviour repeated by several other motorists as I made my way up and down the centre of Ferrymead Avenue in search of assistance.

It was at this point that I became aware of another pedestrian on that stretch of road – a pedestrian bending, as it seemed to me, to unlock the door of a parked car. This other person – a female person – who, because of her age, cannot be named for legal reasons – is the person who has since become known in the media as 'Miss B'.

I cannot, at this stage, remember precisely which of us initiated the conversation that now took place. It may be that Miss B, as I shall also call her, hailed me in a jocular spirit, or I may have approached her. It is not, in any case, a relevant detail. I naturally assumed her to be the owner of the vehicle beside which she was standing, or at any rate a person authorized by the owner of the vehicle to drive that vehicle away, or, at the very least, the holder of a current UK driver's licence. I also accepted at face value her explanation that the vehicle was mechanically defective, and therefore needed to be started by the unorthodox procedure of opening the bonnet and connecting certain cables in the ignition, a technique which, my right honourable friend the Home Secretary informs me, is known as 'hot-wiring'.

Some will no doubt accuse me of naivety in this matter. That is for the House and the country to judge. The essence of the situation is that I asked a person whom I assumed to be a competent driver to give me a lift, that she at first demurred, that I then offered her as payment the wristwatch to which I made reference earlier, and that she then agreed to drive me wherever I wished to go. The whole case is now in the hands of the Crown Prosecution Service and I am advised that it would be prejudicial for me to comment further on a situation where legal action may be pending.

It was, I should estimate, approximately 7.20 p.m. when, with Miss B at the wheel, we pulled out of Ferrymead Avenue at the start of what was to prove an eventful journey. By this time, unknown to me, British Telecom engineers had pin-pointed the precise location of the telephone box from which I had contacted the Downing Street Press Office, my Principal Private Secretary had been alerted, and the Head of Special Branch and the Director-General of the Security Service, in consultation with the Commissioner of the Metropolitan Police, had issued orders for the area to be sealed off. The emergency services had responded immediately with their usual superb professionalism. The stations of Greenford, South Greenford, Drayton Green and Hanwell had all been closed, and a rudimentary vehicle checkpoint (VCP) was aleady in operation, blocking access from Oldfield Lane South to the Greenford Roundabout.

It was towards this VCP that Miss B now accelerated.

Journey into London

My precise recollection of what followed is hazy. According to Miss B, as quoted in yesterday's News of the World, I shouted 'Go, go, go.' I believe, in fact, that my actual words were 'No, no, no' and that, in the heat of the moment, she misheard me. The truth may never be known. What is not in dispute is that an offence was now committed under the provisions of the 1972 Road Traffic Act, in that our vehicle failed to stop when requested to do so by a police officer. I deeply regret this.

In her account of the night's events, as related in the News of the World, Miss B asserts that she had no idea that I was the Prime Minister. I believe this to be true. She certainly did not seem to me to be the kind of young person who would follow political events at all closely. When I told her who I was, and that the wristwatch which she was now wearing had been given to me by the President of the United States, she responded with an exclamation of frank disbelief.

I am aware that I have been widely criticized for failing to recognize that she was of school age. It was, however, as I have pointed out, dark; I may well have been suffering the effects of concussion; I had lost a contact lens; and the photographs of Miss

B reproduced in the *News of the World* – even with her face masked to protect her identity – show, as I am sure the House would agree, a person of unusually mature appearance.

Her driving skills were also those of a person many years in advance of her true age. The noise of pursuit soon died away and we found ourselves on the A40 heading east, back towards central London – the very road along which I had been travelling to Chequers a bare ninety minutes before.

Honourable Members may perhaps imagine the thoughts which were running through my mind. I was beginning to see that my actions could indeed be open to widespread misinterpretation, as my Chief Press Officer had warned me they would be. It was now clear that a considerable police operation was underway in the Greenford area. I had obviously inconvenienced many people. Given the numbers involved, there was little chance of what had happened not becoming public at some stage. I needed to think quickly what I should do. Miss B took the view, and expressed it forcibly, that continuing on our present course along the A40 would foreshorten that thinking time considerably. I concurred. Accordingly, we left the A40 at the Hanger Lane interchange and joined the North Circular Road.

Perhaps I might now quote to the House from Miss B's account in the *News of the World*:

'I said to him, "Are you really the Prime Minister?" He said he was. He seemed like a nice bloke. He'd gone very quiet. He said he was worried he was going to get me in to a lot of trouble. He said the papers were going to come after me. I said, "No way. You're kidding me." He said, "You've no idea what they're like."

'He asked if I lived with someone who would look after me? Did I have a husband? I said no way: my dad was inside and my mum had done a runner and I lived with my gran. He said, "So how old are you then? Eighteen? Nineteen?" I said, "Fifteen", and he kind of groaned and went very quiet again. I thought I'd turn on the radio to cheer him up.'

Mr Speaker, it has been asked – and fairly asked – why, at this stage of the evening, I did not simply direct Miss B to pull off the road, and await the inevitable arrival of the police. With hindsight, of course, this is what I should have done. I was in a vehicle clearly being driven by someone not qualified to do so. But my situation at the time appeared to me more complicated. Miss B has been kind enough to indicate, via the *News of the World*, that I seemed like 'a nice bloke'. May I, across the havoc of the past few days, return the compliment, and say that she seemed a nice young woman?

And there was something more. In the drama of the preceding minutes, a bond had sprung up between us – a purely platonic bond, I hasten to add – but a bond nonetheless, which meant that I now felt acutely responsible for the situation in which I had placed her. I knew only too well what was likely to happen to her, a vulnerable schoolgirl, if her part in the night's events became known to the media. Could some means be found of extricating her from this sorry tangle? Our best hope was surely to remove ourselves as far as possible from the scene of police operations, and it was for this reason, as much as any other, that we continued our journey across London, eventually leaving the North Circular Road at the Brent Cross Shopping Centre, and travelling south down North End Road towards the borough of Hampstead.

'Mr A'

I have quoted Miss B as telling the *News of the World* that it was her idea to switch on the car radio. I was frankly curious to know whether any word of the night's dramas had yet reached the media. As it happened, the owner of the vehicle – to whom I have since written a letter of apology – had left the radio tuned to a news station, and immediately I found myself listening to an interview regarding my recent performance as Prime Minister. The House will perhaps understand if I say that I felt a sudden sensation of dread. My political life, if not exactly passing before my eyes, seemed at any rate to be passing rapidly before my ears. However, as the broadcast continued, I realized that the interview, which was part of a regular political programme, had in fact been pre-recorded. The tone of the comments being broadcast was one of characteristically lofty abuse and I recognized at once the voice of the speaker: a columnist whom I knew personally, and whose work appears regularly in a number of publications, among them the *Guardian* and the *Observer*. His name will be familiar to members on both sides of the House. For legal reasons, I shall call him Mr A.

Honourable members who take the trouble to consult the weekly press summary which I have had placed in the Library will see that it contains several quotations from Mr A's recent journalism. By a curious coincidence, I had been re-reading these quotations earlier in the evening, at around the moment when I was stricken with nausea. In the *Guardian*, for example, he had written:

'The Prime Minister is, by common consent, a little man: "a pettyfogging political pygmy", was how one of his Cabinet colleagues described him at a private meeting last week. The gap between his personal qualities and the importance of the office he holds grows daily ever more embarrassingly apparent.'

And in the *Observer*:

'It should surprise no one to learn that the Prime Minister is a liar. Lying, after all, is the essence of the politician's craft. What should surprise us – and what alarms his colleagues – is that he is such a bad liar. He is a true phoney: an authentic fraud. As one senior Cabinet Minister recently remarked: "He's the sort of man who, if he kept a brothel, would bring prostitution into disrepute."'

There is more in a similar vein, but perhaps the House will excuse me if I confine myself to these two, fairly typical illustrations.

As I said at the outset of my statement, I have always believed strongly in the tradition of robust press comment as an essential part of our democratic system. I have nothing against journalists as such. Far from it. I had seen Mr A socially on a number of occasions, both before and after I became Prime Minister. I had been to his house. He had been to mine. He had sent me his books when they were published. I had presented his recent award at the annual *What the Papers Say* lunch when he was made Columnist of the Year. I had always made efforts to be friendly towards him. His position in the political spectrum was roughly the same as mine. He should have been, if not a friend, then at least an ally. Yet in print, for reasons I had never understood, he adopted a stance of unwavering criticism. I return to the account given by Miss B:

'This posh guy on the radio was really slagging him off, so I said something like, "Sounds like this f***er really hates your guts." And he said, "Yes, but he's always very nice to my face." So I said, "You mean to tell me you know the guy?" And he said, yes he did, that he used to see him a bit. And I said, "Well, it's none of my business, but don't you think he's due a sorting, the way he's going on?" And he looked out of the window and he thought about it for a bit, and then he said that funnily enough the f***er lived somewhere around here.'

Incident in Hampstead

In deciding to visit Mr A at his home I was aware that I was embarking on a potentially hazardous course. On the other hand, I took the view that I was by this stage

'. . . in blood
Stepped in so far that, should I wade no more,
Returning were as tedious as go o'er.'

By which I do not mean to imply that I consciously intended to do Mr A any actual physical injury, but rather that I had by now concluded that my recent actions would, regardless of what I did, become public knowledge very soon. Once that happened, it did not require much effort on my part to imagine what Mr A himself would have to say about my conduct. The prospect of for once seizing the initiative – of, to use Miss B's phrase, giving him 'a sorting', whatever that may mean – held a certain undeniable appeal.

As I have already told the House, our route from Greenford had now carried us as far as Hampstead, the district in which Mr A has for many years lived. I know the area well. As a backbench MP, I had lived around the corner from Mr A in a basement flat. His own, substantial, four-storey house was familiar to me, and I directed Miss B to the appropriate street. For a moment, after we had parked outside, I hesitated. Was this, on reflection, really a sensible course? But then I resolved that I would continue. The media, after all, had frequently turned up uninvited on my doorstep over the years. Why should I not do the same to one of them? I left the car and rang the bell. Mr A himself answered the door.

Mr Speaker, I cannot claim to have the events of the next few minutes arranged with perfect forensic clarity in my mind. I recall that Mr A greeted me with his usual civility, and that he was carrying a bottle of champagne and a half-full glass. He did not seem particularly pleased to see me. He was, he said, expecting dinner guests at any moment, and made a general indication of regret that he was therefore unable to invite me in. Perhaps, he suggested, my office could contact his secretary and we could arrange a suitable date for an appointment the following week.

It was at this point that Miss B left the car and joined me on the doorstep. Her appearance on the scene seemed to affect Mr A's composure. She began quoting back to him several of the points he had been making earlier on the radio, and invited him to step over the threshold and repeat them. He seemed both confused and alarmed by her presence. I explained that she had recently come to work at No. 10 as part of a work experience scheme. This statement, which was part of my continuing efforts to protect her identity, was misleading, and I regret it. He finally agreed to admit us, and asked us to go upstairs and wait for him in his study, while he made arrangements, he said, for one of his domestic staff to greet his guests in his place.

The suggestion in various newspapers that, once in his study, I 'ransacked' his desk is absurd. The truth is that the room was relatively small and it was almost impossible for me to avoid glancing at his computer screen and seeing what was written there – namely, his column for that Sunday's issue of the *Observer*. It included the following passage:

'Unable, it seems, to tolerate even the mildest criticism, the Prime Minister is said by close colleagues to be exhibiting worrying signs of mental instability. "All Prime Ministers go mad eventually," one of his senior Cabinet colleagues told me privately last week. "The difference is that this one was mad from the start."'

I was still reading when Mr A entered the room.

I now proceeded to make a number of points, of which perhaps four stand out in my memory: first, that it was a pity, given his obvious genius for public administration, that he had never seen fit to offer himself for election; secondly, that it was richly ironic for a journalist, of all people, to accuse all politicians of habitually lying, as I had yet to read any article in any newspaper on any subject of which I had any knowledge that didn't contain at least one factual inaccuracy; thirdly, that I considered it morally contemptible of him to quote anonymous so-called 'senior colleagues' who, I was sure, had better things to do than pass the time of day with him; and, fourthly, that if I was mad – and I was beginning to suspect that I might be, for choosing to be a Prime Minister when I could have been a newspaper columnist –

then I had surely been driven mad by him, and by people like him.

Mr A responded that he had, indeed, considered a political career during his time at Oxford, but had concluded that real power no longer resided in this House, which was full – I believe I am quoting him correctly – of 'little people'; secondly, that he had no views as to the respective merits of journalism and politics, except to observe that nowadays the former offered better rewards, in every sense, and therefore attracted individuals of greater talent; thirdly, that no journalist ever reveals his sources; and finally that he had no particular animus against me personally, but took the impartial view that all politicians were mad and liars, and therefore that whoever was Prime Minister at any given time was, by definition, likely to be the biggest and maddest liar of the lot.

I am not sure precisely how long this conversation lasted. As the House will recall, I no longer had a watch. Nor can I say for certain when I first realized that Mr A was deliberately keeping me occupied. But I should say that roughly twenty minutes had elapsed when Miss B, who had taken up a position by the window, suddenly interrupted our discussion to report that the street below was filling with policemen and photographers. It was then that Mr A disclosed that he had misled us. He had not, in fact, left us alone in order to speak to one of his staff, but rather to alert the picture desk of a national newspaper.

The House will appreciate that, until the Crown Prosecution Service has decided whether or not to initiate criminal proceedings, I am not at liberty to describe as fully as I would wish to do exactly what happened next. No party has yet been charged with a criminal offence, and unless and until that happens, Mr A has a right to anonymity. Miss B's published account is, frankly, incoherent. What is not in dispute is that witnesses heard voices raised, and that at some point Mr A and myself both fell, entwined, down the stairs, landing in the hall at exactly the moment when, as luck would have it, the front door opened to admit the first of Mr A's dinner guests, my right honourable friend the Chancellor of the Exchequer.

Conclusion

Mr Speaker, I have tried to set out the facts as clearly and unemotionally as possible. Someone – I think it may have been Abraham Lincoln, or possibly it was Winston Churchill – once wrote that a night in a police cell is good for any man, and I feel that I have personally benefited from this experience. I have been treated as any other citizen would have been under the circumstances, and that is all I have ever sought.

To have been allowed to serve this country has been a great privilege. Over the course of the next few hours, I shall be having further discussions with my ministerial colleagues and others, and later this evening I hope to have an audience of Her Majesty the Queen. After that my own personal position will be clearer.

No doubt much more will be said on these matters in the days and weeks to come. In the meantime, it only remains for me to thank you, Mr Speaker, and through you the House, for the courtesy you have shown in listening to my personal statement.

THE WONDER SPOT

MELISSA BANK

eth talks me into going to a party in Brooklyn. He says that we can just drop by. I tell him that a party in Brooklyn is a commitment. It takes effort. It's like a wedding: You can't just drop by.

'We can just drop by,' he says again, in a tone that says, *We can do anything we want.*

This will be our first party as a couple.

He says, 'It'll be fun.'

My boyfriend is a decade younger than I am; he is full of hope.

We drive to Brooklyn in his old Mustang convertible, with the top down. Because of the wind and because I'm on the side of Seth's bad ear, we can't really talk – or I can't. But he tells me that we're going to Williamsburg, the section of Brooklyn that's been called the New Downtown. After the party we can walk around and have dinner at a restaurant his friend Bob is about to open there. Bob has offered to let us try everything on the menu-to-be if we'll help him name the restaurant; the finalists are The Shiny Diner, Bob's and The Wonder Spot. 'Start thinking,' Seth says, and I do.

Across the bridge and into the land of Brooklyn, we go under overpasses and down streets so dark and deserted you know they're used only to get lost on. I get this pang for Manhattan, where I am never farther than a block from a bodega, never more than a raised arm from a cab. But then we turn a corner and – lights! people! action! – we park.

Walking to the party, I tell Seth about the Williamsburg I've already been to, the one in Virginia. I expect him to have heard of it – he's from Canada and knows more about the US than I do – but he hasn't. I tell him that I was five or six at the time, and I didn't understand the concept of historical re-enactment. I thought that we'd just found a place where women in bonnets churned butter and men in breeches shoed horses. I tell him the real drama of the trip: I lost the dollar my father had given me for the gift shop.

'What period do they re-enact?' Seth says, teasing.

'You know,' I say, 'colonial times.'

'When was that exactly?'

'Sometime before 1910,' I say.

I'm having such a good time that I forget about the party until we're on the elevator up. I say, 'Maybe we should have a code for "I want to go."'

He starts to make a joke but sees that I'm serious and squeezes my hand three times. I OK the code.

The elevator door opens right into the loft. I was counting on those extra few seconds of hallway before facing the party, the party we are now part of and in, a party with people talking and laughing and having a party time. I think, *I am a solid, trying to do a liquid's job.*

I am only a third joking when I squeeze Seth's hand three times. He squeezes back four, and before I can ask what four means, our hostess is upon us. She is tall and slinky, with ultra-short hair and a gold dot in one of her perfect nostrils; I feel every pound of my weight, every year of my age, until Seth tells her, 'This is my girlfriend, Meg.'

I'm not sure I've ever had a boyfriend who introduced me as his girlfriend. I smile up at this ghosty-pale sweetie-pie man o' mine.

As soon as our hostess slinks off to greet her next arrivals, I say, 'What does four mean?'

'It means, "I love you, too,"' he says.

I want to be happy to hear these words – it's the first time we've squeezed them – but I feel so close to him at this moment, I say the truth, which is, 'I feel old.'

He puts his coat around my shoulders and says, 'Is that better?' and I realize that I've spoken into his bad ear.

I nod, and we move deeper into the party. He introduces me as his girlfriend to each of the friends we pass, all of whom seem happy to meet me, and I think, *I am his girlfriend, Meg; I am girlfriend; I am Meg, girlfriend of Seth.*

I'm fine, even super-fine, until he goes to get a glass of wine for me. Now I look around, trying to pretend, as I always do at parties, that I could be talking to a fellow party-goer if I wanted to, but at the moment I am just too captivated by my own fascinating observations of the crowd.

The women are young, young, young, liquidy and sweet-looking; they are batter, and I am the sponge cake they don't know they'll become. I stand here, a lone loaf, stuck to the pan.

It is at this moment that I see Vincent – only from behind, but I know it's him. Vincent is my ex-boyfriend, or X7, if you count all the times we broke up and got back together.

I've told Seth almost nothing about my ex-boyfriends. Now he'll meet the one who told me my head was too big for my body.

When Seth returns with my wine, he says, 'Still cold?' and he rubs my shoulders and arms and back warm. 'Better?' he says.

I do feel better, and I say so.

A small crowd gathers around us – the drummer in Seth's band, and his entourage – girlfriend, brother, and girlfriend of brother. They try to talk to me, and I try to talk back. One of the girlfriends, I'm not sure whose, works in public radio. Since I'm a public-radio lover, I can keep this conversation going, program to program, until she asks me what I do.

I say, 'I'm a weaver,' and both girlfriends look at me like they're not sure they've heard correctly.

'I weave,' I say, and this leads to an almost post-nuclear silence, the usual effect.

But the one who works in public radio says, 'Do you like weaving?'

'Except for the stress,' I say. She laughs, and we are insta-friends.

Then we girlfriends return to them boyfriends. I plant myself beside Seth like a fire hydrant, my back to where I imagine Vincent to be.

But he's not; he's right across the room, his arm slung like a belt around the hips of a girl who I can tell right away is a model. She has the long, straight hair I used to wish for and sky-high thighs you can see through her mesh stockings.

Just like the bad old days, Vincent doesn't seem to recognize me. Then he gives me a look of mock shock.

I inadvertently squeeze Seth's hand, and he smiles without looking at me, like we have a secret language, and I wish we did.

I watch Vincent steer his girlfriend toward us.

He's grown his hair long and now sports a weird beard and mustache, Lucifer-style. Plus, he's wearing a shirt with huge pointy collars jutting out like fangs over his jacket.

When he reaches us, I say, 'Happy Hallowe'en.'

'Hello, Meg,' he says, Dr Droll.

I say, 'Seth, this is –'

Vincent interrupts and introduces himself as 'Enzo'.

'Enzo?' I say.

He doesn't answer, and I remember his New Jersey friends calling him Vinnie, and his firm correction: 'Vincent'.

He pulls his model front and center and says, 'This is Amanda.'

'I'm Meg,' I say to her. Then I get to say, 'This is my boyfriend, Seth.'

'Hi.' She is both chirpy and cool, an ice chick. 'We know each other,' she says about the man I've just introduced as my boyfriend, and she kisses him – just his cheek, but so far back that her pouty mouth appears to be traveling neck- or ear-ward.

I stare at her, even while I am telling myself not to. I fall under the spell not of her eyes but her eyebrows, which are perfectly arched and skinny and make me aware of my own thick and feral pair; mine are a forest and hers are a trail.

When I blink myself out of my trance, Vincent is saying, 'Whenever anyone would say, "Small world," Meg used to say, "Actually, it's medium-sized."'

I say, 'I was about eleven when I knew Vincent.'

Then, like the hostess my mother taught me to be, I say, 'Vincent is a musician, too.'

'I used to be,' he says, and names the best-known of the bands he played in, though I happen to know it was only for about fifteen minutes. Then he asks Seth, 'Who do you play with?'

I can tell Vincent's impressed by Seth's band and doesn't want to be; he fast talks about starting up a start-up – an on-line recording studio, a real-time distribution outlet, a virtual-record label – he goes on and on, Vincent style, grandiose and impossible to understand.

I say, 'Basically, you do everything but teach kindergarten?'

Vincent says, 'There is an educational component.'

Seth comes off as gentle, even meek, but I know he's intolerant of talk like this. He squeezes my hand three times.

'Oh, shoot,' I say, looking at my wrist for a watch I'm not wearing, 'we have to go,' and I love the sound of we, and I love that it's Seth who wants to go and I love that we are going.

Vincent says they're headed to another party themselves. He kisses both my cheeks – what now must be the signature Enzo kiss – and he looks at me as though he cares deeply for me, a look I never got when we were together, a look that Seth notices, and I think Phew: Seth will think another man loved me; he will think I am the lovable kind of woman, the kind a man better love right or somebody else will.

Vincent says, 'You look great, Meg,' and I think of saying, Whereas you look a little strange, but I just say, 'See you, Vinnie.'

A few more pleasantries and we're in the elevator.

As soon as the elevator doors close, I say, 'Good thing she was just a model.' I am giddy just to be out. 'I think that would've been really hard if she were a supermodel.'

Seth looks at me, not sure what I mean.

Out on the street, I say, 'How do you know her, by the way?' and instantly regret how deliberately off-handed I sound.

'I don't really know her,' he says. 'She came up to me after a show a few weeks ago.'

I think, Came up to you or on to you? but I give myself the open, amused look of a bystander eager to hear more about one of life's funny little coincidences.

'She asked me if I would help her celebrate her half-birthday,' he says, and his tone tells me I would be crazy to think he'd ever be attracted to her.

Unfortunately, now I am crazy, and I have to stop myself from saying a tone-deaf and tone-dumb, So you're saying you didn't eat her half-birthday cake?

Suddenly I feel like I'm Mary Poppins floating with an umbrella and a spoonful of sugar into the city of sexual menace, population a million Amandas with ultra-short and long straight hair and pouty mouths and thighs you can see through mesh stockings.

From there I go straight to This will never work. He has models coming on to him after his show. He'll be forty-nine when you're turning sixty. He is young and hip and you don't even know the hip word for hip any more. You belong at home in bed with a book.

I remind myself that this is what I always say and what I always do. As soon as I'm in a relationship, I promote fear from clerk to president, even though all it can do is sweep up, turn off the lights and lock the door.

I am so deep in my own argument that I almost don't hear Seth say, 'Meg'.

He stops me on the pavement, and turns me toward him. His face practically glows white; he is a ghost of the ghost he usually looks like.

He says, 'When did you go out with him?'

'So long ago,' I say, 'he had a different name.'

'Beelzebub?' he says. Then: 'Sorry.'

I tell him that I hadn't seen Vincent for ten-plus years – he was still in purgatory when I knew him.

'But it was hard for you to see him with somebody else, tonight?'

'No,' I say, a little surprised.

He nods, not quite believing. 'But the thing you said about her being a model?'

'Models are always hard,' I say. 'And it was hard to see her necking with your cheek.'

After I've said this, I want to say that I don't usually use the word 'neck' as a verb, it's a fifties word, my mother's word, but he is shaking his head and I can see he is not thinking about how old I sound or look or am.

'Obviously he still has a thing for you,' Seth says, and shakes his head and swallows a couple of times, like he's trying to get rid of a bad taste in his mouth. 'The way he looked at you.'

My *Phew* gives me an Indian burn of shame. 'That look was for Amanda's benefit,' I say, and I know it's true. For a second, I am an older sister to my younger self. 'And if she brings it up later,' I say, 'he'll tell her she's crazy.'

'Very nice,' Seth says, and his voice tells me that he doesn't want to hear any more about Vincent and Amanda, he doesn't care about them, and that he's wishing he didn't care so much about me.

It scares me. But then I get this big feeling, simple but exalted: He's like me, just with different details.

His eyes are closed, and I think maybe he's picturing me with Vincent or other men he assumes I've slept with or loved. Maybe he's telling himself that he's too tall or doesn't hear well enough. Usually, he pulls me in for the hug, but now I do it. I pull him in and we stay like this, his chin on my head, my face on his chest.

I find myself thinking of Amanda at another party with Vincent, and feeling sorry for her. It occurs to me that if I were as beautiful as she is, every passing half-birthday would be harder to celebrate. But mostly I am just glad I am not her and glad we are not them, and glad just to be out here on the curb, breathing the sweet air of Williamsburg and post-colonial freedom.

We are quiet for a while, walking. I begin to see where we are now. We pass the Miss Williamsburg Diner. Little bookstores I could spend my life in. We pass a gallery with black-light art hung above a reflecting pool.

Then we're standing in a parking lot, outside of what Seth tells me is Bob's restaurant. I'm saying that living in Manhattan gives you a real appreciation of parking lots, when Seth takes something out of his pocket and puts it in my hand. It's a dollar. 'For the gift shop,' he says. 'Don't lose it now.'

With my dollar hand, I squeeze Seth's about thirty-seven times, telling him everything I feel.

He says, 'What does that mean?'

I say, ' "I'm hungry." '

What I feel is, *Right now I am having the life I want, here outside The Shiny Diner, Bob's or The Wonder Spot, with my dollar to spend and dinner to come*. We will try everything on the menu. Then we will drive through Brooklyn and cross the bridge with the Manhattan skyline in front of us, which looks new to me every time I see it, and we will drive right into it. We'll find a parking space a few blocks from my apartment on Tenth Street, and we'll pick up milk and tomorrow's paper. We will undress and get into bed.

LAST REQUESTS

GILES SMITH

ork chop – nice and thick, kidney still in – with sprouts, a carrot-and-swede mix, mashed potatoes and gravy. Now, that's a proper meal. And after, fruit pie and custard or cream. A proper, home-baked pie, mind you – none of your tins and packets. Proper, wholesome, homely food – what my husband Derek used to call 'a bit of all right'. The way to a man's heart is through his stomach and that was certainly true with Derek.

But a lot of them, these days, they don't want that. It's all burgers and fries. Milkshakes, some of them. Well, that's not a proper meal, is it? Not what I call a proper, sit-down meal. With my three, every night, there was meat and vegetables and a pie afterwards, never fail. Or sometimes a crumble, or a jam tart, or a trifle, but always a pudding. Always. Not like these mothers now, with their yoghurts and their fruit if you're lucky. And the kids all picky and refusing to eat. I'd have them eating soon enough, I'd crack the whip. No getting down until that bowl's clean. Come on: chop chop, eat up, or you'll waste away. No danger of that with my Stephen. He had a good appetite. Went to Singapore for the bank but he phones at Christmas. Carl, my younger one, he ate well, too, though he's smaller since he left home. He drops in from time to time. Brings the kids, but never for long. I always ask, 'Will you stay for a meal?' But he says he's busy and I'm sure he is.

Steak – that's popular. Quite a few of them ask for steak, and when they do, I try to get a nice one in, which is normally possible. I do a good steak. It was one of Derek's favourites. Steak and kidney pudding, too, but sometimes just a nice, simple, lean, fried steak. A nice layer of oil and the pan at the right heat, which is as hot as it will go. The problem with steak is, it's quite a long way from the kitchen to the Row. You've got to go out of the canteen block then across 'Y' yard and up three flights. It can take a few minutes, what with the security grilles. Really, with a steak, that's not the best thing. 'I won't think it's rude if it spits at me,' Derek used to say and he was right. A steak should be out of the frying pan and on to the plate and then straight into your mouth, all hot and melty. You don't want to wait around for a steak. In a way, they might be better off with a stew or a pie. Something that keeps its heat. I don't think any of them think about that – though why should they? It's not like they haven't got plenty on their minds already, my God. The chips will be OK, though. Most of them want chips. Or 'French fries', they write. Well, the educated ones do. I think a chip should be thick, but if that's what they want, I'll do them stringy. I'll do what they want.

I've been doing it for two and a bit years now, and I suppose you get into something like a routine. Especially recently. At first it was dribs and drabs, but of late, particularly with the bombings, it's been more like a steady stream. There was all sorts of fuss when they brought it back. People say, we didn't used to need it. But you'd have to say it was a more innocent world then. There wasn't the terrorism, for one thing. Or there was, but not nearly so much of it. And you never heard about people having guns, the way you do now. And all the business with the children, which people got very worked up about. I don't know why, as time goes by there just seems to be more wickedness generally. Like the one they sent off last night. Nineteen years old. Climbed a tree by a playground in a park and started firing. Eleven little ones he killed, and three mothers and an au pair girl, a Swiss girl, I think. They asked him why and he said, 'I wanted to see them scared.' Well, what are you going to do with someone like that? No, on the whole, I think they had to bring it back.

Soon after they did, the governor called me in and we had a chat about it. 'Repercussions at catering level,' he called it, because he's a one for the jargon. I said I was happy to take charge of it. He said it would mean some late evenings, and how would that be at home, and I said I was on my own now, so it wouldn't make any difference. I don't mean to sound funny, but it was nice for me in a way because I got to do some cooking again. The thing about running the kitchens is, like all these jobs, it gets to be mostly administration in the end. I write up the menus, do the orders and the store cupboards, the fridges and freezers, and obviously I keep an eye during lunch, or what have you. But in terms of actually cooking, I don't think I'd done any for about seventeen years, all told. Obviously with the burgers being so popular, the fast food, there's some weeks when I don't do much now, either. But not always, not by any means.

Some people think they don't deserve anything. Jean from next door to me, she's said to me before now, 'Maggie, I don't know how you can bring yourself. Cooking a special tea for someone who's evil.' And I know what she means, except I don't really see it like that. That doesn't mean I'm soft about it. I know the kind they get up there. They've done awful things, wicked things, it's unimaginable what they've done, some of them. They wouldn't be in here if they hadn't. Except, obviously, the mistaken identity ones. But even so, I think there's human standards and you've got to treat them right. I said this to the governor when he asked me what my attitude would be. I said I thought something special was appropriate at the end and I haven't changed my mind. You've got to remember, they've been up there for months, some of them – except the political ones, who go through a bit quicker. But for most of them, there's months of sitting around, thinking about what's coming. It's a difficult time for them. And they don't get any special treatment up there, day to day, far from it, just the same food as the rest, which, between you and me . . . I mean, we do our best, but the budget's tight and anyway you're cooking for nineteen hundred. There's not exactly going to be the personal touch, is there?

I don't know what it must be like, to know you're going to die. I mean, we all do know that, but we don't know when, like they do. And how. And I don't think a decent tea is out of order, in that circumstance. Actually, I think it's the least you can do. We know they've done wrong and we know we can't forgive them, but at least we can give them their dignity at the end. I think they appreciate that, most of them. It makes them feel they weren't just sent packing, they were cared about. I think they deserve that much. Well, that's how I see it. I said to Jean, 'You'd want the same if it was you, Jean.'

The form goes up to them the day before and they have to fill it out by midday. That can't be easy for them. It's hard to say, just after breakfast on one day, what you're going to feel like eating for tea the day after. Maybe you thought in the morning you'd want, say, lasagne but then it turned out on the day that you couldn't face mince and you wanted, say, a lamb cutlet. Too late then, of course. But we've got to plan ahead, so there it is. They can have what they like, within reason, up to a maximum of three courses, with coffee or tea and a piece of confectionery or a biscuit if they want it. No alcohol, for obvious reasons. Obviously, you'll get the jokers, like the one who said he wanted a whole roast pig with an apple in its mouth. Or the governor's head, one of them said he wanted. The wardens tell me about those, because they read them while they're up there and tell them there and then if they're wasting their time. The boy in the tree wanted cauliflower cheese. Which, to be honest, I think of more as a snack than a proper supper. But rather that than a burger.

I don't take the meals up. One of the wardens will do that. It might be Dave or John or sometimes it's Dudley. Deadly Dudley, we call him, on account he's so slow. I reckon even the stews must be cold by the time Deadly Dudley gets up there, never mind the steaks. Normally, with the wardens, there's a bit of a lark, which I enjoy. Especially with John, who's a one. He'll say something rude about that day's lunch and I'll tell him he's a yard of pump-water who's obviously never had a decent meal in his life. And he'll say he'd be all right if he had a woman like me to take care of him and I'll say it's a good job his wife can't hear him talking like that. 'The first Mrs Reynolds' he calls her. Maybe it's a funny time to be making jokes, or a funny place, but you have to, don't you? I think we'd go mad otherwise. There's a different atmosphere on execution nights, and I think it gets to everyone. It doesn't mean you're not respectful. Even the wardens. When it's soup, you'll see them pick up the tray really slowly and you'll know they're being really careful not to slop it.

With the McDonald's, we ring up and a taxi brings it. I don't know who pays. It must be an account or something. The taxi comes in the tradesman's entrance and the driver comes in the kitchen with the bags. They come in sometimes and say, 'Grub up!' I don't think they know who it's for. Maybe they think it's for me, though Lord knows it's not my idea of food. I often say, it wouldn't be the first thing I ate, let alone the last. I take out the packages and check everything against the form, and I might just run it through the micro if anything seems to have gone a bit cool. Whatever it is, it might as well be hot. And then it all goes back in the bags and goes up like that.

It has to be in the packages. One time, I didn't do that. I got a plate all ready on a tray and put the two burgers on there, the chips beside them in a pile. I took the little sachet of ketchup and squeezed it out on the side of the plate. And the apple dessert thing that comes in a cardboard tube – I halved that and put it in a dish. And I tipped the Coke out in a glass. Except we only have those little Duralit canteen water glasses and I needed five of them. The amount they put in those cardboard cup things: enough to float a navy. And I set it all out with a knife and fork and a napkin, as you would. Well, apparently he went mad. He wasn't having it. Threw the lot on the floor. Screaming, he was. They had to hold him down. I just thought it would be nicer. Make it seem more like a meal. I don't know. It's what you're used to, I suppose.

There's quite a call for curries. In fact, after burgers, that's probably the most popular request. It's fine by me. Derek enjoyed a curry – not often, but every now and again, maybe with the left-over lamb, and hot as you like, until he was sweating like a donkey sometimes. I had a little run-in with Dave over curries, early on. He came in the kitchen one day, looking a bit edgy, which he does when he's got something to say, and he wondered if maybe, when they asked for a curry, what they were expecting was a takeaway from one of the local Indians. I told him straight away not to be so daft. Why would you want a takeaway when you could have something fresh from the kitchen? Especially these days, when the trimmings – the poppadoms, the nan bread, the difficult things to do on your own – you can just phone up the wholesaler for, along with everything else. So I knocked that idea right on the head. There's nothing anyone can tell me about cooking a curry – a good, wholesome, home-made one, and hot, if that's what's wanted, which very often it seems to be.

'Thai-style dipping sauce' though: that was an odd one. 'Spring rolls and a Thai-style dipping sauce.' Well, spring rolls was fine, because we get a fair number of Chinese through generally, so there tend to be some in the freezer. But Thai-style dipping sauce . . . I think he was mucking me about, to be honest. I asked John if he'd ever heard of Thai-style dipping sauce and he said his wife wouldn't let him watch those kinds of videos, but seriously, no he hadn't. In the end, I sent out the Thousand Island and he had to make do.

There's some that are so negative, I don't pretend to understand. '20 Marlboro Light, one packet of chewing gum.' A particular brand, it was. I don't remember it now – White Ice or something. A shame, really, when you think what he could have had. But there's quite a number, in actual fact, who only want cigarettes or biscuits. Or bowls of cereal, even. Sugar Puffs, Shreddies – and that's it. It's as if they've already given up, in a way. And you wouldn't believe the writing on some of those forms. It's a good job the wardens go through it with them first, because some of them, frankly, I wouldn't be able to read. Big letters and small letters all jumbled. I'll tell you what it's like, it's like what you might do if you were right-handed and you had a go with your left. And as for spelling . . . It's all they can do, some of them, to write their names. There's one came down not long ago, just two words on it in big, block capitals: 'JAFFA CAKS'.

John thought that was hilarious. I had to tell him to calm down.

Some really know what they want, though. There was this lawyer who murdered his wife. It was in the paper. He did it for the insurance. His mistress had helped him set it up and for months he got away with it. He'd done the whole thing – appeared at the funeral in tears, appealed for information with the police on the telly, where he'd actually broken down. He was a hero for a while – a tragic hero. And then they found the mallet, wrapped in a bin-liner on a pleasure boat he owned, moored down at Mersea. They asked him why he hadn't ditched it, thrown it overboard or something, and he said an odd thing. He said, 'I couldn't bear to.' He was through here about a month ago. I remember his handwriting. It was very elegant. As for what he wanted . . . Dave brought the form down and said, 'You're gonna love this.' It was asparagus to start, tips only. Two guinea fowl, wrapped in bacon and roasted, with buttered green beans and mashed celeriac which, I'll be honest with you, I had to look up. And to finish, a crème brûlée. Honestly, I felt like going up there and saying, you want fancy French food, you'd better come down here and make it yourself. Then there were all these cheeses. And special biscuits, not just Jacob's. 'Filter coffee' he put. And at the end – I'll always remember this – he wrote 'Five toothpicks of good quality'. We had a good laugh at that. He got it, though, or nearly all of it, including the toothpicks. It needed a bit of guesswork here and there – especially cooking the guinea fowl – but I did it. I don't know what he wanted with those guinea fowl. There was no meat on them worth speaking of.

I think, with some of the others, the fact you could have anything kind of paralyses them in a way. It's almost as if they'd be better off with a menu, a range of options, so they could choose. There was one the other week who just wanted a sandwich. They'd gone up at midday to collect the form and he was just sitting there, hadn't written anything. He was this middle-aged man who'd killed his children, four of them, at breakfast one morning, with a rifle – for no real reason, apparently. He just got angry and that was that, and the next thing he was phoning the police and asking them to come and get him. And Dave, I think it was, said to him, 'You must be able to think of something.' And he said, 'I'll just have a sandwich.' When they asked him what he wanted in it he just said, 'Whatever.' Sad, really, but I think it's true of a lot of them on the Row that they don't really know their own minds by the end. I made him a cheese and pickle one, because nobody ever objects to that, and I put it on the tray as usual. John said, 'He's not going to get fat on that, is he?' and I said, 'Shush now.'

Derek's last meal – that was a sandwich. I was thinking about it last night when I was doing the cauliflower for the boy in the tree: what was the last thing that Derek ate? And it must have been that sandwich. That's the trouble with hospitals. They order a day ahead, so if you get there after the cards have been round, chances are you'll get the meal the person who was in before you asked for. By the time we got through Emergency and then up on the ward, it was lunchtime and the person in Derek's bed had obviously ticked egg and cress sandwich, which was not Derek's favourite by a long way. I tried to say to him, you'd better get that inside you, Derek, because you don't know when they'll be round again, or what with. He did his best, a couple of mouthfuls, but he was very ill by then. I don't think he knew much after that. He was so grey. That's what I remember most of all. Him so grey and the noise of the breathing.

I've never met any of the ones I've done the meal for. They don't let them in the canteen area, so I never set eyes on them. I suppose I am curious sometimes, to know what they're like. Thai-style dipping sauce – I'd like to have seen him. And the one who killed his children. I'd have liked to try and tempt him into something more than a sandwich. I do feel I know them, in a way. I feel close to them. I wonder if they feel the same about me. And it's funny because the next morning they're gone. And we never even spoke. Sometimes the wardens will pass something on; either 'That went down well,' or 'He looked happy with that.' John sometimes says, 'There was someone up there wanted to marry you last night, Maggie, but you missed your chance.' And as I'm always telling John, 'Flattery will get you everywhere.' The lawyer sent a note down saying 'My compliments to the chef'. No one had ever done that before. I blushed when I read it, I was so pleased. I think everyone likes a compliment. It makes you feel appreciated.

The meal goes up at 8.00 and the executions are directly after midnight. There's some legal reason for that, I think. But that's four hours between the meal and the end of it and I often wonder if they get peckish again. Every now and again, you'll send the meal up and they'll eat it, and then the phone call comes through from the judge and they get a reprieve. All very dramatic. Well, good for them. But often it's only temporary and, a month later, you're cooking the same meal for them all over again. This can go on a while. There's one up there now who's had his last meal five times. Always the same: roast beef with Yorkshire pudding and all the trimmings, vanilla ice cream afterwards with two boudoir biscuits in it and a cup of tea. You'd think he'd be bored of it by now and fancy a change. One time I'd done a chilli con carne for someone. Deadly Dudley took it up, but by the time he got up there, the reprieve had come through and they'd already taken the prisoner off the Row. So Deadly Dudley turns round and comes back in and sets the tray down on the counter. And then he starts hovering, the way he sometimes does. 'Seems a pity to waste it,' he said. 'Oh, go on, then,' I said, and he sat down and tucked in. Men and food, honestly.

I can be away by 8.30 which is plenty of time for the bus. Normally, I'll go home and do myself something from the freezer. One of those individual cottage pies – Sainsbury's do a good one. Imagine: me eating croquettes out of a packet. I wouldn't have dreamed of it while Derek was alive. It was always fresh vegetables then. But somehow, to peel a potato for yourself . . . When you're on your own, it doesn't seem worth it.

There's often a crowd outside when I leave. People come to the gates when there's an execution. Often it's the same people. I notice them. There's a man with a big black parka and a Woolworth's carrier bag. He's always there. I don't know why. It's not like there's anything to see. There isn't even a clock that chimes. It just gets to be after midnight, and at that point they all go away again. So the wardens tell me. Sometimes, when I leave, there might be some banners and there might be a bit of shouting going on. But more often than not they're just standing there quietly, like they're waiting for something, I've no idea what.

Last night was odd, though. I hadn't quite managed to get the monthly freezer check done during the day, so after they'd taken up the cauliflower cheese for the boy in the tree, I finished the job off. It must have taken about an hour and a half, all told. And I'd got my coat on and I'd got my bag together and I was just tying a scarf around my head, because it was a filthy night, when Dave came back with the tray. He looked a bit embarrassed when he saw me and I didn't know why at first. And, of course, ordinarily I wouldn't get to see the trays because usually, by the time I get in the next day, they've been cleared away by the overnight cleaners. And Dave didn't say anything, just put it down and turned away and I got a good look then and I wished I hadn't because, do you know what, he hadn't touched it.

PETER SHELLEY

PATRICK MARBER

Where was I when Kennedy got shot?
Between my mother's legs, getting born.
Georgia thought this was the coolest thing.

It's summer, 1978. We're both fourteen.
We're at the same school in the same class.
She hates me. Because she does.

She's got three items of clothing: a cotton slash-neck dress down
to her knees and a pair of black brogue lace-ups.
She says underwear's for hippies.
She has three dresses: one black, one pink, one white.
Each month she dyes her hair one of these colours.
She also has different coloured laces.
I like her best when she has white hair, a black dress and pink
laces.
That's what she's wearing the day school breaks up.

I've gone to the record shop to buy the new Buzzcocks single.
Last winter they'd done a single called 'Orgasm Addict'.
The sleeve was screaming yellow with a collage of a naked woman
on it.
She had mouths on her breasts and instead of her head she had an
iron.
If I could be anyone I'd be Pete Shelley.

Georgia's coming out as I go in.
'What've you bought?'
She says, 'New Buzzcocks single.'

' "Love You More"?'
And she says, 'Yeah . . . you like Buzzcocks?'
And I say, 'What's more, they like *me*.'
She smiles a bit, showing her funny, gappy teeth and I wonder
what it would be like to slither my tongue around in her mouth.
She's not so good looking but she has this way of being her which
is just her thing. But I'm no oil painting either, I suppose.

She thinks about something and then she says, 'Do you want to
come back to my house and listen to it?'
I say, 'Maybe,' and she says, 'Well, fuck off then.'
I say, 'Maybe I will fuck off,' and she says, 'If you want to come
with me I live above that pub.'
She points.
'The Swan?' I say.
'Go to the black door at the side and push the buzzer saying
"Murphy".' So I say, 'OK, I'll just go and buy it myself.' And she
says, 'OK', and I say, 'See you.'

I go into the shop and buy the record and I also buy her a copy of
'Gary Gilmore's Eyes' by The Adverts in case she doesn't have it.
The B side is better than the A side. It's called 'Bored Teenagers'
and the chorus goes, 'We're just bored teenagers, see ourselves as
strangers', or something like that and at the end the lead singer
(T.V. Smith) goes, 'We're just bored teenagers, bored out of our
heads bored out of our MINDS', and the way he screams 'minds'
is really quite passionate.

I buy her this record for two reasons: first, I think she'll be
impressed that I've even heard of it and the second reason is that
on the collage on the front cover it says, 'One rural oaf in Georgia
even sent me a hunk of rope'. I don't know why. But I know from
geography that Georgia is a state in America. I think Georgia will
like seeing her name in print.

*

So I press that buzzer and she lets me in and I follow her up a long flight of dark stairs. They have red lino on them and steel edges so you won't slip. It stinks of old smells and some new smells, too. As she goes up I look at the creases in the backs of her knees.

We go into the kitchen and she gets two cans of beer out of the fridge and throws me one. The fridge is full of beer. She opens her can and I open mine and we both drink. Georgia sits on the table dangling her legs and I lean in the doorway, just leaning and drinking my beer. We don't say much.

She says, 'You got a fag?' and I say, 'No, I don't smoke.' Georgia looks disappointed and then she calls down the corridor, 'Mum, you got any fags?' and a voice (Irish sounding) comes back, 'Yeah, in here.'

In our house, our flat, no one smokes and everything is clean, plus if I invite someone round for tea my mum will always be there fussing around and making sure we've got enough food and stuff. Georgia gets up from the table and says, 'Come and meet my mum.'

We go down a corridor full of old newspapers, beer crates and musical instruments and speakers all in their black suitcases. The carpet is like fungus on cheese.

In her mother's room the curtains are closed and she's in bed. The TV's on showing the horse racing. She makes a shushing noise to us. The race ends and as it does she goes, 'Ahh, shite.'

Georgia sits on the bed and gives her mum a kiss. Her mum says, 'That's your father in a filthy mood all night. Someone gave him a tip, this "dead-on certainty" and he's rushed off to the bookies like greased arse lightning. Get us the cigs would you love, they're on the table.'

I thought she was talking to Georgia and then I realize, when nothing happens, that she's talking to me.

I go over to the table. It's a round, Formica pub table with a rectangular mirror propped up against the wall. The wallpaper has strange yellow flowers on it. I give her the cigarettes. There's a book of matches, 'The Swan' matches, tucked into the cellophane. I say, 'Here you are', and she says, 'Have a seat then.'

There are no chairs in the room so I sit on the bed, on the other side from Georgia with her mother in between us.

The sun is coming in through a gap in the curtains and wherever the sun touches in the room it looks clean and everywhere else looks like it's been smeared with dishwater.

'So, Georgia, who's your friend? Are you going to introduce us?'

Georgia lights a cigarette.

'This,' she says, 'is my friend, Peter Shelley. Peter Shelley, this is my mum.'

We shake hands.

I say, 'Pleased to meet you, Mrs Murphy', and she says, 'Call me Claire.'

Then she takes a drag and says, 'Now, if you'll forgive me for a while I need a snooze before we open this evening. Will we be seeing you later, Mr Shelley?'

'I don't know, maybe.' Her calling me 'Mr Shelley' gives me a little snigger inside.

'Well, you're welcome to stay if you want, have you far to go?'

'The Attlee. On the other side of the park.'

'I've heard it's quite nice, the Attlee.'

'It's OK.'

'Good. Georgia, give him some tea, he's wasting into thin air.'

'Bye, Peter.'

'Bye.'

On the way back to the kitchen Georgia has her hands behind her back. She quickly clenches and unclenches her hands; three pulsebeats.

*

In the kitchen she makes tea. She says 'How many sugars?' and I say three please.

I tell her I like her mum and she says she does too. She says her mum lets her do whatever she wants. I say my mum lets me do whatever she wants me to do.

Georgia smiles and gives me a funny look.

I ask her why she said I was Pete Shelley and she says, 'Because I want you to be'; and I say, 'So do I', and she replies, 'So, there you are.'

We go into her bedroom. Ads from the *NME* are stuck on the walls, posters of The Clash, Buzzcocks, Sex Pistols, Siouxsie and the Banshees, Ian Dury, Dead Kennedys and some others. Records everywhere. Two dresses on a clothes rack.

I give her The Adverts single and she's pleased. She touches my arm for a second and I go hard. It's the weirdest. It goes down after a while.

So we sit on her bed with the mugs on the floor.

We get our Buzzcocks singles out of their bags. We decide to swap. For a lark you could say. We agree that this cover is better than the last two ('What Do I Get?' and 'I Don't Mind'). It's a pink and purple graphic of nine rooms seen from above.

The Buzzcocks logo (with the second Z raised above the first) is in pink in the bottom left-hand corner. In capitals at the bottom of the sleeve it says UP36433: LOVE YOU MORE.

The back of the sleeve is more complicated: a cartoon man and woman are in the same nine rooms but never together. They're moving speakers around . . . maybe to get the right sound. Who knows?

In the bottom right-hand corner room there's a man holding a board or tray with the letter K on it. It's hard to say what he's up to. It's all quite mysterious.

*

Georgia takes the disc out of the sleeve and because it's brand new it kind of sticks to the paper producing a tiny static crackle. We look at it.

The first thing we notice is how short it is: 1.45.

The B side which they always call '1 side' is 2.49. It's called 'Noise Annoys'.

Georgia holds the side of the record with her finger tips.

Her fingers are pretty chewed up but they look nice all the same.

I sip my tea to be polite. It's evil. The milk's all sour and floating about.

She says, 'Do you think it'll be quite fast or very fast?'

I say that as long as it isn't slow I don't care, but given that it's very short it will probably be very fast.

We examine the inner spiral for more information.

Scratched in capitals it says, 'THE CROSSOVER MARKET'. We don't know what this means.

Then, Georgia says, 'Come on, let's put it on.'

I nod. My mouth is full of tea. She puts her hand on my leg and holds the record with her thumb on the A side and her fingers on the 1 side.

I'm looking at her, my face is three inches from hers and she says, 'Spit it out all over me.' I shake my head. Meanwhile, my cheeks are bulging and my mouth is smiling. She says, 'Dare you.' Her hand is between my legs now and she's beginning to move it further up. I spit my tea in her face and then she buries her face into mine and it's hot and wet. Her mouth tastes of beer and cigarettes and she's waggling her tongue about and I'm doing the same. I can feel her teeth and the gaps between them and I go, 'I like these bits,' and she says, 'They're horrible,' and I say, 'No, I love them.'

We're like two dogs scrapping.

I can't get my hands and mouth in enough places at once.
I'm thinking I might come any second and I don't know if this is
allowed.
Does she know about spunk? She must do, she's got 'Orgasm
Addict'.
I vaguely wonder if she has spunk or some equivalent thing that
would come out.
I hope so.
Suddenly she gets up and puts the record on at top volume and we
start squirming about again.

The record plays over and over because her record player has
something that makes it do that. After about the fourth time we
can make out more of the words in the rushing, relentless noise
and we sing along and we're at each other like mad.
I'm on top of her, her dress is up to her waist and she's got her
shoes on, I put my hand down between her legs and put some
fingers (three) up her and take them out and taste it. It tastes of
God knows what but something interesting.
Georgia licks my fingers and then wrinkles her nose.
'Do you know what to do?'
I say, 'Not certain, do you?'
She says, 'No, but don't stop.'
She puts her hand down my trousers. She begins to wank me just
how I do it to myself and I'm really totally shocked.
How does she know how to do it? How could she *know*?
I say, 'Don't, I'll come,' and she whispers in my ear, 'Go on
then.'
So I do.
She wipes some of it on her sheets and then licks her hand and
then kisses me so I can taste some of it.

'Love You More' is tearing out of her crappy speakers.
The song is so loud and fast it just comes and goes and the ending
is desperately sudden and sad. My trousers are down and her dress

is up to her neck, her chest is as flat as mine. I say too loud right in her ear shouting over the music, 'Now what?'

She nods and suddenly her mouth is on my cock and her cunt is in my face and we're wriggling away like fish. I start to lick all round the area and to be honest I feel a bit stupid for a second because the music stops while the record player does its thing and we're just making these noises. And suddenly I imagine my tongue is painting in a wall where the plaster's broken off, which is quite a nice thing to do but only *quite* nice. And she's kind of gnawing away on some bone I can see out the corner of my eye and it all seems a bit ridiculous. I can't quite concentrate on enjoying what she's doing because I'm having to do the stuff to her and it's really quiet and just these slippy sloppy noises but then the song starts again and it's OK again. So we do that for a bit and then when the song begins again, maybe the sixteenth time, she crawls up to my face and she says, 'Come on, let's fuck.'

I get on top of her and she smiles and Pete Shelley's wailing away. I find the right hole quite quickly and I'm not, to tell the truth, sure it *is* the right one but Georgia says it is and then when it goes in, we're both holding our breath and staring wide eyed at each other and I go, 'Fucking hell,' and she says, 'Jesus fucking Christ', and we're both sort of laughing and it's the most totally weird feeling for me so for her it must be equally if not more weird and I'm also thinking this is what the world makes such a fuss about your whole life and I get it now.

I lie on top of her and it goes all the way in and we're both by this time very sweaty and covered in spit (and tea and a bit of spunk) and we suddenly lie very still. Just contemplating our situation.

I say, 'What does it feel like?'

Georgia says, 'I don't know, full, funny, it feels nice. What does it feel like for you?'

'I don't know, like someone's taken all my skin off and put me in a warm bath.'

She says, 'Move about, like this.'
She begins to move and I move with her very, very fast and she says, 'Tell me when you're coming, I'm coming, tell me when you're coming,' and I say, 'Now, Now' and we come and then collapse in a heap as they say.

After a while she leans over and unplugs the record player just before it starts again.
I stretch with her, still inside her. It's quiet.
We lie in each other's arms and then she says, 'We've lost our virginities.'
I say, 'I thought you hated me,' and she says, 'I do.'
I flick her on the arm and she punches my leg.
And we lie a bit more, doing nothing, contemplating things again.

Then I start going a bit soft so I say, 'Shall I take it out now?'
She says, 'OK.' So I do, quite slowly. We both gasp a little. We really do.
I sneak a quick glance at it and there's some blood. Which is OK I think.
She says, 'You've been in the wars.'
She's actually talking to my nob like it's some other person in the room.
She's holding it very gently, she says, 'You've been in the trenches.' (We did 'First World War' this term).
I say, 'Are you OK, with the blood?'
And she says, 'I'm dandy,' which I just love.
Then she lights a cigarette and says, 'My first post-coital fag.'
'Coital's *fucking* isn't it?'
And she says, 'One hundred per cent.'

After a while we get up. We lie on the bed kissing and stroking each other, listening to her favourite records, discussing the lyrics, talking about school.

She walks me home through the still summer air. I say I won't be able to sleep and she says, 'Wank about me.' I say I will but in fact I won't because I ache like mad down there.

We sit on the kerb near my flat.
My mother comes out on the balcony, it's getting dark.
She shouts down that she's been worried sick about where I was.
I say I'm sorry and that I've been with Georgia and this is Georgia.
My mother knows all about Georgia and she smiles.
She says, 'You must come to tea soon, Georgia.'

We kiss good-bye.
I say, 'I love your hair, I love your dress, I love your shoes,
I love your laces, I love your body.' She says, 'Don't be poxy.'

I go up in the pissy lift feeling like I could eat the world.
I go on to the balcony to watch Georgia walking away but she's still standing in the street, smoking.
She looks up at me and says, 'We forgot to listen to the B side.'
I say. 'Tomorrow?' and she says, 'Tomorrow.' And then she walks away.

THE DEPARTMENT OF NOTHING

COLIN FIRTH

hrough a creepy forest she ran, young Emma in her white nightie; flapping and phantasmic in the gloom of an enchanted night-storm. For it was prophesied that the only way to lift the spell was for her to find the Night Garden and take the ring from the hand of the evil Lucien Lothair who ruled all Sardorf with an iron fist and a nasty climate. In order to do this she had to run through this forest, where darkness had stolen all colour – sucked it like a vampire does.

Something was chasing her. How could she know if she was running towards even greater danger? She couldn't, basically, so she just had to get on with it and run anyway and hope she was running in the right direction. On she strove, scraping her extremities on stumps of mighty oak and frowning yew – whereupon she came upon an ivied wall . . . wildly she fought for passage – and lo! By luck or grace, she fell upon a door which gave on to . . .

The Night Garden:

All moonlit and full of eerie beauty and tranquillity. Here the wind fell silent – and her pursuer seemed not to be around any more. The garden seemed to belong to a great house or castle, now mainly forgotten. All around were crumbling walls and sundials, old statues, rose trees, terrible gargoyles and stone animals. What she didn't see were little real live devilish faces poking from behind rocks. Then suddenly, standing right in front of her, there was a group of weird children. They were staring at her. One of them said, 'Who are you?' And then, before anyone could answer, this big loud honking voice from somewhere else, suddenly shouted 'Henry!!!' which is my name . . .

*

And then there wasn't any garden or children, just me sitting next to my grandma's bed, probably late for school, smelling haddock – wishing Grandma's stories didn't have to be always interrupted. You see how annoying it is? It's more than annoying, it's irksome. In fact, it was twenty to nine and I was about five minutes away from quite a big detention if I didn't go damn sharpish. I still wanted Grandma to go on, but that's always when she gets strict and says, 'No more talking, the session is closed.'

Whenever I'm listening to a story I always turn her bedside clock away so I don't see the time. She says I'm not allowed to, because I have to respect punctuality – but I always manage it. Clocks are definitely on the TTPUYL list. Things That Pants Up Your Life. Grown-ups think they are fantastic – they love minutes and they add them up like they're made of pound coins or something. Our teacher Shitty McVittie (I didn't make up the shitty part, that's what everyone calls him) . . . if you're, like, a minute late then it's like you've stolen a minute off him and so he'll steal an hour off you – after school. Even Grandma says 'chop chop' all the time, in spite of being magic. It's strange, because the place where clocks most can't get you is in her stories. Even after she's told one it's like you go into a kind of slo-mo for ages.

So when I came out of Grandma's room I already knew I'd be thinking about the rest of the story until five o'clock, and I'd probably get in trouble for daydreaming. You always come out with a load of new words and things you can carry in your head until next time – and school would be much worse without these things in your head . . . *my* head.

It can still make you go a bit mental to be torn viciously from a mysterious midnight garden to your mum shouting 'cause you didn't eat your haddock. So your life is made of half-finished stories and games that never actually get added up into a whole thing – unless it's your homework or your broccoli, then you can finish it all, however long it takes.

There's a name for all this: most people call it real life, but actually it's called the Department of Nothing. It's not just one department, but loads of mini departments. The broccoli and haddock and meat with vomity white bits get made in the Kitchen of Nothing. School is the Paper Department, where they have this special *doom-paper* so that anything you write on it is doomed. Then there's the Waiting Room of Nothing where you get told *Not now, I'm busy*, or *You're not old enough yet* and all that, and this is also where all detentions come from. And then the Department Vacuum Cleaner comes and sucks up all the second halves of stories and games, so you can never find them again. Grown-ups think they are the controllers, but they're not really, because it's the Clock Department who have all the actual power; marching grown-ups about like sergeant majors to *one two*, *one two*. Absolutely everyone lives there – unless they get to go to Grandma's room, which is the only way out of the Department – except nobody knows that, even though it's blatant. The trick is holding on to the magic to get you through the Department of Nothing. The luckiest thing is that stories come right at the beginning of the day.

Stories are my best thing in my life. OK so . . . it goes, best things: Grandma's stories, Grandma, Tintin books, the crossword in *The Chronicle*, gobstoppers, weekends and holidays. And days when Mr McVittie's away. But the main best thing is usually Grandma.

Grandma doesn't live in the world any more, because she has to live in her room. She can't do the stairs and her health isn't brilliant. She wishes she could get out, and I wish that too, but her room and the stories are better than any of the places she wants to get out to, and that's where I visit, all the time, even though she's strict and checks if I've washed my hands, and you have to ask her if you can sit down. Going to Grandma's room is like going to thousands of incredible different places. And sometimes when she's doing a story, I look at her hands, which I know are really old and kind of baggy but they make me think of places too. They've got paths that lead where you don't know, like a map of mountains and rivers of countries you wish you could get to.

And when her teeth are out and in the glass they smile at you so weirdly that sometimes you think they are going to burst out laughing about something they know and you don't.

It's not like with the woods at the bottom of our garden, 'cause when you go in them you think it's like this totally wicked place to explore and you can't see further because the bamboo is so thick, but then you always really quickly get to the fence of Mrs Lowescroft's garden, or if you go the other way, you get the fence to Crossways Road, so the whole exploration turns into a total bin. But when you go to Grandma's room, it's like exploring with no fence at the end. Except for when Mum calls you. She makes her room seem bigger than the world outside, which she wants to escape into, and I think it's sad that there's something back to front about it all. I want to escape to her room, and she wants to escape into the Department of Nothing.

Grandma tries to persuade Mum to let her go out – to church or something. That's what she talks about wanting to do, and she talks about it a lot. Mum always says she'll talk to Doctor Morgan and she'll see. Grandma said she felt like Rapunzel, but who everyone's forgotten about. She said, 'My prince would get a bit of a nasty shock if he climbed the walls and saw me now, wouldn't he? He shouldn't have been so blessed long about it.' She always says these kind of things in a cheerful voice, but she only does her cheerful voice when she's not really cheerful. It's a Mary Poppins putting-a-brave-face-on sort of thing. When she's happy she always goes all strict and pretends not to be cheerful.

She's quite a back-to-front lady really.

Max – my older brother, who's not on my list of best things – says it's completely pants to go visiting your Grandma all the time instead of having *proper friends*. He calls me the Prince of Pants and the only reason he hasn't told everyone at school is because he's too embarrassed for everyone to know that his brother's a bell-end. Well, he's fourteen and I found a picture of All Saints inside his Southampton fanzine, and he's got a mail order catalogue under his bed for girls' underwear, and he's only just stopped playing with Pokémon cards and you can't get much pantser than that, and weirdest of all, I found two Barbie dolls in with his Action Men and I think he might be doing pervy things to them.

He says stories are for poofs, but *he's* the one going on all the time about the evil shed. I've always been scared of the evil shed even if I don't know whether to believe him about it. The evil shed is the shed in our garden which no one uses, and Max says that at night the old bags of cement which are in there, turn into bollock-eating midgets. They are exactly the right height to eat your bollocks and there's no escape. The boy who used to live in our house before us, Christopher Creswell, was sitting down on the floor of the shed once, when a midget came up through a rotten floorboard and ate his entire bollocks, his nob and part of his bum, and now he has to wear special trousers. So that's why I don't go down there. It's probably not true but I don't want to chance it and neither does Max – which is funny for someone who thinks stories are for poofs.

But Max isn't even close to the top of the list of things that pants up your life. He isn't even on it really. I don't care actually; he doesn't spoil things. TTPUYL have to be much worse than just irksome. The evil shed would be, but it's probably not true and anyway I can avoid it. TTPUYL have to be hard to avoid. Like clocks. Timetables. Shitty McVittie detention. Sarcasm. This is what Shitty McVittie uses and it makes me wish the cane was legal – 'cause I'd much rather have the cane. Well, not really.

Then there's Uncle Toby. I don't even know if he's evil but he gives me the creeps, even though he used to be a vicar or dean or something, but that just makes him creepier. I think he stopped being a vicar when he got into trouble for walking down Mitford Road with his penis out. But I'm not sure about that; it might just be a rumour. He's my dad's brother, which means he's my grandma's son, and she doesn't like him either but she won't ever say why . . . so maybe it's because of his penis . . . I don't know. She's just always telling me to watch for him.

And then scariest of all, even though I've never met him, is O'Hare – of Brothers O'Hare. He's the undertaker and it's not just 'cause he's the undertaker, I mean, I'm not so pathetic as to say *oh ooey! The undertaker!* It's 'cause he's actually just scary and the undertaking parlour is scary as well. There used to be four Brothers O'Hare, but one's gone away, another one's simple, and one's dead except people say he's still there, as a ghostly partner. The back window of the parlour backs on to the railway line. Max says that *old* Mr O'Hare was found hanging in that window. It's called the Darkling Window of Death. If you go down the High Street, you have to pass *in front* of O'Hare's, and often you see O'Hare watching you through net curtains, thinking of you in his clutches. I saw him driving the Daimler with the box in the back containing Old Mr Hesperson, and you could see he was thinking, 'That's another one for my evil collection.' He first came here to Walden Bridge in 1989, which is the year I was born, and I've always wished he hadn't, because it's as if he came here specially to wait for me. It's probably nonsense, like the shed, but nonsense is a lot scarier than sense.

When I got downstairs, Mum was doing *where's my glasses*, which is where you feel guilty for standing still while Mum runs through different rooms banging drawers and things, with her glasses on her head going 'Where's my glasses?' and she's annoyed 'cause you're not as worked up as she is. She told me to get a move on 'cause I was late for school, and then wouldn't let me go because she had to tell me that she had to go to the Underwoods tonight, and Dad had his *movement* 'cause it was Thursday.

Dad hates it when she calls it a *movement*. He says it's a *society*, not a *movement*. But it's always hard for my dad to argue very well because he's so boring. It comes from not expressing himself as a child. He even used to be a morris dancer but he's stopped that now, because a counsellor told him to have more self-respect. He lives mostly in the toilet when he's not at work. Since he joined

the *movement*, my mum loses her temper and her glasses more
than she used to. The *movement* go in the woods and do wolf
business. It sounds slightly like the Cubs, except someone told me
it's all naked – which I'm not sure it can be because they do it even
in February. Mr Bowyer from the Abbey National goes, and so
does Wing Commander Devonish. I know they play drums and
Mum says they sniff each other's bottoms. That's what I heard her
saying when they were arguing. She said Dad hadn't kissed her in
five years and yet he's sniffed the area branch manager's bottom,
and he sniffs it every Thursday at seven o'clock, after the news.
No one's supposed to mention it. When it was beginning about six
months ago I answered the phone and someone said 'Can I speak
to Romulus, son of Grey Dawn?' and I told them they had the
wrong number. When I told Dad, he got angry and told me to
ruddy well tell him next time, and I said *how was I to know?*
which is answering back but Dad didn't send me to my room
because he can't be bothered, usually.

Mum was still doing *where's my glasses* when Dad came down all
ready for work. He didn't want to stop and talk – just like *I* didn't,
so he said one of his quotes to get through the room and past
everyone, like *he who riseth late must trot all day*, whatever that
means. As he was going out the door, my mum tried to stop him
to talk about the Underwoods and he did a fantastically huge
bottom-cough, and my mum went postal. My dad said he was
only expelling negative Chi. Chi is another thing he's started going
on about since the *movement*. I don't know quite what it means,
but it seems definitely to be negative.

I did get detention. When I got there McVittie had started a
biology lesson and he asked me if I wanted to take the class
because I obviously knew so much about the subject and stuff.
The thing is, at that exact same moment I was quite sure I saw a
Devil Creature from Grandma's story sitting at my desk. I know
you probably don't believe me, but there would be no point in my

lying, seeing as I'm taking so much trouble to tell you all this anyway. He was only there for a second and then he was gone and McVittie was saying, 'Look at me when I'm talking to you', and then he said, 'Don't look at me like that.'

He has a plastic skeleton called Frank, who he always asks what the punishments should be. He goes 'Let's ask Frank, shall we?' and then puts his ear to Frank's mouth. He says that Frank used to be a prurient and beastly schoolboy who was always late and got endless detentions and thus became a skeleton. Frank told him I had to stay for an hour after school. McVittie made me copy a chapter about femurs and humeruses, while he said things like 'Does anything pass through that head of yours, eh? Does anything actually interest you?' And I said things like 'Don't know, sir.' I thought about telling him that I still had to buy Grandma *The Chronicle* on the way home, and if I was late there might not be any left, and she was an old lady and she didn't have much to look forward to apart from *The Chronicle*. But how can you, when you're in the Department of Nothing, and McVittie's the Head of Department?

I got the paper, but I had to run like bugger. I went up the drainpipe into Grandma's window. She hates me coming in that way, because it scares her, so I got quite a long and very boring telling off for it, and also for sitting down without asking, and for being late, and I told her why, so she bollocked me for that as well, and besides my hands were a state . . . You just have to wait for it to be over, and then you can start the crossword. This was a whole ten minutes, and then I realized I had dropped the paper coming up the drainpipe, so I got bollocked quickly for that.

'Who are you, O weird children?' said our intrepid heroine. Their answers were always mysterious. One little girl held in her arms a Devil Creature who was grinning at Emma. 'Who looks after you?'
  'Blind Jack.'
  'Who's Jack?' said Emma, by way of enquiry. But instead of

answering, one of the children took her hand and said, 'Come.'

They led her under vaulted arches, through herbaceous avenues of rosemary and borders until they came upon a little wooden door.

Through it they entered and found themselves in a magnificent hall, full of enchanted people dressed in garb . . . which is period costume . . . except it was from loads of different periods – a ball in mid-flow; a festival of reverberant colour. But that's not the point, the point is that they were all completely still – like statues. All was uncannily quiet and dreamy and Emma was frightfully moved by this strange inert celebration.

'Who are they?' she enquired.

'We don't know them,' said a weird boy.

'Where is Jack?' asked Emma.

'He'll come,' they said.

Then Emma laid eyes on this really good-looking bloke – one of the still people – and fell instantly in love, right there. And before she had time to think 'Oh no, I'm in love with a still person,' she started to feel sleepy – like something had taken hold of her. And the next thing she knew she was asleep on a giant throne- type thing in the Great Hall.

When I woke up, the first thing I saw was some teeth grinning at me like someone taking the micky. Then I saw that they were Grandma's teeth in their glass and I was still in her room, and then I realized that there was a great sound and fury coming from the landing and it was morning and I had slept all night in Grandma's chair.

The door was being banged in a *where's my glasses* sort of way and Mum was going, 'Grandma, why is this door locked?' and, 'What's going on? This is going too far!'

I came out and Mum was purple. Grandma told her to settle down, and I just made a run for it. Mum said, 'Where do you think you're going?' And I said, 'Be on time for school.' I didn't brush my teeth or have breakfast, or anything.

*

Devil creatures have skinny grey bodies, where you can see the bones – except for their tummies and their bums, which are fat, and they have no nobs and they always have a cheeky grin on their faces, with teeth like Grandma's dentures. I did quite a good one on the back of my spelling book – probably because I kept thinking I could see them. There was one under McVittie's chair. Lynne Lassin saw it and asked me what it was, so I told her . . . and it meant telling a bit of the story . . . and you know what? She thought it was very cool indeed. And when it came lunchtime she wanted to hear the rest. I didn't mind, because I sort of, in a way, don't mind Lynne Lassin.

I carried on the story on the school field by Mr Hodkin's room. And Deborah Willis and Zena Whitchurch came and listened as well, which I quite liked, even though I don't like Zena Whitchurch. Roy Hattersley, the school's worst bully (who'll nut you if you say his whole name), loves Deborah Willis but she doesn't love him, and he hates me 'cause I'm pants at football. And now she was listening to my story and looking at me like I'm Ricky Martin, which I didn't mind either.

I wasn't sure about telling Grandma about it all, because I thought maybe I should have asked her permission or something. But when I told her, she acted like she was about seven. She clapped her hands and kept asking what they'd said, and if I'd remembered to put in the bit about the young prince, and how she wished she could have seen their faces.

I said, 'Why don't I bring you to school so you can see them?' And she said; 'You don't bring old ladies to school, Henry.' She said I would take her stories out of here and that was wonderful, because that way I'd be taking her out of her room every day. She did this big smile and said, 'I'm your muse!'

When Emma awoke, everyone in the room had moved. They were all still still but in different positions, and some were facing her like they had been looking at her. She would have liked to see that young man again, but she was feeling not quite the thing and thought she'd better get the hell out. She had seen livelier parties, let's face it.

She found a door but it was locked and the children had gone. Above the door was this inscription which said:

THE FRAGRANCE PURE DOTH PASS THIS WAY BUT ONCE A THOUSAND YEAR.

THE SOUND OF HEART MAY SOON DEPART AND NE'ER BE FOUND BY FEAR.

VAGABONDS WHO LOSE THEIR WAY, SHALL LOSE IT YET AGAIN.

AND SOMETHING SOMETHING DIE TO DANCE, AND SO SHALL DANCE IN VAIN

SO TOUCH THE KEY AND TAKE THE RING, BUT ALL MUST UNDERSTAND,

THAT IF THE HEART BUT HESITATE, THE DOG SHALL BITE THY HAND.

When she looked round for another door she saw that all the people had moved again, like musical statues.

Then she turned again, and right in front of her was the man she had fallen in love with. He was still, but in the courtly position of asking her to dance. He had a golden key glinting upon a chain round his neck and she thought, 'if the heart but hesitate', and she took his hand . . . and as soon as she did it the whole room started to move, and a waltz struck up and they were all suddenly dancing. Whirling and whirling ever faster.

And then she realized that she was no longer dancing with the same bloke, but a very old man with white eyes, who, you could see, was blind.

The next day I had about fifteen people listening to the story. It was brilliant, but I started to get so many questions that it got quite difficult to carry on, and new people kept coming and irksomely wanting to hear the beginning and some of the questions got too difficult without being able to ask Grandma. In the end, when Deborah Willis asked if Emma was scared of the blind man, I said, sort of without meaning to, 'I'll have to ask her about that.' 'Cause if you haven't already guessed, Emma and Grandma are the same person.

That really shut everybody up – for about five seconds. Then it just all broke loose, with everyone saying different things. Some of them wanted to know where she was and why they couldn't see her, and if Jack was real, too. Finally, I told them all about Grandma, and now everyone wants to meet her, which gives me a bit of an arrangement problem, because, well, now I've told them that I *can* arrange it, and they all think I'm really cool. So I decided to bust Grandma out of her room. That way she can see people's faces at last when she tells a story and they can see she's real and maybe see other things are real, too – and the Department of Nothing might not be so nothing.

Emma stood in the Night Garden, the great hall and all its denizens had vanished – and before her stood once again the weird children, but now in their midst stood also the strange blind man. This was Jack. Were he and the fine prince she'd danced with really the same bloke? She wondered secretly.

He spoke to her at length in a golden mellifluous voice, which made her feel all funny and he told her that it had been him who had been chasing her through the forest, but it was the only way to get her to the Garden and so they could all be free from the curse of Lucien Lothair. The children were all doomed to wander lost in the Garden for an extremely long time and only Emma could break the spell. All the people in the great hall were stuck like that, too. What she had to do was climb the wall of the Castle of Ballangree, which is only visible on Thursdays, and in its highest tower stood Lucien Lothair who was frozen like a statue 'cause he had accidentally put a spell on himself. Then she had to get his ring. The trouble was that as soon as you took the ring off he would come back to life and you'd be buggered. And also he was said to be so ugly that people who had had the misfortune to glance at his face for even a second had to do weeks of therapy.

Why her? she asked. ' 'Cause of the prophecy,' they said.

Anyway they waited till Thursday for the castle to become visible. When it came into view, it was quite the most terrible

thing she'd ever seen. Very high with big black spooky windows –
specially the high tower where waited for her the awful ugly
Lucien Lothair.

One by one she hugged the children and she started to climb the
tower by means of creeping vines.

Long they waited below. For long she spent up there doing
goodness knows what.

Friday came and the castle disappeared and she still hadn't
come down, and now it was obvious something bad had
happened, like she was trapped or something.

Grandma did escape, but I didn't bust her out. She bust herself
out, by ambulance.

I noticed something funny was happening to her during *where's
my glasses* on Monday morning. And then the next morning she
didn't look that brilliant – and then after school she had her
stroke. A totally new thing on the list of TTPUYL. The visit to
the hospital was like a visit to the Nothing Department of the
Department of Nothing . . . only more depressing – like a place
where everyone's been in detention for about five hundred years; a
waiting-room you get put in before O'Hare comes for you. So the
point of everything then is so you can end up coming here. It's
why you grow up and try and be good . . . so you can be like these
people – so you can end up in a dustbin like this. And then you're
in O'Hare's box, and that's it.

I went with just Mum. And she was really quiet and actually
nice – which I knew meant something had to be really wrong with
Grandma. She had a kind of secret whispering-chat with the
doctor in the corridor before we went in to see her – and when it
came time I got shaky and went into the loo for ages.

Grandma was in a big lounge full of old loonies. There was an
old lady gargling with tea and an old bloke who kept going 'Just
like that, just like that'.

Grandma's head kept moving about like she had a crick in her
neck and her face was fixed like she was surprised.

Mum said, 'Give her your flowers, Henry.' So I did.

It was ages before she said anything, and then she said – and I remember it exactly – 'How nice. They are so much nicer this way – on the inside without all that trouble . . . they ought to have more like that – I'm glad you gave them to me on the inside.'

Mum squeezed my shoulder. Grandma asked if we wanted to meet her friends and that Mr Hodges had come back from India specially and she said he was an awfully nice man but his toes were too long, which troubled him terribly. My Mum said, 'Why don't you rest?' And Grandma got annoyed then and started saying, 'Rest of my life! Rest! Silly woman! Rest of my life!' I tried to give her the paper and Mum tried to stop me doing it but Grandma didn't take it anyway. She just smiled at me and said, 'Lovely boy – they didn't believe I had a cousin . . .' And then she shouted out, 'Come and meet my cousin Henry, who brings the paper!' and I tried to tell her that I was her grandson and that she had been ill but she was better now. She went quiet for a minute and said, 'You have to be ill if you want to get better.'

I bumped into Roy Hattersley by the school gate with loads of his mates, and then I saw Max was one of them. And it was blatant what must have happened 'cause Roy Hattersley started to say something about fairy stories, and Max must have done a snider and told him about Grandma to suck up to Roy Hattersley, and maybe too because he wanted to seem like he was too cool to give a nob about Grandma, I don't know. But when Luke Burns (who's like a three foot feeb but hangs round with Hattersley so no one can ever get him) started doing loony faces I tried to hit him but I got nutted by Max. It really bloody hurt, in case you've never been nutted. It makes your face feel really far away from your brain. Everyone went, 'Look, he's nearly crying!', which I wasn't, I was probably just red from being nutted. Then when I was still on the ground Roy Hattersley started doing the loony face and then Max nutted him, too, and said, 'Leave him alone!' It's always like that. Max can nut me but no one else can. Anyway, then Roy

Hattersley nutted Max and everyone went away, except Max, who came up and grabbed me by my ears and went, 'Fucking pack it in, all this Grandma stuff, OK?' and you could tell he was nearly crying too. Blatantly.

When I got in I saw Grandma's wheelchair in the hall. I ran upstairs calling her, but I could hear all these upset voices coming out of Grandma's room, with Mum going 'Not now Henry!' and Grandma like she was going to cry, going 'Leave me alone you wicked girl!' I shouldn't have gone in, but I did. Grandma was standing, and Mum was trying to hold her up by the waist. Grandma didn't have any pants on . . . I saw her bum, which looked like a rhino's bum. I ran out again but I couldn't hide in my room 'cause Max was there, so I went to the bathroom. Dad was just coming out, and he looked like maybe he was nearly crying, too. He just said, 'Better out than in', and walked past. I locked myself in and the whole bathroom smelled of negative Chi. A mixture of newspaper and number twos. I sprayed lemon zest and sat on the edge of the bath, but it still really stank. Mum knocked on the door and said I could go in and see Grandma but I said I was doing a poo and she went away.

I went in to see her ages later. I was a bit scared. I didn't know what it would be like trying to talk to her, but I really really wanted to know how the story ended. It was a bit creepy: 'cause she was in bed and only her bedside light was on and I thought she was asleep, but when I got close to her she opened her eyes quickly like a vampire, and looked at me. I said 'Bugger' really loudly and it's the only time I've ever said that in front of Grandma and she didn't tell me off, which was even sadder than her sitting with loonies. I said, 'I came to sit with you for a while, Grandma.' And she said something which was nonsense but it made me feel weirdy anyway: she said, 'That's another ring on your tree of shadows.' I didn't know if it was a secret message, or what. Anyway it seemed very serious and it made me say what normally I would have been embarrassed to, which was, 'I love you, Grandma,' and she said,

'Two more rings.' And then she smiled this huge smile, which started out really nice but then it kept getting bigger until I could see all her dentures and then I realized she wasn't smiling, she was poking out her teeth. She reached up and put them in the glass. This always means no more talking. No more talking. The session is at an end. Anyway it didn't look much like I was going to find out what happened with Lucien Lothair.

She closed her eyes, but her teeth carried on smiling in the glass.

The next day all the people who had listened to the stories, because I couldn't tell the rest, turned into piss-takers, and started saying there was no such thing as my grandma and that the stories were pants anyway – and called me a fairy boy. All except for Lynne Lassin, who said she was my friend anyway. Lynne said maybe Lucien Lothair had put a spell on Grandma because she was giving away too many secrets. I said it's not a spell, it's just how old people always get. She said maybe it's always a spell.

What I reckon is: everyone's a loony. However normal anyone seems, deep down inside they're actually mental, every single person in the world and the whole of your life you have to learn not to seem mental to other people, who are all mental, too. Deep down you speak this different language – you talk in a loony language which doesn't talk in your voice, I don't know. Maybe it screams really loudly or something. I mean we're all born mental aren't we? If you think how babies act – we really don't stop being like that. Everyone wants to scream loudly, and grab things without asking and break them, but it's not allowed is it? So what you have to have is a kind of anti-mental translator-device, which translates all your mentalness into normal speech - and you've got to learn to use it, and it's got to be working properly – or you get found out for being a loony.

Like Grandma.

*

A funny thing happened when I went in to see her with the paper. She lay in bed hardly talking or if she did it was just nonsense. I still sat with her – 'cause it's better than the Department of Nothing and anyway maybe she'll get suddenly better. I know she probably won't, but I decided to do the crossword out loud in case it gave her a clue about words and helped to repair her brain . . . And she gave me a clue while she was asleep! A crossword clue I mean. It was really weird and you might not believe me but I really swear it's true! I was trying to do 9 down which was 9 letters, first letter L and I thought it was LUMINOUS but then her voice said, 'It's LUDICROUS'. I didn't see her lips move and she didn't open her eyes or anything. And when I spoke to her, she didn't reply. She seemed asleep. It might have been a coincidence and she might have just been saying 'it's ludicrous' in her sleep because she thought of something ludicrous. But the thing is, it *was* ludicrous! That was the right answer!

When I got home the next day Mum and Dad were arguing about Grandma. Mum was saying that the old lady would exhaust us into the grave and outlive us all. I couldn't hear what Dad said.

Grandma's room was getting really stinky now. It had always been a bit stinky but this was more toilety now – and it hadn't been irksome before, but it was now. When I went in, she suddenly sat up in bed and said, 'Where am I?'

I said, 'You're here in your room, Grandma,' and then she grabbed my arm and said, 'I'm over there. I'm over there.' And she pointed to her photo on the wall – of her as a young girl (Emma, in other words), and I said, 'Yes that's right, that's you.' And then she pointed to her dressing gown on the back of the door and said, 'There, that's me – there I am.' And her hand got tighter on me, which hurt. Then she started saying my name over and over again, like 'Henry, Henry, Henry' like that: 'Henry, Henry, Henry'. I told her she was hurting me but she was shouting really loudly now. And she started saying nutty things again, like, 'Put my voice under a walnut tree!!! Henry, Henry, Henry.'

That's when Mum came rushing in already all red and worked up going, 'Henry, what have you done?' Then I got free and ran to the door. It's funny 'cause then Mum's face changed and she went over and hugged Grandma quietly and calmed her down. She rocked her like she was two years old. When I came out I saw Dad had been standing at his door listening. He shut it when he saw me.

Later, in my room, Mum did this speech, where she had this patient wise voice that she always uses for talking bollocks, where it's like, 'When you're older you'll understand this is not bollocks.' She said that Grandma needed me to let go of her. Like I had to say goodbye and it would be like permission for her to go. I said I could see what she was up to and that Mum and Dad and Max and everyone might want her dead but I wasn't going to help her conspiracy.

The next morning I heard Mum say to Grandma, 'Are you finding it hard to let go?' and Grandma said, 'Let go of what?' I don't know why they don't just get O'Hare in to measure her up and then hit her over the head with a frying pan.

That evening I fell asleep in Grandma's room and I dreamt that I was doing the crossword again while she was asleep and I heard that funny voice from Grandma. Then I realized in the dream that it wasn't Grandma at all but her dentures talking by themselves in the glass. They introduced themselves as 'A fine set of molars, eight incisors, central and lateral, upper and lower, and four canines with a perfectly sound bite. How do you do.' And they had this really strong Scottish accent.

I asked them if they could finish Grandma's story and they said yes, but not yet. I said why not, and they said 'cause we hadn't got to the end. And I asked when they would tell me, and they said that would be up to me. Then I realized that this was more or less what Mum said about saying goodbye – and I got angry with the teeth and threatened to pour their water out.

I said, 'Are you saying she's definitely going to die?' and they said, 'I don't know, I'm a set of teeth, not the Oracle of Bloody Delphi!'

I was about to leave, when they gave me this mysterious instruction. They said that if I wanted to hear the rest of the story I had to make sure that they weren't buried with Grandma and if I kept them separate they'd finish the story – and that was a promise.

Next day I was in a really crap mood and decided no way was I going to see Grandma any more because everyone was blatantly trying to trick me into making her die and it was like I was the only one who could do it. And anyway what was the point – I mean she couldn't even talk any more except like the Mad Hatter.

I got into such a crap mood that it made me really brave, 'cause I didn't care, so I did an amazing thing: Roy Hattersley told me to piss off by the terrapin huts and so I told him to eff himself and he grabbed me and told me to apologize and before he could nut me I knocked him down. And no one did anything – not one thing!

I felt like the most powerful person in the world, like Colossus, who can turn his flesh to steel, so when I got home I punched Max. But he punched me back, right in the eye.

I've had all these speeches from Mum about how she can't cope any more and if I'm not going to see Grandma then she has to go in a home. She's the one who has to clean her and stuff – which means her bum.

I said I'd see her, and I knew I should have, but I still didn't.

It was another thing without any explanation. I just knew when it happened. I was on the railway line going to school, and it was a windy day, and a bit rainy, and I suddenly got the smell of Grandma's room in a gust of wind. I didn't even think about it; I turned round and ran home. I remember now, I was shouting but can't remember what. But I was thinking how, because it had only just happened, you could go back in time, like rewind – 'cause you wouldn't have to go back that far.

Mum must have just left 'cause the house was locked, so I went up the drainpipe into Grandma's room. She was looking like the cover of *Goosebumps*. Her eyes and her mouth were open and her skin was all stretched and her head was kind of back on the pillow. I stopped looking at her and ran out and right out of the house down to Stoney Lane where the woods start. It was all slippery on the gravel from wet leaves and I kept falling over. It was only about nine o'clock, so I wasn't going to bump into any naked bank managers or my dad in the woods. I got soaked going through the trees.

I could see Mrs Bluck's cottage and I thought it's not fair that she's still alive. I suddenly got a strange idea that Mrs Bluck didn't have blood in her veins but just tea. Then I didn't think for a long time. I tried to think, but instead I just kept seeing my classroom in my imagination – and I could hear a song by Westlife coming from somewhere – and then it was *Teddy Bear's Picnic* and it made me laugh because I thought of Wing Commander Devonish and you really would get a big surprise. And then I cried. For ages.

I went home in the afternoon and I was really hungry. My mum knew that I knew when she saw me. She hugged me and I cried again.

She said, 'She looked lovely – so peaceful. She had a beautiful calm smile.'

I knew that was a lie for a start and it made me stop crying.

I said, 'Can I see her?' and she said no 'cause she was gone and she didn't think it was appropriate at my age to see a dead person. This started me going quite postal. 'Gone where?' I asked her.

'She's gone to O'Hare's, Henry. We're going to bury her on Tuesday.'

I said, 'Were her teeth in?' and Mum said '*What?*'

This is where you'll think I'm mental – I had this thing where I knew the dream was important. After I'd cried by the Stoney Lane

I'd started to think, and I'd thought about the dream and how the teeth had said to rescue them from being buried with Grandma, how they said they'd tell me the end of the story. And I'd remembered too how Grandma had told me to put her voice under a walnut tree, and it all seemed like an important message that I'd buggered up. First I hadn't said goodbye to Grandma and she'd had to go without me, and now I'd let the teeth already go with her to O'Hare's. And there was only one way I could get them back now.

I stood for ages, not quite in front of O'Hare's but a bit to the side and I knew I couldn't do it in a million years. What would I do, just go in there and say, 'Oh hi, Mr O'Hare, can I have my Grandma's teeth back?' The only other way was the Darkling Window of Death, and I wasn't exactly going to do that either.

The drainpipe was quite wobbly but I reckoned, if I even thought about it, *forget it*. And anyway, she would be buried in two days and at least it was daylight and this way I wouldn't have to talk to O'Hare.

One of the panes was boarded up from the inside and it was quite easy to push open.

I don't remember much about going in 'cause I was so scared I could nearly have started laughing like the Riddler out of *Batman*. I remember thinking for a second that I was a total superhero. First I'd punched Roy Hattersley and now I'd climbed into the Darkling Window of Death . . . and then I felt number twos coming on. The room was empty and really spooksville. I must have gone out and down some stairs. I think I just followed myself. I don't know how long it took me but I obviously found the right room.

The coffin was open and I kept thinking of the music from *Pet Rescue* to stop myself from being scared but then that started to sound creepy and then I'd get so scared that I almost wasn't scared, if you know what I mean. I was probably a bit mental to be honest. The room was quite darkish but I could see which end her face was. I just closed my eyes and put my hand right in her mouth.

Her teeth wouldn't come out. They were completely stuck. Then I opened my eyes and saw that it wasn't Grandma but Mrs Wharburton who helps with Oxfam. I didn't even know she was dead.

I turned around and saw that, like a bell-end, I hadn't noticed that there was another coffin in the room.

This really was Grandma. And actually she really did look peaceful and almost smiling. So maybe Mum wasn't lying. So why wasn't it 'appropriate' to see her then? Anyway I got the teeth quite easily and that's when the door opened and O'Hare came in.

I don't know who screamed louder. This was like blatant pant-load hair-fall-out time. I might not have been able to scream if he hadn't have screamed. But he did . . . he screamed the place down. I'm surprised no one came. Actually someone did but only from upstairs.

He was still shaking in his office when he gave me a cup of tea.

I was sitting in this great big comfy leather armchair and he had made me put a blanket round me – I don't know why – and he said (and I think it was Irish, I'm not sure), 'I bet you had to stick your courage through a stick pin to come in there, did you?' He was smiling.

He tried to give me a gobstopper out of his jar but they were all stuck together. 'I hate how they get like that,' he said. 'Sorry.'

Another old man came in and said, 'Will you be needing anything more?'

O'Hare asked me if I wanted more tea, and I asked for some water, and the old man went out.

'That's Ned. He helps me out around here.' I wondered if it was really the ghostly old Mr O'Hare.

'I'll tell you what, you gave me the fright of my bloody life,' he said. 'It's not every day I hear knocking about back there. People don't break into places like this, not since Burke and Hare. No relation.'

He kept asking how I was feeling and I kept saying fine and he said I was made of sterner stuff than him, then.

He asked me what it was all about – was it curiosity? And I said it was. He told me that where he comes from they wouldn't let a little lad run around trying to figure out what's being kept from him. Everyone gets to say goodbye and they have a kind of party and the dead person gets invited and you all get a last look, something to keep in here like a photo, and he tapped his head. 'It's not the same here,' he said. 'Everyone had to creep around like it's a big dirty secret.'

I told him about how Grandma told stories, and how she never got to the end of the last one. I told him loads of stuff in fact. I don't know why, but it all just came out. I didn't tell him about the teeth though, in case he thought I was mental.

Grandma was going to be first up on Tuesday – to be buried, I mean – ten o'clock. Which meant the same limo deposits our lot and has to be back at nine-thirty for Mrs Wharburton. The Wilcoxes are at twelve ('And you thought this was a quiet town?' he said). Mr Craddock he's three o'clock ('He wants a Mercedes Benz, bless him.'). Four shows on one day. That's what he called them – shows. He said he was just a stage manager and the mourners were the actors – temperamental. He told me to come and see him again sometime and not wait to be brought in a box. He'd have fresh gobstoppers.

It's strange but when I came out I felt better than I'd felt for absolutely ages.

I went straight home and filled up a glass of water and went to the bathroom and put the teeth in and waited. I waited for quite a long time.

But they didn't speak, and by now I knew they wouldn't, and it had been a piss-take. The whole thing. A big racket. Doing what you're supposed to do, being rewarded for being brave . . . It's all bollocks to get you to do it. Like Mum's wise voice . . . That's why it's in all the stories, to hypnotize you into thinking you'll get something out of it – like there's a bargain. But there isn't a bargain. You pass tests, which in stories always end up with you becoming king or Lord Mayor or you rescue a princess or find a pot of gold – but in the Department of Nothing you do it all and nothing happens. Your Grandma dies and everything stays the same. And you never get to hear the end of the story. I knew we had a walnut tree, so I decided to bury them there. It's not 'cause I thought anything would happen. It was just 'cause . . . what else was I going to do with them? Put them back?

During the funeral I kept trying to think up an ending for the story. I still haven't managed to. I'm sure Emma will have got out of that tower, but bugger if I know how. Maybe she gets the ring and Lucien Lothair turns out to be a really nice bloke and gives her a cup of tea – and then she goes off happily ever after with Blind Jack who's not blind any more . . .'cause it's a story. Actually, you know what? Jack could rescue her, 'cause with being blind it wouldn't make any difference, the castle being invisible! That's not bad is it? So maybe that's the ending.

I was thinking that if I told a story about *my* life, everyone would boo at the end.

So it's back to the Department of Nothing. The house is calmer now. Dad's gone back to morris dancing instead of his *movement* and that calms Mum down a lot. Mrs Foster reported the *movement* for moral turpitude and they all got arrested. I go and see O'Hare quite a lot now. He tells jokes. They're not that funny, but if you don't laugh it hurts his feelings. Going in there makes Roy Hattersley more scared of me. O'Hare told me I had one or two tales to tell myself now, and maybe I should try them out. So that's what I just did.

And the session is now closed.

I'M THE ONLY ONE

ZADIE SMITH

She was my sister and she was sleeping late. She's a lot older than me and at the time she was about to break into films, directing them, so everybody was indulging her. She was the only girl, too. If something didn't work out in her life and she had to come home for a while, it was a big deal. It mattered more than if I fucked up in one way or another. When Kelly was at home you had to creep around the house and keep your voice down even if it was the middle of the afternoon. Our mother's Canadian – I don't know why I say that, except maybe it helps explain her opinion about Kel: *Smarts Needs Special*. It was this little crappy phrase she had made up and it meant that clever people, people with special talents, need special treatment. Like they have a disease. You have to meet the Canadian side of our family to understand how cute she thinks that phrase is. I remember thinking that it was bullshit when I was fourteen and it still smells bad now. But to my mother, Kelly was this asteroid that had landed in our lives and no one knew how she got there or what size hole she was going to leave. I've never been very good at school, and Pete, our older brother, is the same. Then along comes Kelly. So my mother had us all pussy-footing around like a family mime troupe, waving our hands, taking our shoes off.

I'm thinking of a particular morning. I was creeping around trying to make a silent breakfast, opening cupboards quietly, acting like I didn't exist. I'd been doing it for a couple of weeks since Kelly got back. It felt like I'd been doing it my whole life. The situation came about because earlier in the year Kelly had moved in with this guy called Aidan. They bought furniture, the whole works. Then she cheated on him and he left her. Apart from Kelly being back in our house, it was also a shame because Aidan was the only man she ever went out with, before or since, whom I've had any time for whatsoever. Aidan was a top man, a good guy. The thing I liked about him was that he was smart, but he didn't need so much of this special treatment. He was Irish, from Dublin, and he could be funny, he could talk football and he liked to see other people's mouths open and close besides his own. It was good knowing someone like him. I needed it; what with Dad not being around, Pete married and gone; and me in a house full of women. That was the year I was praying for a few more inches on my height and shaving the bare space under my nose hoping that something might turn up. So it was good to know Aidan, six foot three and hairy as a bear. He was hairy back and front and Kelly would tease him about it, and he would laugh her off or tell her she could do with losing a few pounds which, between you and me, was nothing but the truth. She was a fat little thing back then. And he went and told her, straight-up; didn't care that she was almost, sort of, famous. He told it how it was. That was the way he loved her. She never appreciated it, though, and then she had this fling with some pretty boy in the film industry. But you could see she realized what she'd lost when he left her because she slunk back home and holed herself up in Pete's old room that I'd been using for weights. She took it over and lay in there all day in the dark curled up in a stinking duvet watching old black-and-white films. I remember asking her, 'Why can't you use your own bedroom?' She had a small bedroom upstairs that used to be covered wall to wall in her school friends' graffiti until she went off to university and Mum whitewashed the whole thing. I asked her again, 'Why can't you use your own bedroom, that's what it's there for.' She said, 'I can't sleep and work in the same room. I need a *study*.' She said it as if a study is one of those things you can't do without, like clean water. I said, 'But I need to exercise.' She said, 'You're fourteen. Your body isn't even developed. The only thing you need to do is stop beating the bishop before you go blind.' This was classic Kelly. She always knew how to make you feel four inches long in every direction.

So she came back, and I had to move out all my weights and spread them around the house wherever there was space. I put the bench press in my room along with the free weights. I put the Abdominizer in the lounge. I stuck the chin-up bar at the top of the stairs which lead down to the front door. And even though I was pissed off with Kelly for taking the spare room, having the weights all over the place did make it more like circuit training and doing circuits made me feel I was Rocky. It's what they do in the middle of *Rocky* movies; a two-minute sequence to show that over a number of months he got fit and pumped up. You pray for that kind of speedy, magic-time when you're working out, the same way you wish your adolescence would pass like it does in a TV serial: a school scene, a sex scene and a graduation. It's slower and faster than that. And some events become still and solid, and turn into a *thing* in your life, an object like a lampshade or an ironing board. They hang around; you could reach out and touch them. This day I'm trying to tell you about is like that.

So: my exercise. I'd start in my room, and do about four sets of twenty. Then I'd run downstairs and start on the Abdominizer. If you've never seen one, they're like half of something fun, half a bike or half a swing. You lie down in them and you do sit-ups. You spend good money trying to make sit-ups something else. In the end, a sit-up is a sit-up. But I'm as big a mug as anyone and I'd try and do two hundred sit-ups on that thing in sets of fifty. The pain was very bad. So I'd think of something that pissed me off, usually Kelly, and the anger would help me push out the last fifty. I wanted to show her that I could develop if I wanted to. Because there was always this thing between her and me that we were both kind of overweight, and always telling the other one that they were obsessed with it. So if Kelly didn't eat lunch, I'd be like 'For fuckssake, you're not *dieting* are you? You're not even *fat*.' Trying to make her feel pathetic. And if she caught me with the Abdominizer (it was hers, she never used it), she'd say something like, 'Jono, you're not even *developed* yet. It's just puppy fat, for fuckssake, give it a chance.' We used to swear like troopers. And we liked to make each other feel bad about things. Around that time she was also giving me a lot of shit about girls. All about how she didn't want me to sleep with girls because I was too young and under-developed. She was more a mother in that way. And the fact that I started exercising, working-out – that really irritated her. She'd find me with a weight in my hand and start shouting. She'd say I was a boy trying to be a man too soon. I know I'm meant to be the stupid one, but I could work out for myself that it was all about Aidan, not me. Most days, I just did my best to avoid her.

Anyway, when I'd finished the sit-ups, I'd normally do about twenty-five press-ups before going to the top of the stairs and doing my chin-ups. The way the bar was positioned meant I could see people passing in the street. That was deliberate. To be honest, I've never been a natural exercise freak and you need something to distract you, take you away from the *reality* of it, otherwise you go mad. So I'd watch people without them knowing and then occasionally someone would spot me through the glass pane in the door, spot my head going up and down, and you could see them double-take, trying to work out what was going on. From out there it looked like magic. Levitation. A nice way to end a heavy-going routine.

Now, on this morning that I'm talking about, I really wanted to see the street and pull my own weight – I didn't care about the rest. I skipped the press-ups, went straight to the bar and hooked my hands round it. I don't know how much you know about it, but when you do a chin-up you meet your own fingers in a position you don't usually come across. With the nails facing you, like somebody's else's hands are reaching out to touch your face. I remember looking at my fingers, all white, all the blood gone travelling elsewhere, and thinking that this was OK, doing this with your fingers. Do you know what I mean? It wasn't holding a camera or writing a concerto, but it was OK. It made them tingle. It got the blood going, and that's the whole point, isn't it? Whatever gets the blood pumping. Whatever makes you feel high; unreal.

And then I saw Cole coming down the street, heading for our front gate. You couldn't miss Cole because he was black, six foot nine and a half inches and fourteen years old. I had only met Cole a month earlier, after I joined this new school for my re-takes. I failed practically everything the summer before and it was one of those schools where they cram a lot of stuff into a little time to get you ready to re-take your exams in December. Cole was re-taking practically everything too. But weirdly, between the two of us, we'd managed to fail a lot of totally different subjects. I remember thinking that was hilarious, at the time. Two people being so stupid, but with no overlap. Stupid in two completely different ways. So Cole and I were only in one class together, Performing Arts, a course that had a lot less performing in it than we'd hoped. We'd both taken it because we thought it'd be an easy option. In fact, it was mostly reading about the history of the cinema and the theatre. Really dry stuff. I was bored out of my mind until Cole turned up, late and slow as usual, two weeks into the course. Six foot nine and a half. I remember when I first saw him I couldn't believe it. I asked him all the usual questions. I said, is it weird being that tall? Do you have to buy different clothes? Are all your family like that? And Cole said, 'No, mate, I'm the only one.' You could tell how often he got asked the lame stuff I'd just asked him. I didn't want to bore him, but it's a hard thing to get used to. Harder than you'd imagine. It still hadn't worn off when I saw him loping up the path, a magic giant, while I levitated, a genie. He spotted me, and looked surprised, and I laughed and dropped down from the bar. For some reason I always felt so happy to see Cole. So happy! And this was the first time he'd come round to my house so it was like a stamp on our new friendship. It was a green light. I didn't want to be a big girl about it, but to be honest with you, I kind of skipped down the steps.

'Whatsup Cole?' I said, opening the door. I greeted him how we always greeted each other. In ways I can't really describe; low handshakes and a kind of slouchy walk we picked up off MTV, the videos, the rap shows. We liked to be American about it. But it was still very personal to us. We added something to it, is what I'm trying to say.

Cole grinned like a madman. 'Hey, brother, you were floating! Where's your magic carpet?'

I pointed to the chin-up bar.

'Oh, I see. Getting fit for the ladies,' he said, even though I had no success with the ladies and he knew it. 'Can I come in?'

I said, 'Yeah, but be quiet on the stairs. My sister's asleep. And be careful, bro. You know these ceilings are low! Good to see you, man.'

We went up to the lounge and talked about some stuff, stuff that was happening in school. Cole was one of those people who's always trying to put the best spin on things. All you got from him was, 'Of *course* she likes you', and 'Don't worry about *that*, he won't give you any trouble', so by the end of a conversation with Cole you sort of felt you were the king of the world, even though he was the one with his head in the heavens. I remember he was talking, flattering me and everything, and I kept looking at him and feeling this strange pride, as if the fact that he was so tall was something to do with me. Then I got this burning urge to show him to Kelly.

'Wait here,' I said, 'I want to get somebody. Just a minute. Just stay here.'

I knocked on Kelly's door a few times but of course she didn't answer so I pushed it open a crack. It smelt like shit in there. I don't think the sheets had been changed since she moved back. She was asleep but she had an old black and white film that she'd been watching, *The Philadelphia Story*, playing on the video. Sometimes she'd watch this film three times in a day. If I walked in she'd always say something like, 'Now, you see Jimmy Stewart? There was a man. There was a tall, handsome man.' Or if the other guy was on screen, she'd be like, 'That's how a man should wear a suit. Can you see the cut of that suit?' I didn't give a shit about the film or anybody in it. Kelly was always telling me about stuff I didn't give a shit about. But for some reason, I wanted her to see Cole. I didn't know if it was me or her who would get a buzz out of it. Maybe neither of us. But I wanted it. I was persistent. I said, 'Kelly! Kelly, I want to show you something.'

She didn't move. But I kept on. I wanted her to see Cole so much it surprised me. She was asking me, 'What is it? Just tell me what it is. What is it?' But I wanted her to see Cole without warning, the way I first saw him, coming into a room like a moving statue – something great and still that had been given life. Finally, Kelly moved her great big fat butt out of that duvet, but she was only wearing a pair of knickers. 'OK,' she said, 'OK, I'm up. This better be good.' You're fourteen. You don't want to see your sister naked. Not under any circumstances. I told her that. I said, 'Kel, you've got to put something on.'

She cut her eyes at me and moaned a bit more, but in the end she put a dressing gown on and followed me into the lounge. She kept on muttering, 'This better be good', and I kept on telling her to shut up and see.

I know that people say *I won't ever forget your face when such and such happened* . . . and half the time they don't mean it, but I *mean* it. I can see her face now if I close my eyes. It was fantastic! I saw this amazing curve, like a piece of fruit, right across her face. She smiled like I hadn't seen her do since she moved back, like I'd never seen her do before. I don't want to say I won't see it again. That would be a jinx. There's a line from that film she was always watching – *The time to make your mind up about people is . . . never*. Generally, I don't enjoy films like that – nothing happening, everything slowed down – but I always thought she had a point, the thin-lipped woman who says that. And it's not my business to say it won't ever happen again – what do I know? – but it *felt* like a one-off. It wasn't only the smile, it was her eyes as well, which were watery like she wanted to cry. A week earlier I'd read about the Lumière brothers – so was this what they looked like, the people who saw those first films, in Paris or wherever? In the dark – watching the flat people walk, watching the flat trains move and the fake steam – were they smiling? Kelly's face. I said I'll never forget it and I won't. Then it changed. As if she'd remembered something she'd forgotten; leaving the lights on or the key in the door; and then this look I'm talking about was gone.

There was silence for a while and then in the gap I said, 'Look how tall my friend Cole is!'

Cole said, 'Hello.' I could tell he was embarrassed, Kelly in her dressing gown and everything with these fat calves on display. He just looked at the floor.

She said, 'Fucking hell, you're *tall*.'

Cole laughed.

'How tall *are* you? Six seven?'

'Six nine and a half,' said Cole, and he shrugged as if he wished that just at this moment it wasn't true. I wondered whether he'd felt that before.

Kelly shook her head and whistled. 'And how old are you?'

'Fourteen.'

Kelly whistled again. 'That's unbelievable. Are the rest of your family like that?'

'No, I'm the only one. My Mum's only five seven.'

'Well, you're a very big fellow, Cole.'

'Yep.'

'Do they make you play basketball at school?' asked Kelly, which was the stupidest question ever and kind of racist and I was worried Cole would be upset. But instead he grinned.

'They try but I'm no good, mate. I'm terrible.'

'Six foot nine and a half. Fucking *hell*.'

She reached over to touch his elbow and then moved back. It was a weird thing to do. Her eyes were full of water. 'Fourteen years old. I didn't think they made them like you any more. You're a very big fellow, Cole,' she said again like a broken record.

Cole looked at the floor, getting more and more awkward and I wished to God I'd never brought her in the room in the first place.

'Yes, I am. I'm big. I don't know how it happened, it just happened.'

Then out of the blue Kelly said, 'You know, I make films.'

I see now that she had to get the conversation back over to her side of the fence, to where she knew what everything looked like, how everything felt and what everything meant. I do it a lot myself these days. But at the time, I hated her for it. She couldn't let him just *be*.

Cole raised his eyebrows. 'Really?'

'Yeah, really. I'm about to make my first feature film, would you believe.'

Cole said, 'Cool, cool, I believe it,' but he looked like he didn't.

Then she said, 'Well, a man your height, I'll have to find a place for you in my next film, won't I?'

Cole shrugged again, like it would be nice if she did, but then again it would be just fine if she didn't. Such a big man, Cole, but fluid as water. To look at him you'd think he couldn't fit anywhere – actually he fitted everywhere. That's how I remember him.

'I can think of a hundred roles,' she said, 'I can think of a hundred things you could be.'

She said that, and then she pulled her dressing gown round her and sort of nodded to herself and left, and in a few minutes I could hear the film starting up again, from the beginning with the opening title music.

'She's nice,' said Cole, because he always tried to say the right thing. 'Let's go upstairs,' he said, 'spin some tunes!'

I think Cole did me a great service that day. But every time I try to pin it down, all I have is the image of his long, sleek calves in front of me as he climbed the stairs, his massive hand on the banister.

NIPPLEJESUS

NICK HORNBY

They never told me what it was, and they never told me why they might need someone like me. I probably wouldn't have taken the fucking job if they had, to tell you the truth. And if I'd been clever, I would have asked them on the first day, because looking back on it now, I had a few clues to be going on with: we were all sat around in this staff-room type place, being given all the do's and don't's, and it never occurred to me that I was just about the only male under sixty they'd hired. There were a few middle-aged women, and a lot of old gits, semi-retired, ex-Army types, but there was only one bloke of around my age, and he was tiny – little African geezer, Geoffrey, who looked like he'd run a mile if anything went off. But sometimes I forget what I look like, if you know what I mean. I was sitting there listening to what this woman was saying about flash photography and how close people were allowed to get and all that, and I was more like a head than a body, sort of thing, because if you're listening to what someone's saying that's what you are, isn't it? A head. A brain, not a body. But the point of me – the point of me here, in this place, for this job – is that I'm six foot two and fifteen stone. It's not just that, either, but I look . . . well, handy, I suppose. I look like I can take care of myself, what with the tattoos and the shaved head and all that. But sometimes I forget. I don't forget when I'm eyeballing some little shitbag outside a club, some nineteen-year-old in a two-hundred-quid jacket who's trying to impress his bird by giving me some mouth; but when I'm watching something on TV, like a documentary or something, or when I'm putting the kids to bed, or when I'm reading, I don't think, you know, fucking hell I'm big. Anyway, listening to this woman, I forgot, so when she told me I'd be in the Southern Fried Chicken Wing looking after number 49, I never asked her 'Why me? Why do you need a big bloke in the Southern?' I just trotted off, like a berk. I never thought for a moment that I was on some sort of special mission.

I took this job because I promised Lisa I'd give up the night work at the club. It wasn't so much the hours – ten till three Monday to Thursday, ten till five Friday and Saturday, club closed on Sunday. OK, they fucked the weekends up, and I never saw the kids in the morning, but I could pick them up from school, give them their tea, and Lisa didn't have to worry about childcare or anything. She works in a dentist's near Harley Street, decent job, nice boss, good pay, normal hours, and with me being off all day, we could manage. I mean, it wasn't ideal, 'cos I never really saw her – by the time the kids were down and we'd had something to eat, it was time for me to put the monkey-suit on and go out. But we both sort of knew it was just a phase, and I'd do something else eventually, although fuck knows what. Never really thought about that. She asks me sometimes what I'd do if I had the choice, and I always tell her I'd be Tiger Woods – millions of dollars a week, afternoons knocking a golf ball about in places like Spain and Florida, gorgeous blonde girlfriends (except I never mention that bit). And she says, no, seriously, and I say, I am being serious, and she says, no, you've got to be realistic. So I say, well what's the point of this game, then? You're asking me what I'd do if I had the choice, and I tell you, and then you tell me I haven't got the fucking choice. So what am I supposed to say? And she says, but you're too old to be a professional golfer – and she's right, I'm thirty-eight now – and you smoke too much. (Like you can't play fucking golf if you smoke.) Choose something else. And I say, OK, then, I'll be fucking Richard Branson. And she says, well you can't just start by being Richard Branson. You have to do something first. And I say, OK, I'll be a bouncer first. And she gives up.

I know she means well, and I know she's trying to get me to think about my life, and about getting older and all that, but the truth is, I'm thirty-eight, I've got no trade and no qualifications, and I'm lucky to get a job headbutting cokeheads outside a club. She's great, Lisa, and if you think about it, even her asking the question shows that she loves me and thinks the world of me, because she really does think I've got choices, and someone else is going to have as much faith in me as she does. She wants me to say, oh, I'd like to run a DIY shop, or I'd like to be an accountant, and the next day she'd come back with a load of leaflets, but I don't want to run a DIY shop, and I don't want to be an accountant. I know what my talent is: my talent is being big, and I'm making the most of it. If anyone asks her what I do, she says I'm a security consultant, but if I'm around when she says it, I laugh and say I'm a bouncer. I don't know what she'd say now. Probably that I'm an art expert. You watch. Give her two weeks and she'll be on at me to write to *Antiques Roadshow*. I don't know what world she lives in sometimes. I think it's something to do with the dentist's. She meets all these people, and they're loaded, and as thick as me, half of them, and she gets confused about what's possible and what's not.

But like I said, it wasn't the hours at the club. There were a couple of nasty moments recently, and I told her about them because they frightened me, so of course she did her nut, and I promised her I'd pack it in. See, the trouble is now, it doesn't matter how handy you are. I mean, half of those kids who went down Casablanca's, I literally could pick them up by the neck with one hand, and when you can do that . . . Put it this way, I didn't need to change my underpants too often. (I do anyway, though, every day, in case you're thinking I'm an unhygienic bastard.) But now everyone's tooled up. No one says, I'm going to have you. They all say, I'm going to cut you, or I'm going to stab you, and I'm going, yeah, yeah, and then they show you what they've got, and you think, fucking hell, this isn't funny any more. Because how can you look after yourself if someone's got a knife? You can't. Anyway, about a month ago I threw this nasty little piece of work out of the club because he'd pushed it too far with a girl who was in there with her mates. And to be honest I probably slapped him once more than was strictly necessary, because he really got on my fucking nerves. And the next thing I know, he's got this . . . this thing, this . . . I've never seen anything like it before, but it was a sort of spike, about six inches long, sharp as fuck and rusty, and he starts jabbing it at me and telling me that I was dead. I was lucky, because he was scared, and he was holding this thing all wrong so it was pointing down at the ground instead of towards me, so I kicked his hand as hard as I fucking could and he dropped it, and I jumped on him. We called the police and they nicked him, but when they'd gone I knocked off. I'd had enough. I know what people think: they think that if that's the sort of job you choose, you're asking for whatever you get, and you probably want it, too, because you're a big ape who likes hurting people. Well, bollocks. I don't like hurting people. For me, a good night at Casablanca's is one where nothing's happened at all. I mean, OK, I'll probably have to stop a couple of people coming in because they're underage, or bombed out of their brains, but I see my job as allowing people to have a good time without fear of arseholes. Really, I do. I mean, OK, I'm not Mother Teresa or anything, I'm not doing good works or saving the world, but it's not such a shitty job if you look at it like that. But I'm a family man. I can't have people waving rusty spikes at me at two in the morning. I don't want to die outside some poxy club. So I told Lisa about it, and we talked, and I packed it in. I was lucky, because I was only out of work for a fortnight. They wouldn't let me draw the dole because I'd left my previous employment voluntarily. 'But this geezer had a rusty spike,' I said. 'Well, you should have taken it up with your employers,' she said. Like they would have offered me a desk job. Or given the kid with a spike a written warning. It didn't matter much, though, 'cos I found this one pretty much straight away, at an employment bureau. The money's a lot less, but the hours are better. I was well chuffed. How hard can it be, I thought, standing in front of a painting?

So. We had the induction hour, and then we were led through the gallery to our positions. On the way I was trying to work out whether I'd ever been in an art gallery before or not. You'd think I'd remember, but the trouble is, art galleries look exactly like you think they're going to look – a load of corridors with pictures hanging on them and people wandering around. So how would I know if I've been to one before? It feels like I have, but maybe I've just seen one on the telly, or in the films – there's that bit in *Dressed to Kill*, isn't there, where that bloke's trying to pick her up, and they keep seeing each other in different rooms. I can say this for sure, though: I've never had a good time in one. If I have ever been, it was on a school trip, and I was bored out of my skull, like on just about every school trip I was taken. The only one I remember now is when we went to some Roman ruins somewhere, and I nicked a few stones out of this mosaic thing. I stood on the edge and loosened a few with my foot, and while the teacher was talking, I crouched down as if to do up my shoelace and slipped a few in my pocket. And when we got back on the coach, I showed all the other lads what I'd done, and it turned out they'd all done exactly the same, and we were holding half the fucking floor in our hands. And the next thing we knew the bloke in charge of the place was chasing the coach down the street, and we all had to go to the front and put what we'd nicked into a carrier bag. We got in a lot of trouble for that. Anyway, what I reckon is we did go to an art gallery somewhere, and I don't remember because nobody walked off with a painting.

The thing is, this gallery's like the normal sort of gallery for the first few rooms – pictures of fruit and all that, and then it starts to go weird. First we went through a couple of rooms where the pictures aren't pictures of anything, just splodges, and then when we get to our bit, the new exhibition, there aren't many pictures at all. There are bits of animals all over the place, and a tent, and ping-pong balls floating on air currents, and a small house made of concrete, and videos of people reading poetry. It looks more like a school open day than an art gallery. You know, biology here, science there, English over at the back, media studies next to the toilets . . .

'I could have done any of these myself,' said this miserable old git called Tommy who'd already moaned once about the length of the coffee breaks. 'Yeah, you could now, you old cunt,' I said to him. 'Now you've seen them. Anyone could now. But you didn't think of it. So you're too late.' I was pleased with that. I pinched it off of a teacher at school, apart from the 'you old cunt' bit. That's mine. We were reading this poem at school, and some kid said exactly the same thing as Tommy – 'I could have done that.' Because it was an easy poem. It was short, and we knew all the words, and it didn't rhyme. And the teacher said, 'No, you couldn't. You could now, because you could just copy it out. But you didn't think of it.' I thought that was smart. Anyway, Tommy hasn't spoken to me since I called him an old cunt, and I'm glad.

I don't give a fuck about whether it's art, or who could do it. The thing is, it isn't boring, our gallery. The other rooms, with the pictures of cows in, they're boring. But our rooms, with the actual cows in, all cut up, they're not. There's got to be a lesson in there somewhere, hasn't there? It wouldn't work for everything, though, I can see that. I mean, it works for cows and tents and small houses, but it wouldn't work for, like, the fucking river. You'd still have to do a painting of that.

Anyway. Our group was getting smaller and smaller, because the woman taking us to our positions was sort of dropping us off, like we were in her bus. And it turned out that I was the last passenger. Like when me and Lisa went on a dodgy package holiday to Spain, years and years ago, before the kids came, and there was a coach to pick us all up at the airport, and every other bastard got dropped off at their hotel before we did, because it turned out that our hotel was two miles from the fucking beach. My painting was sort of the same thing as that. It was off to the side, in a room all of its own, and there was a curtain across the entrance, so it was separate from the others. Outside, there was a sign that said: 'WARNING! This room contains an exhibit of a controversial nature. Please do not enter if you feel you might be offended. Over 18s only'. The woman didn't say anything about that. She just ignored it – never asked me if *I* might be offended.

'You're in here,' she said. 'Watch out. We're expecting trouble.' And then she went off.

I went behind the curtain, and there on the far wall was this massive picture of Jesus. I'd say it was probably ten feet high, five or six feet wide, something like that. It's kind of like the pictures you've seen before – eyes closed, the old crown of thorns on his head. That was when he was on the cross, wasn't it? It's sort of a close-up, head and shoulders, so you only see a bit of the cross, but what this picture has that the normal ones don't – not to me they don't, anyway – is that you can really tell just how much it must have fucking hurt, being nailed up. Usually, it looks like he's having a kip, but this one, his face is all screwed up in agony. You really wouldn't want to be in his shoes, I'll tell you. So the first thing I thought was, bloody hell, that's a good picture. Because it makes you think, and I don't often think about things like that. I haven't been anywhere near Jesus since Lisa's sister got married, three years ago.

And the second thing I thought – I'd forgotten about the sign and the curtain and all that for a moment – was, who the fuck would get offended by that? Because you can go into any church and see the same sort of thing. Not so realistic, maybe, a bit more PG than R, but, you know, basically the same sort of stuff: moustache and beard, crown of thorns, sad. Because you can't tell how it's done from a distance, see. When you step behind the curtain, you just see the picture, and the face. You have to get quite close up to see anything else. So I couldn't understand it, why there was all the fuss. I just thought: religious people. Nutters. 'Cos they are, most of them, aren't they? I mean, to each his own and everything, but you wouldn't want to marry one, would you?

There's a chair in front of the picture, and I walked towards it to have a sit-down. And as I got closer, I could see that the picture was made up of hundreds – thousands, maybe millions – of little squares, like the mosaics I pinched from the Roman ruins. And when I got really close, I could see that these millions of little squares were actually little pictures, and every single little picture had at least one female breast in it. So . . . you know those pictures that are made up of dots? Well, that's how this Jesus picture was done, except all the dots are nipples. And that's what the picture's called – *NippleJesus*. There were big breasts and small breasts, and big nipples and small nipples, and black breasts and white breasts. And some of the pictures had as many as four breasts in them, and I could see then that all of the pictures were stills from porn mags, and he'd cut them all up and stuck them on. Must have taken him years. So now I understood what the sign was about.

I hated the picture then. Two minutes ago I'd liked it, now I hated it. And I hated the bloke who'd done it, too. Wanker. I went to have a look at the name of the artist, and it turned out to be a woman. Martha Marsham. How can you be a woman and do that? I thought. I could have understood some bloke doing it, some bloke with too many dirty magazines and no girlfriend. But a bird? And I hoped that someone did manage to fuck the picture up somehow, and if they did, I said to myself, I wouldn't try to stop them. I might even give them a hand. Because that is offensive, isn't it, a Jesus made out of nipples? That's out of order.

One thing I forgot to say before: this was about six o'clock in the evening, and the exhibition hadn't opened to the public yet. It was opening the next day, but we'd been called in to do the first-night party. I was actually still looking at all the little pictures when the first people came in, holding wine glasses. I felt a bit of a tosser, like I'd been caught looking at dirty pictures, which is actually what I was doing, if you think about it. Or even if you don't. I stopped looking, quick, and stood by the chair with my hands behind my back, looking straight ahead, like I was on sentry duty, while these two people, a man and a woman, looked at the picture.

'It's rather lovely, isn't it?' said the woman. She was about my age, short hair, quite posh.

'Is it?' The bloke didn't seem too sure, so I decided I liked him more than her, even though he had floppy hair and braces and a suit.

'Don't you think?'

He shrugged, and they left the room. There was none of that stuff, the stuff they take the piss out of in TV comedies, where they stroke their chins and talk bollocks. (There never is, in my experience, which has now lasted two days. Most people don't say anything much. They look and they go. If you ask me they're scared of talking bollocks, which pisses me off, because once I was sat here for a while I wanted the bollocks. Something to laugh at. But there isn't any.) The next couple were younger, early twenties, studenty types, and they were more interested in me than the picture.

'Fucking hell,' said the bloke.

'What?'

'Look at him.'

And the girl looked at me, and laughed. It was like I was part of the exhibition, and I couldn't hear what they were saying.

'Well,' she said. 'Can you blame them?'

And then they went, too. By this stage, I was starting to feel a bit sorry for this Martha woman. I mean, you spend fucking who knows how long doing this thing and people come in here, look at me, laugh, and then fuck off again. I might ask her for half her royalties, or whatever it is she gets.

The moment the students left, the curtain swished back, and I heard this woman's voice going 'Ta-ra!', and then a whole group of people came in – two younger guys, an older couple, and a young woman.

'Oh, Martha,' the older woman said. 'It's amazing. That'll get them going.' So I looked at the group, and straight away I guessed it was her mum and dad, her boyfriend, and maybe her brother. Martha is about thirty, and she doesn't really look like I thought she'd look – no dyed hair, no pierced nose, nothing like that. She looks normal, really. She was wearing this long, green, sort of

Indian skirt and what looked like a bloke's pinstripe jacket, and she's got long hair, but . . . she's nice-looking. Friendly.

I wondered for a moment whether her mum and dad knew about the nipples and all that, because I liked the picture when I first came into the room. But then I realized that was stupid, and she would have told them something about it before they came, or ages and ages ago. So what kind of parents were these? I know what I would have got if I'd told my dad I was making a picture of Jesus out of women's breasts. He probably would have wanted to see the breasts, but he would have given me a pasting for the Jesus bit. So I looked at Martha's mum and dad and tried to work them out. Her dad was tall, and wearing jeans, and he had long grey hair in a ponytail; her mum was wearing jeans too, but she looked a bit more like somebody's mother than he looked like somebody's father. They all looked like they were artists, though. They looked like they all sat around at home smoking dope and painting. Which was why no one had given her a back-hander for making a Jesus out of porn, probably.

'I want a photo,' Martha said. 'With all of us in it.' And then she looked at me. 'Do you mind?'

'No,' I said.

'I'm Martha, by the way.'

'Dave.'

'Hello, Dave.' We shook hands, and then she gave me her camera, and I took a picture of them all, standing there grinning and pointing, and I didn't know whether it was right, what with the kind of picture it was. But at that precise moment, I wished that I knew them better, or people like them, because they seemed nice, and happy, and interesting. I wanted a dad with a grey ponytail instead of a miserable old git who was always going on about the fucking Irish and the fucking blacks; it seemed to me that if I'd had a dad like that, I wouldn't have ended up going into the Army, which was the worst mistake I ever made.

I wanted to ask them questions. I wanted to ask her, Martha, why she'd wanted to do what she'd done, and why it had to be nipples, and why it had to be Jesus, and whether she actually wanted to upset people. And I wanted to ask them whether they were ashamed of her, or proud of her, or what. But I didn't ask anything, and nothing they said made me any the wiser; after the photos they talked about where they were going to eat, and whether someone else that they knew had come to the party, and then that sort of thing. Before they went, Martha came over to me and kissed me on the cheek, and said, 'Thank you.' And I went, you know, 'Oh, that's OK.' But I was really pleased that she'd done it. It made me feel special, like I had a proper, important job to do.

Martha smiled, and I was left on my own again.

I told Lisa about the picture when I got home that night, after the party. She couldn't believe it – she said it was disgusting, and how come it was on the wall in a famous gallery. For some reason I found myself sort of defending it, taking Martha's side. I don't know why. Maybe I fancied her a bit, maybe I liked the look of her family – maybe I trusted them, and, like, took my lead from them. Because I knew they were nice people, and if they didn't see anything wrong with *NippleJesus*, then maybe there wasn't anything. And anyway, the stuff that Lisa was coming out with . . . It was just plain ignorant. 'You should take it outside when no one's looking and smash it to bits,' she said.

'After all that work she's put in?' I said.

'That's got nothing to do with it,' she said. 'I mean, Hitler put in a lot of work, didn't he?'

'What harm is she doing you?' I asked her. 'You don't have to go and look at it.'

'Well, I don't like knowing it's there,' she said. 'And I paid for it. Out of my taxes.'

Out of her taxes! How much of her taxes went towards *NippleJesus*? She sounded like one of those lunatics you hear on radio phone-ins. I got twopence out of my pocket and threw it at her. 'There,' I said, 'there's your tax back. And you're making a profit.'

'What you gone all like this for?' she asked.

'Because I think it's good,' I said. 'Clever.'

Lisa didn't think it was clever. She thought it was stupid. And I thought she was stupid, and told her, and by the time we went to bed we weren't speaking to each other.

So yesterday morning, I get on the bus to go to work, and I pick up the paper that someone's left on the seat, and there it is, my painting, all over page seven. 'PROTESTERS TARGET SICK PICTURE', it says, and then there's all this stuff about what a disgrace it is, and people from the Church and the Conservative party going on about how it shouldn't be allowed, and someone from the police saying that they might want to interview Martha and maybe press charges of obscenity. And I read it, and I think, I've never been in the news before. Because it is me, sort of. That's my room there, my private space, and I've even started to think of the picture as mine, in a weird sort of way. Probably no one apart from Martha has spent as long looking at it as I have, and that makes me feel protective of it, kind of thing. (Which is just as well, when you think about it, seeing as that's my job.) I don't like these people saying it's sick, because it is and it isn't, and I don't like the police saying they're going to charge Martha with obscenity, and I don't like the idea that they're going to take it out of the exhibition, because it says outside the door that you shouldn't go in if you think you might not like it. So why go in? I want people to see what I saw: something that's beautiful if you look at it in one way, from a distance, and ugly if you look at it in another, close up. (Sometimes I feel that way about Lisa. When she walks into the room when we're just about to go out, and she's got her make-up on and she's done her hair and that, you'd think she could be a model. And sometimes I wake up in the night and I roll over and she's an inch away from me, and she's got bad breath and she's snoring a bit, and you'd think . . . Well, never mind what you'd think, but you wouldn't think she'd make much of a model, anyway. So maybe Martha's picture, it's sort of like that a bit.) But if these people have their way, no one's going to see anything, and that can't be right. Not after all that work. All that cutting up and sticking on.

Did you know you couldn't smoke in an art gallery? Neither did I. Fucking hell.

When I got there, there was already a crowd outside. Some of them were people queuing to see the exhibition, and some of them were protesters – they had placards and they were singing hymns – and there were TV crews, and photographers, and it all looked a bit of a mess. I just pushed through them and knocked on the front door and showed my pass through the glass and one of the guys let me in.

'You're in for a busy day,' one of the others said when I went to change into my gear, and I thought, yeah, I'm looking forward to this.

Nothing much happened at first. A steady stream of people came in and looked, and a couple of them sort of clucked, but what's really clever about the picture is that you have to get close up to get offended, because if you stand at the back of the room you can't see anything apart from the face of Christ. So it makes the cluckers look like right plonkers, because they have to go and shove their nose up against the painting to see the nipples, and you end up thinking they're perverts. You know, first they have to ignore the sign on the door telling them not to go in, and then they have to walk the length of the room, and then they go, 'Oh, disgusting.' So they're really looking out for it.

After about an hour, I got my first nutter. He looked like a nutter: he had chunks missing from his hair, like he'd been eaten by moths, and he wore these huge specs, and he kept blinking, like some demented owl. And he dressed like a nutter too: even though it was a hot day, he was wearing a winter coat covered in badges that said things like 'DON'T FOLLOW ME – I'M LOST TOO' and 'I'M A SUGAR PUFFS HONEY MONSTER'. He stank, and all. So it wasn't like he was hard to spot. He wasn't an *undercover* nutter, if you know what I mean.

He stared at the picture for a couple of minutes, and then he dropped to his knees and started praying. It was all, 'Heavenly father who gave his only son Jesus Christ to us so that we might be saved please deliver us blah blah blah', but what was weird was, you couldn't work out whether he was praying because he was looking at Christ, or whether he was praying like they prayed in *The Exorcist*, to get rid of the demons in the room, sort of thing. Anyway, after a little while I got pissed off with it and made up a rule.

'I'm sorry sir. We don't allow kneeling in the galleries,' I said.

'I'm praying for your immortal soul,' he said.

'I don't know about that, sir, but we don't allow kneeling. No flash photography, no sandwiches, no kneeling.'

He stood up and carried on muttering, so I told him praying was out, too.

'Don't you care?' he said.

'About what, sir?'

'Don't you care about where you are going?'

'And where's that?'

'To hell, man! Where serpents will suck on your eyeballs and flames will lick your internal organs for all eternity?'

'Not really, sir.' What I meant was, I didn't think I was going to be sent to hell. Not for standing in front of a picture, anyway.

You don't really want to go down that road, the eyeball-sucking road, do you? It's not very . . . *cheerful*, is it? I mean, what must it be like to be this geezer? And what's he doing here? Does he just wander around looking for stuff that's going to make him blink and drop to his knees and mutter away? Does he spend all his life wandering around Soho and King's Cross? Because if he does, then no wonder he's a nutter. If you don't spend any time playing with your kids (and I'll tell you, this is not a bloke with kids), or drinking with your mates (and I'll bet mates are a bit thin on the ground as well), or watching *Frasier* (I like *Frasier*) . . . you're going to end up like him, aren't you?

Just as I was wondering what I was going to do with him, a couple of women came in and he scuttled off, and things went quiet for a while. But then just before my lunch break, just as I was starting to think that it was going to be an aggro-free day after all, a bloke walks in wearing a dog-collar. A fucking vicar! He was younger than most vicars, and a bit trendier, too – he had a sort of Hugh Grant floppy haircut, and he was wearing jeans. He came into the room and stopped and stared, and I knew, because I knew all the angles and distances by now, that he couldn't see anything from where he was stood. Or rather, he could see Christ, but he couldn't see the nipples. So when he started to walk down towards the picture, I started to walk towards him, to block him off, and we stood there almost nose-to-nose.

'Why do you want to do that, your honour?' I asked him. 'Why don't you just stay where you are?'

'I have to make up my own mind,' he said.

'You know what's there,' I said. 'Everyone knows what's there now. Why do you have to go and look at it? Stay where you are. Look. It's beautiful.'

'How can anything made out of pornography be beautiful?'

For a moment I wanted to get into a whole different argument. This isn't porn, I wanted to tell him. This is just page 3 stuff. Porn is what we used to watch in the Army, with dogs and lesbians with strap-ons and all that, but you don't want to be talking to a vicar about sex with dogs, do you? I didn't, anyway.

He moved to his right to get by me, so I moved to my left, and then we did the same dance the other way round. He was getting annoyed now, and in the end I had to let him through; otherwise I swear it would have all gone off, and I would have been fired for decking him.

'Happy now?' I said after he'd been there a while.

'Why did she do it, do you think?'

'I wouldn't know, your honour. But she's a very nice young lady.'

'That makes it even sadder, then.'

Not to me it doesn't, I thought. If it had been made by a seedy old git whose hobby was looking up women's skirts, then that's one story, but it's different when you've seen what Martha is like, the kind of person she is. You end up sort of trusting her, and trusting what she does, and why. I did, anyway. I can see that wouldn't work for everyone. It wouldn't make a lot of difference to the nutter, for example.

'I think you've been here long enough now,' I said to the vicar. This was completely out of order, of course, but the truth was I was sick of him, and I didn't want him in my room any more.

'I beg your pardon?'

'We've been told to watch out for people who stay here more than five minutes. You know, perverts and that.' That did the trick.

If I'd just read about *NippleJesus* in the paper, or seen it on the news, I'd have thought it was wrong, no question. Sick. Stupid. Waste of taxpayers' money. (You always say that even if you've got no idea if taxpayers pay for it or not, whatever it is, don't you?) And then I'd never have thought about it again, probably. But it's more complicated when you actually stand by it all day. And now I still don't know what I think of it, really, but what's so great about the nutter and the kinky vicar and all the other people who came to have a look that first morning is that they make up your mind for you about whose side you're on. I'm not on theirs, that's for sure, and the longer I have to spend with these wankers the more I hate them. It's so simple, really. The nice ones like the picture, and they get it, and they have a look at how it's done but that's not why they're staring; the horrible ones come in, gaze for hours at the tits, moan to each other (or, if they're really mad, to themselves) . . . You don't need to work out what you think. You just need to have a look at what other people think. And if you don't like the look of them, then think the opposite.

No sooner had the vicar gone than a whole fucking zoo turns up. I recognize a couple of the monkeys in it: there's this woman politician I'm sure I've seen on TV, that fat one who's always banging on about the family and all that, and she's brought a TV crew with her. The interviewer is that bloke who does the local news on the BBC. You'd probably recognize him too – smoothy, sharp suits, fake tan. Anyway, you should have heard this woman. She was calling for Martha to be sent to prison, for the people who put on the exhibition to, I don't know, have their licence taken away or something . . . And the smoothy geezer was just egging her on. 'You've been campaigning very hard for a return to family values, and presumably this kind of thing doesn't help your cause . . .' Stuff like that. When they'd finished I wandered over to the interviewer and had a word with him, just to wind him up, sort of thing.

'So,' I said. 'You getting someone else to say something?'

'How d'you mean?'

'Well, you can't have just her, can you?' She was standing about two feet away, having her microphone taken off, so I knew she could hear me. She turned round and looked at me.

'We'll be talking to the artist, too,' said the presenter. 'She should be here in a second.'

'Did you do a close-up of the painting?'

'I would imagine so,' he said. All sarcastic, like I was being thick.

'So you're going to show thousands of nipples on the local news? My kids watch that.'

'Do they?' he said, like he didn't believe me. Like no one with a skinhead haircut could have kids who watched anything but football. Cheeky bastard. OK, my kids don't watch the news, but that's because they're too young, not because they're too thick. Wanker.

When Martha turned up, I realized I sort of had a crush on her. She looked great – fresh, and friendly, and young, and she was wearing this bright lime-green T-shirt that added to the freshness. The politician was wearing this dark suit, and she had a hard face anyway, and Martha makes her look old and cruel. She said hello to me, and asked me how it was going, and I told her about the nutter and the vicar, and she just smiled.

The interviewer didn't like her, I could tell. He asked her whether she minded offending so many people, and she said she didn't think she had, only one or two. And he asked her what the point of the picture was, and she said that she didn't want to have to explain it, she thought it could explain itself, if she could tell everyone what it meant then she would have just written the meaning down, she wouldn't have gone to all the trouble of sticking all the nipples on the paper. And the interviewer said, well, some people wish you hadn't bothered, and she said, well, it's a free country.

I was disappointed, to be honest. I was hoping she'd talk about how beautiful the picture was – how holy, sort of thing. And I wanted her to explain that if you wanted to see the nipples you really had to get up close, like the vicar had to, and what kind of vicar you were if you wanted to do that. And I wanted to hear why she'd done it, too. I mean, there had to be an idea behind it, didn't there? A meaning, kind of thing. It's not just something you'd wake up in the morning and do, is it? You know, 'What am I going to do with all these pairs of breasts I've been cutting out? Oh, I might as well turn them into a picture of Christ on the cross . . .'

Maybe they should have interviewed me. Like I said, maybe I've thought more about this picture than anyone. Because she doesn't know, Martha. She hasn't seen it in action, like I have. And she hasn't spent any time standing in front of it, watching people looking at it. Perhaps she should; then she'd be able to say things about it in interviews.

*

Just before we closed, the smelly nutter with the badges came back with an egg, and tried to throw it at the picture. I saw it coming a mile off, and I grabbed his arm just as he was raising it, and the egg travelled about two feet and landed splat on the floor. It was so pathetic it made me laugh, and I remembered the kid with the rusty spike outside the club, and why I'd packed that job in; it's hard to be scared by a scrawny weirdo with an egg. I was still angry though, so I didn't let go of him after he'd thrown it – I pinned his arm behind his back with more violence than I needed, and he started yelling. I marched him out, and down the corridor towards the front entrance. I hated the fucker so much that I got carried away a bit – I was twisting his arm and calling him all the names under the sun, and he said he was going to sue me and report me to the police and he wasn't going to pray for my soul and he hoped that all the agonies of damnation were heaped upon me. Pillock.

But he knew what he was doing. As I was shoving the nutter down the corridor, there was a commotion behind me, shouting and crashing and alarms going off and then the sound of running. I let the nutter go and went back to my picture, and a couple of the other security guards were in there staring at the floor. Someone had fucked *NippleJesus* over good and proper. They'd taken it off the wall and stomped all over it and then fucked off. There wasn't hardly anything left of it.

I felt like crying. Really. I'd let Martha down, and I'd been stupid to leave the room, and it was only when I saw the picture smashed up on the floor that I finally realized how much I loved it. But I'll tell you something else, something really weird: seeing Christ on the floor with his face all smashed in like that . . . It was really shocking. What they'd done was much more blasphemous than anything Martha had done. I wonder if they'd thought about that when they were doing it? Whether they'd had any moment of doubt, or fear? Because, I'll tell you, if I was religious, and I thought that there was a hell where serpents suck your eyeballs out and all that, I wouldn't go round stomping all over Jesus's face. Jesus is Jesus, isn't he? No matter what you make him out of. And maybe that's one of the things Martha was trying to get at: Christ is where you find him.

Some people from the gallery turned up, people I'd seen at the party the night before but no one who'd ever bothered to speak to me. And I told them about the nutter and the egg, and how I shouldn't have left my post but I did, and they didn't seem to blame me much. And then a copper came, and I told him the same stuff. He seemed to think it was funny, though. He didn't laugh or anything, but you could tell that it was low down on his list of crimes to solve.

And then Martha came in. I walked towards her because I wanted to hug her, but I worked out just in time that my relationship with her was not the same as her relationship with me, if you see what I mean. I've spent a lot of time over the last couple of days thinking about her, because of my job, but she couldn't have spent much time thinking about me, could she? Anyway. I didn't hug her. I just went over to her and said, you know, I'm sorry and all that, but she didn't seem to hear me. She just stared at the picture on the floor, and said, 'Oh my God', which considering the circumstances was about right.

And when she looked up again, her face was all lit up. She was thrilled to bits, excited like a kid. I couldn't believe it.

'This is perfect,' she said. 'Brilliant.'

'How d'you mean?' I said, because I didn't get it.

'Who did this? Did you see?'

So I told her about the smelly nutter with the egg, and how I thought he'd done me, wound me up to get me out of the room so his nutter mates could do their stuff, and she loved it. She loved the whole story. 'Perfect,' she kept saying. 'Fantastic.' And then: 'I can't wait to see the video.'

And I was, like, 'What video?', and she pointed out the CCTV camera up in the corner of the room.

'That's part of it,' she said. 'That's part of the exhibition. What I was hoping was that someone would come in and do this on day one, and on day two we could show the film, and . . . I'm going to call it *Intolerance*.'

And I thought about the vicar, and the politician, and all the other people who'd come in and stuck their noses up close and then said how disgusted they were and how shocking it was and I could see that it would be a bit of a laugh for people to see them on the telly. But that was all it was, really, a bit of a laugh.

'So that was the idea?' I said. 'Someone would come in and smash it up?'

'Put it this way,' she said. 'I'd have been stuffed if they hadn't. I'd have been stuck with a portrait of Jesus made out of breasts, and what use is that to anyone? It's Dave, isn't it? Well, Dave. Art is about provocation. Getting a reaction from people. And I've done it. I'm an artist.'

I remembered the party, when she thanked me, and I asked her why she'd done that if all she wanted was for someone to smash it up. But she didn't remember thanking me. So I said, you must remember, last night, at the party. When I took your photo, and you came over and kissed me on the cheek and said 'Thank you'. And she shrugged, and said, 'Oh, yeah. I was thanking you for the photo, I think.' Like it wasn't a big deal. Which it clearly wasn't, I can see now. I suppose if you're an artist, it doesn't mean anything, kissing someone on the cheek. They do it all the time. 'Twenty Marlboro Lights, please.' Kiss. 'Leicester Square, please.' Mmmmwa. It doesn't mean, oh thank you for the important and dangerous job you're doing, obviously. Silly cow. I should have just stood there. I shouldn't have gone out with the smelly nutter with the egg. Because, if you think about it . . . The only reason it got smashed up was because I cared about it too much. I could have just stood there, stopped the egg, got rid of the nutter; but he'd got on my nerves, he'd tried to damage my picture – *my* picture – and I wanted to make sure he left the building, maybe give him a couple of digs at the same time. Which is why I wasn't in the room when it got broken. So. She wouldn't understand this, but she needed me for her film as much as she needed them.

When I went home last night, I felt stupid. I felt like I look, if you like: a six-foot-two, fifteen-stone bouncer with a shaved head who doesn't know anything about art. I'd spent two days thinking something was, you know, beautiful, and worth protecting, and all the time it was a piece of shit, stuck on the wall because some bird thought it would be a laugh if someone smashed it to pieces. So everyone's a prat, aren't they? The nutters are prats for doing what they were supposed to do, and I was a prat for trying to stop them . . . The only one who isn't a prat is Martha. She's watching us and having a laugh. Well, fuck her.

Except maybe she isn't as clever as she thought she was. Because the film's showing now, up the corridor, and no one looks at it. It's too long, so most of the time nothing's happening, and you can't see very much anyway – they cocked up the angle of the camera, so you see the painting coming off the wall, but you don't see anyone jump on it. And it's not beautiful. It's just a CCTV film, like you see in a petrol station when you're waiting to get served. And that's what you get instead of the face of Christ in his agony. So who's the prat, eh Martha?

I've got an onion now. A fucking onion. And some other stuff, beds, and tents and shit, because I'm not in a room by myself any more; the CCTV film isn't controversial, so they don't need anyone to keep an eye on it. But my chair's by the onion, and it bores me shitless, because there's nothing to think about onions, is there? So I don't. I just sit here and think about what I'd like to do, apart from be Tiger Woods or Richard Branson.

AFTER I WAS THROWN IN THE RIVER AND BEFORE I DROWNED

DAVE EGGERS

Oh, I'm a fast dog. I'm fast-fast. It's true and I love being fast I admit it I love it. You know fast dogs. Dogs that just run by and you say, 'Damn! That's a fast dog!' Well, that's me. A fast dog. *Hoooooooo!* I'm a fast fast dog. *Hooooooooooooooo!* You should watch me sometime. Just watch how fast I go when I'm going my fastest, when I've really got to move for something, when I'm really on my way – man do I get going sometimes, weaving like a missile, weaving like a missile between trees and around bushes and then – pop! – I can go over a fence or a baby or a rock or anything because I'm a fast fast dog and I can jump like a fucking gazelle.

Hoooooooo! Man, oh man.

I love it, I love it. I run to feel the cool air cool through my fur. I run to feel the cold water come from my eyes. I run to feel my jaw slacken and my tongue come loose and flap from the side of my mouth and I go and go and go my name is Steven.

I can eat pizza. I can eat chicken. I can eat yogurt and rye bread with caraway seeds. It really doesn't matter. They say, 'No, no, don't eat that stuff, you, that stuff isn't for you, it's for us, for people!' And I eat it anyway, I eat it with gusto, I eat the food and I feel good and I live on and run and run and look at the people and hear their stupid conversations coming from their slits for mouths and terrible eyes.

I see in the windows. I see what happens. I see the calm held-together moments and also the treachery and I run and run. You tell me it matters, what they all say. I have listened and long ago I stopped. Just tell me it matters and I will listen to you and I will want to be convinced. You tell me that what is said is making a difference, that those words are worthwhile words and mean something. I see what happens. I live with people who are German. They collect steins. They are good people. Their son is dead. I see what happens.

When I run I can turn like I'm magic or something. I can turn like there wasn't even a turn. I turn and I'm going so fast it's like I was still going straight. Through the trees like a missile, through the trees I love to run with my claws reaching and grabbing so quickly like I'm taking everything.

Damn, I'm so in love with all of this.

I was once in a river. I was thrown in a river when I was small. You just cannot know. I was swimming, trying to know why I had been thrown in the river. I was six months old, and my eyes were burning, the water was bad. I paddled and it was like begging. The land on either side was a black stripe, indifferent. I saw the grey water and then the darker water below and then my legs wouldn't work, were stuck in some kind of seaweed or spiderweb and then I was in the air.

I opened my burning eyes and saw him in yellow. The fisherman. I was lifted from the water, the water was below me. Then shivering on their white plastic boat bottom, and they looked at me with their moustaches.

I dried in the sun. They brought me to the place with the cages and I yelled for days. Others were yelling too. Everyone was crazy. Then people and a car and I was new at home. Ate and slept and it was dry, walls of wood. Two people and two girls, thin twins who sleep in the next room, with a doll's house between them.

When I go outside I run. I run from the cement past the places and then to where the places end and then to the woods. In the woods are the other dogs.

I am the fastest. Since Thomas left I am the fastest. I jump the farthest too. I don't have to yell any more. I can go past the buildings where the people complain, and then to the woods where I can't hear them and just run with these dogs.

Hoooooooooooooooooo! I feel good here, feel strong. Sometimes I am a machine, moving so fast, a machine with everything working perfectly, my claws grabbing at the earth like I'm the one making it turn. Damn, yeah.

Every day on the street I pass the same people. There are the men, two of them, selling burritos from the steel van. They are happy men; their music is loud and jangles like a bracelet. There are the women from the drugstore outside on their break, smoking and laughing, shoulders shaking. There is the man who sleeps on the ground with the hole in his pants where his ass shows raw and barnacled and brown-blue. One arm extended, reaching toward the door of the building. *He sleeps so much.*

Every night I walk from the neighbourhood and head to the woods and meet the others. It's shadowy out, the clouds low. I see the blues jumping inside the windows. I want all these people gone from the buildings and moved to the desert so we can fill the buildings with water. It's an idea I have. The buildings would be good if filled with water, or under water. Something to clean them, anything. How long would it take to clean all those buildings. Lord, no one knows any of this. So many of the sounds I hear I just can't stand. These people.

The only ones I like are the kids. I come to the kids and lick the kids. I run to them and push my nose into their stomachs. I don't want them to work. I want them to stay as they are and run with me, even though they're so so slow. I run around them and around again as they run forward. They're slow but they are perfect things, almost perfect.

I pass the buildings. Inside, the women are putting strands of hair behind their ears, and their older children are standing before the mirror for hours, moving tentatively to their music. Their fathers are playing chess with their uncles who are staying with them for a few months while things are straightened. They are happy that they are with each other, and I pass, my claws ticking on the sandpaper cement, past the man laying down with his arm reaching, and past the steel van with the music, and I see the light behind the rooftops.

I haven't been on a rooftop but was once in a plane and wondered why no one had told me. That clouds were more ravishing from above.

Where the buildings clear I sometimes see the train slip through the sharp black trees, all the green windows and the people inside in white shirts. I watch from the woods, the dirt in my nails so soft. I just cannot tell you how much I love all this, this train, these woods, the dirt, the smell of dogs nearby waiting to run.

In the woods we have races and we jump. We run from the entrance to the woods, where the trail starts, through the black-dark interior and out to the meadow and across the meadow and into the next woods, over the creek and then along the creek until the highway.

Tonight is cool, almost cold. There are no stars or clouds. We're all impotent but there is running. I jog down the trail and see the others. Six of them tonight – Edward, Franklin, Susan, Mary, Robert and Victoria. When I see them I want to be in love with all of them at once. I want us all to be together; I feel so good to be near them. We talk about it getting cooler. We talk about it being warm in these woods when we're close together. I know all these dogs but a few.

Tonight I race Edward. Edward is a bull terrier and he is fast and strong but his eyes want to win too much; he scares us. We don't know him well and he laughs too loud and only at his own jokes. He doesn't listen; he waits to speak.

The course is a simple one. We run from the entrance through the black-dark interior and out to the meadow and across the meadow and into the next woods, along the creek, then over the gap over the drainpipe and then along the creek until the highway.

The jump over the drainpipe is the hard part. We run along the creek and then the riverbank above it rises so we're ten, fifteen feet above the creek and then almost twenty. Then the bank is interrupted by a drainpipe, about four feet high, so the bank at eighteen feet is gapped for twelve and we have to run and jump the gap. We have to run and feel strong to make it.

On the banks of the creek, near the drainpipe, on the dirt and in the weeds and on the branches of the rough grey trees are the squirrels. The squirrels have things to say; they talk before and after we jump. Sometimes while we're jumping they talk.

'He is running funny.'

'She will not make it across.'

When we land they say things.

'He didn't land as well as I wanted him to.'

'She made a bad landing. Because her landing was bad I am angry.'

When we do not make it across the gap, and instead fall into the sandy bank, the squirrels say other things, their eyes full of glee.

'It makes me laugh that she did not make it across the gap.'

'I am very happy that he fell and seems to be in pain.'

I don't know why the squirrels watch us, or why they talk to us. They do not try to jump the gap. The running and jumping feels so good – even when we don't win or fall into the gap it feels so good when we run and jump – and when we are done the squirrels are talking to us, to each other in their small jittery voices.

We look at the squirrels and we wonder why they are there. We want them to run and jump with us but they do not. They sit and talk about the things we do. Sometimes one of the dogs, annoyed past tolerance, catches a squirrel in his mouth and crushes him. But then the next night they are back, all the squirrels, more of them. Always more.

Tonight I am to race Edward and I feel good. My eyes feel good, like I will see everything before I have to. I see colours like you hear jetplanes.

When we run on the side of the creek I feel strong and feel fast. There is room for both of us to run and I want to run along the creek, want to run alongside Edward and then jump. That's all I can see, the jump, the distance below us, the momentum taking me over the gap. Goddamn, sometimes I only want this feeling to stay.

Tonight I run and Edward runs, and I see him pushing hard, and his claws grabbing, and it seems like we're both grabbing at the same thing, that we're both grabbing for the same thing. But we keep grabbing and grabbing and there is enough for both of us to grab, and after us there will be others who grab from this dirt on the creek bed and it will always be here.

Edward is nudging me as I run. Edward is pushing me, bumping into me. All I want is to run but he is yelling and hitting me, trying to bite me. I am telling him that if we both just run and jump without bumping or biting we will run faster and jump farther. We will be stronger and do more beautiful things. He bites me and bumps me and yells things at me as we run. When we come to the bend he tries to bump me into the wide hard tree. I skid and then find my footing and keep running. I catch up to him quickly because I am faster and overtake him and we are on the straightaway and I gain my speed, I muster it from everywhere, I attract the energy of everything living around me, it conducts through the soil through my claws while I grab and grab and I gain all the speed and then I see the gap. Two more strides and I jump.

You should do this sometime. I am a rocket. My time over the gap is a life. I am a cloud, so slow, for an instant I am a slowmoving cloud whose movement is elegant, cavalier, like sleep.

Then it all speeds up and the leaves and black dirt come to me and I land and skid, my claws filling with soil and sand. I clear the gap by two feet and turn to see Edward jumping, and Edward's face looking across the gap, looking at my side of the gap, and his eyes still on the grass, exploding for it, and then he is falling, and only his front paws land above the bank. He yells something as he grabs, his eyes trying to pull the rest of him up, but he slides down the bank.

He is fine but in the past others have been hurt. One dog,

Wolfgang, died here, years ago. The other dogs and I jump down to help Edward up. He is moaning but he is happy that we were running together and that he jumped.

The squirrels say things.

'That wasn't such a good jump.'

'That was a terrible jump.'

'He wasn't trying hard enough when he jumped.'

'Bad landing.'

'Awful landing.'

'His bad landing makes me very angry.'

I run the rest of the race alone. I finish and come back and watch the other races. I watch and like to watch them run and jump. We are lucky to have these legs and this ground, and that our muscles work with speed and the blood surges and that we can see everything.

After we all run we go home. A few of the dogs live on the other side of the highway, where there is more land. A few live my way, and we jog together back, through the woods and out of the entranceway and back to the streets and the buildings with the blue lights jumping inside. They know as I know. They see the men and women talking through the glass and saying nothing. They know that inside the children are pushing their toys across the wooden floors. And in their beds people are reaching for the covers, pulling, their feet kicking.

I scratch at the door and soon the door opens. Bare white legs under a red robe. Black hairs ooze from the white skin. I eat the food and go to the bedroom and wait for them to sleep. I sleep at the foot of the bed, over their feet, feeling the air from the just-open window roll in cool and familiar. In the next room the thin twins sleep between their doll's house.

The next night I walk alone to the woods, my claws clicking on the sandpaper cement. The sleeping man sleeps near the door, his hands praying between his knees. I see a group of men singing on the corner drunkenly but they are perfect. Their voices join and burnish the air between them, freed and perfect from their old and drunken mouths. I sit and watch until they notice me.

'Get out of here, fuck-dog.'

I see the buildings end and wait for the train through the branches. I wait and can almost hear the singing still. I wait and don't want to wait any more but the longer I wait the more I expect the train to come. I see a crow bounce in front of me, his head pivoting, paranoid. Then the train sounds from the black thick part of the forest where it can't be seen, then comes into view, passing through the lighter woods, and it shoots through, the green squares glowing and inside the bodies with their white shirts. I try to soak myself in this. This I can't believe I deserve. I want to close my eyes to feel this more but then realize I shouldn't close my eyes. I keep my eyes open and watch and then the train is gone.

Tonight I race Susan. Susan is a retriever, a small one, fast and pretty with black eyes. We take off, through the entrance through the black-dark interior and out to the meadow. In the meadow we breathe the air and feel the light of the partial moon. We have sharp back shadows that spider through the long gray-green grass. We run and smile at each other because we both know how good this is. Maybe Susan is my sister.

Then the second forest approaches and we plunge like sex into the woods and take the turns, past the bend where Edward pushed me, and then along the creek. We are running together and are not really racing. We are wanting the other to run faster, better. We are watching each other in love with our movements and strength. Susan is maybe my mother.

Then the straightaway before the gap. Now we have to think about our own legs and muscles and timing before the jump. Susan looks at me and smiles again but looks tired. Two more strides and I jump and then am the slow cloud seeing the faces of my friends, the other strong dogs, then the hard ground rushes toward me and I land and hear her scream. I turn to see her face falling down the gap and run back to the gap. Robert and Victoria are down with her already. Her leg is broken and bleeding from the joint. She screams, then wails, knowing everything already.

The squirrels are above and talking.

'Well, looks like she got what she deserved.'

'That's what you get when you jump.'

'If she were a better jumper this would not have happened.'

Some of them laugh. Franklin is angry. He walks slowly to where they're sitting; they do not move. He grabs one in his jaws and crushes all its bones. Their voices are always talking but we forget they are so small, their head and bones so tiny. The rest run away. He tosses the squirrel's broken form into the slow water.

We go home. I jog to the buildings with Susan on my back. We pass the windows flickering blue and the men in the silver van with the jangly music. I take her home and scratch at her door until she is let in. I go home and see the thin twins with their doll's house and I go to the room with the bed and fall asleep before they come.

The next night I don't want to go to the woods. I can't see someone fall, and can't hear the squirrels, and don't want Franklin to crush them in his jaws. I stay at home and I play with the twins in their pyjamas. They put me on a pillowcase and pull me through the halls. I like the speed and they giggle. We make turns where I run into door frames and they laugh. I run from them and then toward them and through their legs. They shriek they love it. I want deeply for these twins and want them to leave and run with me. I stay with them tonight and then stay home for days. I stay away from the windows. It's warm in the house and I eat more and sit with them as they watch television. It rains for a week.

When I come to the woods again, after ten days away, Susan has lost her leg. The dogs are all there. Susan has three legs, a bandage around her front shoulder. Her smile is a new and more fragile thing. It's colder out and the wind is mean and searching. Mary says that the rain has made the creek swell and the current too fast. The gap over the drainpipe is wider now so we decide that we will not jump.

I race Franklin. Franklin is still angry about Susan's leg; neither of us can believe that things like that happen, that she has lost a leg and now when she smiles she looks like she's asking to die.

When we get to the straightaway I feel so strong that I know I will go. I'm not sure I can make it but I know I can go far, farther than I've jumped before, and I know how long it will be that I will be floating cloudlike. I want this so much, the floating.

I run and see the squirrels and their mouths are already forming the words they will say if I don't make it across. On the straightaway Franklin stops and yells to me that I should stop but it's just a few more strides and I've never felt so strong so I jump yes jump. I float for a long time and see it all. I see my bed and the faces of my friends and it seems like they already know.

When I hit my head it was obvious. I hit my head and had a moment when I could still see – I saw Susan's face, her eyes open huge, I saw some criss-crossing branches above me and then the current took me out and then I fell under the surface.

After I fell and was out of view the squirrels spoke.

'He should not have jumped that jump.'

'He sure did look silly when he hit his head and slid into the water.'

'He was a fool.'

'Everything he ever did was worthless.'

Franklin was angry and took five or six of them in his mouth, crushing them, tossing them one after the other. The other dogs watched; none of them knew if squirrel-killing made them happy or not.

After I died, so many things happened that I did not expect.

The first was that I was there, inside my body, for a long time. I was at the bottom of the river, stuck in a thicket of sticks and logs, for six days. I was dead, but was still there, and I could see out of my eyes. I could move around inside my body like it was a warm loose bag. I would sleep in the warm loose bag, turn around in it like it was a small home of skin and fur. I could look every so often through the bag's eyes to see what was outside, in the river. I never saw much through the dirty water.

I had been thrown into the river, a different river, when I was young by a man because I would not fight. I was supposed to fight and he kicked me and slapped my head and tried to make me mean. I didn't know why he was kicking me, slapping. I wanted him to be happy. I wanted the squirrels to jump and be happy as we dogs were. But they were different than we were, and the man who threw me to the river was also different. I thought we were all the same but as I was inside my dead body and looking into the murky river bottom I knew that some are wanting to run and some are afraid to run and maybe they are broken and angry for it.

I slept in my broken sack of a body at the bottom of the river, and wondered what would happen. It was dark inside, and musty, and the air was hard to draw. I sang to myself.

After the sixth day I woke up and it was bright. I knew I was back. I was no longer inside a loose sack but was now inhabiting a body like my own, from before; I was the same. I stood and was in a wide field of buttercups. I could smell their smell and walked through them, my eyes at the level of the yellow, a wide blur of a line of yellow. I was heavy-headed from the gorgeousness of the yellow all blurry. I loved breathing this way again, and seeing everything.

I should say that it's very much the same here as there. There are more hills, and more waterfalls, and things are cleaner. I like it. Each day I walk for a long time, and I don't have to walk back. I can walk and walk, and when I am tired and can sleep. When I wake up, I can keep walking and I never miss where I started and have no home.

I haven't seen anyone yet. I don't miss the cement like sandpaper on my feet, or the buildings with the sleeping men reaching. I sometimes miss the other dogs and the running.

The one big surprise is that as it turns out, God is the sun. It makes sense, if you think about it. Why we didn't see it sooner I cannot say. Every day the sun was right there burning, ours and other planets hovering around it, always apologizing, and we didn't think it was God. Why would there be a god and also a sun? Of course God is the sun. Simple, good.

Everyone in the life before was cranky, I think, because they just wanted to know.

LUCKYBITCH

HELEN FIELDING

The last thing I want anyone thinking is I fell over because I'm old. I'll be able to move this arm in a minute, and then I'll get the other one out from under me and press the panic button and some divine young man will turn up in a uniform and I'll tell him I pressed the button by mistake and I'm simply looking for a contact lens! Sometimes I'm so uniquely resourceful and clever I actually feel quite overcome.

Christ, though, I could murder a Mai Tai. I was drunk! That's right. I'll tell them I was bloody well drunk and dropped my contact lens on the floor and I'm looking for it.

I've just had a frightful thought. I look like one of those ads in the Sunday supplements – 'Mrs Hope knows help is coming' – with some ghastly grey-haired old dear lying prone, with her tweed skirt riding up over a pair of elastic stockings.

Ugh. Grey hair. Why would any woman let herself go like that? It's like wearing a sign on your head saying 'Old lady'! Obviously everyone thinks I'm a natural blonde and quite frankly it was a godsend when I went grey – not that I am grey, obviously – but hypothetically speaking, should I not have been a natural blonde and should I then have had the misfortune to turn prematurely grey it would have been a godsend, because then you don't have to bleach and if you run ivory highlights through you can leave the roots for six to eight weeks and nobody notices a thing.

The panic button was not actually installed for this sort of carry on, of course. It was Lisa who made me fit it. It's not in case I fall over and wet myself. Hmm. But now I come to mention it . . . well, at least I'm in the bathroom and it's a tiled floor. But, as I told Lisa when she insisted, 'I'll only have a button if it's strictly for intruders.' I mean – imagine! A man could burst in here and do anything he wanted with me! Anything! I'd be helpless. A fragile, helpless creature in the power of a ruthless brute, hell-bent on getting what he wanted and only wanting ONE GODDAM THING.

Mark used to call me the Hampshire Grace Kelly. She gave the best blow job in Hollywood. The bed was my stage, darlings. And if one has to take repeated bows . . . then one simply does! But one doesn't have to swallow.

That's what I say to Lisa when she goes on about boundaries this and boundaries that: 'I know, darling, one doesn't need a self-help book to have boundaries – I never swallowed!' I don't know what happened to the poor girl's sense of humour. You'd think with a combination of my genes and Jean-Paul's she would have been able to raise a smile.

Christ, this is boring. What I don't understand is how I ended up down here in the first place. It's still light so it can't have been that long – unless it was dark when I fell. At least I'm wearing Escada, but you see that must mean I was going somewhere, so surely whoever I was meeting would have thought to drop by. Unless it was to shop? If I could get one of my hands up I could see what colour lipstick I've got, but you see one of my bloody arms is underneath me and for some reason the other one won't move. My mouth feels so strange . . . I . . . oh . . . I'm so thirsty . . . maybe I'll sleep.

It's dark. What's happening? I'm going to die . . . die . . . DIEEEEE. I've been here for ever. I'm dying. Dying. Aaaargh!

Now come along, you delirious fool. There's absolutely no point in being histrionic if there's no one around to buy one a trinket. I must have been asleep or something. There are worse places to sleep. I remember Claude and I sleeping on the railway station platform at Arles and being pissed on by a filthy French guard. We made love under a coat! Imagine! It was jolly good, actually. Bit cold on the *derrière*. In fact, the whole scene was bizarrely similar to this one, give or take Claude and his persistent erection. It was so heavenly that year. I remember sitting in the square in Saint-Paul-de-Vence with chèvre and a bottle of San Remy, and Claude accusing me of sleeping with Matisse on the construction site for his chapel.

'Don't be absurd,' I said. 'It's a consecrated site, and besides, I'd have got all painty.'

Actually, it was in a room at the Colombe d'Or and I knew it was naughty.

I do worry about Lisa, inasmuch as one ever actually worries about anything. I always consider worrying as utterly pointless as feeling guilt or expecting gratitude for one's largesse. I remember Ernest remarking to me when he'd taken a bunch of ghastly people to a bullfight that gratitude actually doesn't exist: only the expectation of gratitude. Oh dear, I do wish I hadn't fallen on my front. This is awfully hard on the neck, really, and so ungainly! Maybe a doctor will come. I do so adore doctors. What was that boy called when I was first expecting Lisa? Dr someone or other. Those hands! Now that was one instance when I did hold myself back. I mean, my unborn child! The Hippocratic oath! Frankly, I always regretted it.

You see, one never wants to be overly maternal – hasn't one done enough by giving birth? It was like passing a grapefruit. No, I've merely tried to give her a sense of joy and life and refrain from bossing her about. After the nightmare I had with my own bloody mother, I always said I'll never be the sort who gives advice when it isn't asked for. Or worse, who gives advice whilst pretending not to. So why the bloody hell does she do it to me? Boss, boss, boss. It's the oddest thing – she couldn't have had more fun when she was small, bobbing about in the back of the car, racing round and round the Cap from one *terrasse* to another, when half the girls in her school had never even been on the continent. But does she have fun? No. She works, she works, she works. I've never smelt a whiff of perfume on the girl. And the whole delightful frisson of sex and flirtation and the illicit affair seems to have disappeared in a fug of angsting about the whys and wherefores and respect and independence and blah blah blah. I mean, of course, I realize I should never have flirted with that banker fellow she brought round here, but really, it was the slightest thing – I was merely sounding him out to check his responses. How was I to know he was going to start calling me?! Daphne and I used to have a little code: YELS. Young enough to be legal son. But I bet Daphne wishes she had lived long enough to wrestle with a YELG – Oh goodness, I wish I could call Daphne. Darling! Young enough to be legal grandson – is that too young? Is it? You don't think so? Oh, whizzo! Must dashloveyoubyeeeee!

I could murder a bit of ham. People survive for days in the desert. It's the water that kills you. Oh Christ, I hope I'm not going to be some sort of ghastly stroke victim with a lopsided mouth . . . Maybe Collagen could sort it out . . . and incontinence pads . . . Baaah!! Now I'm not going to think about that. There's nothing to be gained. I shall tell them I was drunk and stick to it. Drunk drunk drunkety drunk.

Oh, the fun I've had when I've been drunk. Now, you see, Lisa never seems to drink a thing except cups of hot steam. I can't understand why she makes such a meal over men. She seems to expect them to behave like – like women. She's always trying to get them to 'talk about relationships'. She goes, 'I called him and I said, "We're going to have a serious talk . . . I need to talk about how it's going."' What are the poor things going to say? They simply don't have the vocabulary.

I don't think I heard her father say one word about his feelings ever – unless he was drunk, and then I'd just pat him on the arm and put him to bed. Oh, I tell a lie. When he died – it was the drink, of course, his liver was completely shot. Not that he was an alcoholic – he was French. When he died, he said, he held my hand, he said, 'Lucky,' he said, 'you were *formidable*, formidable!' He said it the French way and then the English way. And then he died.

Oh, my Christ alive. I'm not going to have any last words. I'm going to die here – alone! – on this cold floor in an ungainly position like an incontinent geriatric. Alone! And dead and not looking pretty. Aye. Help me. HEEEELP!

Look. I'm not going to die here and that's that. It's simply not the way for one to go. I should be strangled in a sports car with a long silk scarf. Or beheaded in a coupé. Of course, Jayne Mansfield wasn't actually beheaded. It was a wig. Her wig was on the dashboard and the reporters thought it was her head. Silly boys.

And the last Lisa had before the banker – what was his name? Frankly, he was wet as a drip. What was his name? Lisa's boyfriend? Peter or something. Steve. Ken. Frankly, I'd rather sleep with a North Sea halibut. But I do want her to be happy. I really do. She seems to think she has to carry the burden of the whole world and its woes on her shoulders. I say to her, what is one here for if not to be happy? I don't mean that one doesn't care about others . . . the poor! And then she goes on about principles and the meaning of life. It just makes me want to drag her into Fenwicks to shut her up. The thing is, she never understands quite how profound I actually am. Making oneself happy doesn't make one selfish. Well, except it does. One just takes care of oneself and assumes everyone else is taking care of themselves, and then if someone actually can't help themselves one helps them to do so, but goodness me all these causes and principles and angsting and ugh. What was that banker chap's name? James or Jeremy. Something terribly *Anglais*. Do you know, the other day I actually found myself trying to remember who it was whose name I had forgotten. James, I think it was. He was really quite an attractive boy. Do you know who he reminded me of? Sinatra. Now that was something I never told any of them except Daphne. He was really quite rough with one, though. No finesse. And having seen him so . . . close to, I've been completely convinced ever since I saw her that Mia Farrow was Frank's daughter. Think about it. They are virtually identical. Of course Lisa says its nonsense and people always date people who look like them but why else would they have got divorced so quickly?

James . . . so like Frank, in a funny way. I suppose it was the suits. He didn't have Frank's swagger, of course. But you know there they were, he and Lisa coming round here straight from work with their briefcases and her all sort of busy and carrier bags from the supermarket sort of thing. She's a very attractive girl but she doesn't use it.

Well, of course the minute he saw the cocktail shaker and I put the music on and . . . oh, my shoes! He loved the shoes. I've had them for forty-five years and they never fail. It's the way they elongate the foot, I think, and one's leg looks so delicate. Afterwards she said, 'Mother, why on earth did you have to put on those shoes? It's an old people's home.' Now that was cruel. It really isn't a home. It's more like – well – a condominium, as Frank would say. They have them in Palm Springs. I fully intend to go there. Fully. Once I'm up from this floor. I'm going. I don't care what she says. Actually, this James only called a couple of times and took me out once. And I used it as an opportunity to do some research. I always say if one's seriously interested in a man, never ever let them maunder on about their girlfriend or their ex-girlfriend or prospective girlfriend. When he's on a date with you, no one else should exist!

But I broke the rule because obviously with one's daughter's boyfriend one can't really consider it a 'date'. Now I wasn't going to say anything ridiculous like 'How's it going with Lisa?', so I merely mentioned her name *en passant*. So then immediately it was like opening some sort of floodgate and off he went: 'Well, you see my last girlfriend's still very keen and I think Lisa's looking for commitment and . . .'

'Stop right there!' I said. 'I haven't come out to listen to you boasting and whingeing. Fetch me a martini.'

So, of course a mimosa martini led to a whisky sour, which led to dinner, but I left him at the door and – loyal to the last – immediately got on the phone to my daughter. I mean that one sentence was enough – 'she's looking for commitment'. Deary me! What did he think he was saying? 'She wants to marry me'? It was absolutely insufferable assumptiveness, but more to the point, categoric proof that she was doing something dreadfully wrong. Of course, it was fine to give this James a slice of tongue pie. I mean I'm not his bloody mother, am I? And I'd no intention of dating him after that. Besides, he's dating my daughter.

'So how did it go with James?' she said, icily. (You see this is what she does to these men. I bet when James has seen this dreary ex-girlfriend she goes, 'So how did it go with what's her name?' in that same martyrish accusing tone, when really she should be talking a bit racy and putting all thought of the other one clear out of his mind.)

'Mother?' she said. 'How did it go?'

'How did what go?' I said. 'What is *it*?' You see I hate this *it*. *It*. *It* assumes.

'The drink with James, Mother. Remember? Earlier this evening.'

I mean, really, when she talks like this, slowly and loudly as if I'm deaf or something, it really brings out the worst in me. 'And who are you?' I said in a sort of wavery dotty voice, as if I'd got Alzheimer's all of a sudden.

'It's Lisa, Mum, remember? Lisa?' Anyone would have thought I was Outer Mongolian and stone deaf. 'It's Lisa. Your daughter.'

'Of course I know who you are, you bloody fool,' I rasped, and then suddenly, I don't know what happened, I suppose it was the drink: 'I've just spent four hours with that puffed-up young chap of yours, and really, darling, if you don't change your tack a bit he'll be bailing out with a head the size of an inflatable dinghy!' And then out it all popped – I was like a bottle of Crystal that's been left in the freezer: 'You've got the whole thing completely wrong, darling. It's all very well saying you shouldn't use your attractiveness to get what you want, but look at the amount of time you spend trying to get what you want using your bloody lawyer's training and arguing the silly boy into the ground about commitment, when if you had the first clue how to play your cards right he'd be pursuing you round the Ritz bar with a Tiffany's box because he simply can't get enough of you. What about mystery? What about allure? What's the point of marching the poor boy round Sainsbury's in a filthy mood when you could be sliding your toe up his thigh in the Caprice while he slips his Gold Card to the *garçon*. You're a woman, darling, not some sort of Chinese co-worker in a communist cooperative. You're not supposed to be his equal, you're supposed to be his empress.'

I told her to get herself out of those ghastly stiff suits and buy herself something slinky. Oh dear, I really can't remember what I said. I think some of it might have been really rather louche. I feel so ashamed. I always said I'd never never lecture her. Was it the day before yesterday? Has it been dark once? Before this. It's coming light now. Maybe that's why she hasn't come. Oh dear, and I was always complaining about her ringing every day and 'popping round' as if I was on the verge of death and now . . . oh dear.

Anyway, after my little outburst there was the most filthy silence. 'Mother,' she said eventually, in a clipped little voice, 'have you been reading the rules?'

'What rules? Don't be silly, darling. I don't need to read any rules. I've known them since I could walk.' And then she was maundering on about some dating book and 'retrogressing' and setting back the cause of feminism five hundred years, which as I said, '. . . is all very well except that a woman has her needs and what's the point of being a feminist if you spend 90 per cent of your time trying to turn a man into one too? Besides, if one doesn't get one's needs met it makes one frightfully crotchety and frustrated, so how can one function effectively in the world?'

But all the time I was thinking the reason I knew what to do with men was that my mother drummed it into me like the bloody sergeant major of Divas, but then the whole phone call with Lisa turned into a really quite dreadful, dreadful scene, and I knew, I knew I had somehow deeply hurt her and I never . . . I never, never wanted to hurt my little . . . my sweet, my sweet little . . . oh God, please don't let me die. Please don't let me die and I'll go to church in a veil and really cut down on the spirits – I won't drink a thing except champagne. But please, don't let me die and leave my little one like this. Please, I'd rather be a stroke victim with a saggy mouth. I really don't want to die. She put the phone down on me for the first time ever in our lives and then I went for a bourbon and . . . oh my God, that's what it was. I was drunk! Oh, thank God, thank God and all his saints above, I was bloody drunk! That's why I'm wearing the Escada, because I'd been out with Jeremy or whatever his name is, and then I came in here and sort of lurched at the basin and then I suppose I sort of toppled off my lilac Diors.

Oh Christ, what a ridiculous bloody fuss I've been making. I must have simply broken my arm, because I really can move the other, so if I haven't had a stroke then everything's marvellous and all I've got to do is sit – or maybe shit! haha! – it out and try not to starve to death and then everyone will make the most enormous fuss of my plaster cast and sign it and things – maybe I could have it in pale, pale pink with a frill! Oh! It's the telephone! The telephone! And I can't get to it. If I could just get my other arm from under me – oh, the answerphone – oh, it's Lisa! It's Lisa!

'Mummy, it's me.' She hasn't called me Mummy for so long! 'I'm so sorry I was angry on Friday and I haven't called round. I thought about what you said and you really do have a point. So I've shopped – you should see what I bought, and I wore them with James on Saturday night, and do you know, it's Monday morning now and we've only just stopped shagging! So I'm just pulling up outside your block now – I'm on my way to work. I'm not checking up, it's just I've got a little something for you. If you're not there I'll just let myself in and slip it on the table. Oh Christ, Mother, I can hardly walk and I've got a clouting hangover but I'm so bleeding happy.'

There, you see! Sometimes I'm so uniquely intuitive and clever, I really feel quite overcome . . . oh, here she is! There's the bell! There's the key in the door!

'Lisa! Lisa darling, I'm in the bathroom. I've fallen over, but you mustn't think it's because I'm old. I was drunk, darling! Absolutely bloody steaming!'

THE SLAVE

RODDY DOYLE

Terry is forty-two. He sits on a stool at a kitchen counter. He wears a towelling dressing gown and slippers, no pyjamas. He has a cup of coffee and a book, Cold Mountain *by Charles Frazier, in front of him. It's very early, still dark outside.*

My very educated mother just showed us nine planets. My very educated mother just showed us nine planets. My, Mercury. Very, Venus. Educated, Earth. Mother, Mars. Just, Jupiter. Showed, Saturn. Us, Uranus. Nine, Neptune. Planets, Pluto. All of them, in the right order. It was brilliant. The only problem was the two M's, Mercury and Mars. Mixing them up. Except for that, it was plain sailing. Simple. And that was what I liked about it. All that complicated business straightened and tidied into one sentence. Even if the sentence itself was stupid. My very educated mother. Just showed us nine planets. Mind you, that bit is good. Because there *are* nine of them. So it fits and helps you remember.

And it's about the only thing I do remember learning in school. I must have learnt more, I'm not saying that. A lot more, actually. I can read, for fuck sake.

He nods at the book.

I'm a two-a-week man. I eat the fuckin' things. So, yeah. But I don't remember learning how to read. And I do remember my very educated mother. Like it was now. The first week of secondary school. And the teacher, God love her. Miss something. O'Keefe, I think it was. Something like that. Her name was on the timetable, 'O'Whatever it was. Miss'. And we were hoping that a nice bit of stuff would come walking in the door. But in marches your woman. Older than our ma's. And as ugly as our da's. With a box of chalk. Holding it up in the air, like a cup or something. A trophy, and she waits till there's absolute silence.

'What is this?' she says, and she points at some poor cunt at the front. Me.

'A box of chalk,' I say, and wait to be told that I'm wrong.

But, 'Yes,' she says. 'It *is* a box of chalk. And what type of chalk is it?'

I look at the box.

'Coloured,' I say, and I'm right again. Twice in a row, for the first time in my life. And the last.

'Yes,' she says. 'It is coloured chalk. And it is mine.'

She goes over to the desk. The teacher's desk, like, the high one at the front. And she opens the drawer, and in goes the chalk.

'I am Miss' – whatever it was – she says. 'And I am your geography teacher. We will meet three times a week. And three times a week I will open this drawer and I will find my chalk exactly as I left it. I have information to impart but I cannot do this to my satisfaction if I do not have my coloured chalk.'

And then she says – you've guessed it: 'Do I make myself clear?'

'Yes, Miss,' say the saps at the front, *mise** here included.

'A stick of coloured chalk is the geography teacher's essential tool,' she says, God love her. 'The box contains ten sticks and it will contain ten sticks when we meet again on Wednesday.'

'Wed-nesday' she called it. Some hope, the poor eejit. The other teachers took it, every fuckin' stick. It was all gone by lunchtime.

Anyway, she took a stick of the ordinary white off the tray at the bottom of the blackboard, and then she wrote *my very educated mother* down the board instead of across, and the names of the planets that the words stood for beside them. And she told us to copy it all into our copies, after we'd done the margin and the date. And I've remembered it ever since, and nothing else. Precious little. Damn-all, really. The only other thing I remember clearly is the Latin teacher – I did Latin, believe it or not, for three years. And I remember none of it. But I *do* remember him. He went round the room every morning, putting his hand down our

* *mise* ('mish-eh') – me.

jumpers to make sure we were wearing vests. A Christian Brother he was, and I can remember *his* name. But I'll keep it to myself. Yeah, I remember him all right. Every morning, right through the winter. Feeling my chest. Leaving his hand there for ever. Freezing. Rough palms – old cuts gone hard, years of swinging a hurley. That was my only experience of abuse. His hand. He's still alive as well. So I'm told. I should report him, I suppose. Only, (a) I don't think I could handle the humiliation, and (b) I'd hate anyone to know that I used to wear a vest. And it's harmless enough when you hear about some of the things that went on. And he did it to all of us; he wasn't just picking on me. Hang on –

He listens, staring at the ceiling.

No; it's grand. One of the kids, or herself shifting in the bed, that's all.

He stares at the ceiling for a few seconds longer, then at floor level, around the kitchen. He starts to talk again as he looks, searches.

It's one of the things I like about getting up at this hour, before the rest of them. The coffee and the book, yeah, but I love hearing the house wake up, d'you know what I mean? The toilet flushing, them yapping at each other, their feet on the stairs. I love it.

Used to, at least.

And I will again. It's a matter of time, I reckon. Just a matter of time.

He drinks.

Cold. Fuck it. Better than nothing, though. It's the caffeine I'm after, not the heat. No, I can't remember a word of Latin. Not a word. I'm not blaming the Brother, mind you. No. Not at all. I've no French either, barely a word – maths, history. Tiny bits, only. 1916. 1798. Black '47. Irish? Ah, good night. *Oíche mhaith.** Very, very little. The *cúpla focail*† only. I can hardly help the kids with their homework and the eldest left me behind years ago. No, the

---

* *oíche mhaith* ('ee-heh wah') – good night.
† *cúpla focail* ('coop-la fuck-ill') – a few words.

only thing I remember, consciously remember, is that thing, my very educated mother. But she was a clown, the teacher, God love her. We ate the poor woman after we got the hang of her. 'Is there life on Uranus, Miss?' 'No, indeed.' She was fierce enough the first day, with her box of chalk. Scary. Worthy of a bit of respect. But then, I suppose it was when she said about the chalk being her essential tool, we realized then she was just a mad ol' bitch, and we made her life a misery. I'd say sorry to her now if I ever met her; I would, no bother. We ended up throwing the chalk at her every time she turned her back. She was getting on the bus in front of me once and there were coloured chalk marks all down her back. God love her, whatever her name was.

But. It has to be said. She taught me the only thing I remember. So, that's something. And it's not just that I remember it now and again, when I hear one of the words, say, 'mother' or 'very', or there's something on the telly about astronomy or anything to do with geography. No, I remember it every day. It's not a memory, no more than the names of my children are; d'you know what I mean? One of your kids comes running up to you with its head split open, you don't have to think of its name. The names are always there. And it's the same with my very educated oul' one.

It's like this. Every day, every working day I walk down to the Dart station – like I'll do this morning. I'm on a job in town. Have been for the last eighteen months. And there's another year in it, I'd say. On Westmoreland Street there. We're converting a bank into another bank. It's huge. Years of work in it. So, I don't bother with the van. I leave the tools in a strong box on the job. So, I don't need the van. I've given up doing the nixers, except for the odd one, for a friend, say. And the traffic in town is desperate. So I go in on the Dart. And *she*'s driving the van. She doesn't mind. I thought she'd hate the idea, it not being a car, like. But she's grand. It beats walking, is her philosophy. 'I love a walk,' she says, 'but only when I'm going for a walk, not when I'm hauling the shopping.' And the kids love rolling around in the back. Except the eldest. She wouldn't be caught dead looking at it, never mind being driven in it. So, I walk down to the station every morning, and there's a bit of a hill just before it and when I get to the top there's the Pigeon House chimneys in front of me. God's Socks, the eldest used to call them. In the days when she used to talk to us. And every time, *every* time I hit the top of the hill it goes through my head, the same thing every day: my very educated mother. Don't ask me why, but it's like clockwork. Just showed us nine planets. I don't expect it or anticipate it, or whatever. I don't wait for it to happen or even remember that it always happens when I'm going over the hill. It just pops into my head, new every morning, when I see the chimneys. And it stays, lodged in there, until I get into the station. My ver-y ed-u-cay-ted mo-ther just –. Every morning. Rain, wind or hail.

And that was what went through my head the morning I found the rat.

He says nothing for some seconds.

I shut the kitchen door. And I leaned back against it. I had to force myself to breathe. To remember – to *breathe*. In, out. In, out. My heart was pounding, Jesus, like the worst hangover I'd ever had, pounding, pounding, pounding. It was sore. Really sore, now – like a heart attack or something. Huge in my chest. And I leaned against the kitchen door.

He points.

Just out there, out in the hall. In, out. In, out. My very educated mother. My very educated mother. And when I got the breathing together, I went back in. I braved it. I went in and I had another look, to make sure I'd actually seen what I'd seen. I was half-sure there'd be nothing there. It was a bit of brown paper, a wrapper or something, one of the baby's furry toys. Or even nothing at all. A shadow. It was just about dawn, the blinds were open. Any of the things on the windowsill could have made a shadow – the washing-up liquid, the dishwasher powder. At that hour of the morning. Still half-asleep. Just showed us nine planets. I took the long way. Just showed us nine planets.

He stands up, to demonstrate his movements.

Instead of going straight to the fridge. The direct route. I couldn't. I came around here, to this side of the counter. I was scared, yeah, fine. I'm not going to *not* admit that. But that wasn't just it. I wanted to *see*, to be absolutely sure. To see it from a distance and an angle. To be absolutely positive.

And, yeah, it was there. Of course it was. In under the pull-out larder. A rat. A dead fuckin' rat. A huge fucker. Huge, now. Like a, like a teenage cat, d'you know what I mean?

Lying there.

And I still couldn't accept it. I couldn't – comprehend it. I was staring at the fuckin' thing. There was nothing else, in my head, in the world, just that thing lying there, under my pull-out larder, that I installed myself – that was my own fuckin' idea – and I couldn't get to grips with the situation. I couldn't say to myself, 'That's a rat there, Terry, and you'd want to think about getting rid of it.' No. I couldn't organize myself. I couldn't *think*. I walked out and shut the door again. And I was going to go back in and go through it all over again, gawk at it and hope to fuck it would be gone or was never there in the first place. And I was on my way back in.

And then I heard him. Little himself. The baby. Inside in the sitting room.

And I kind of cracked up. I began to think, properly think, for the first time, really. Since I found the thing on the floor. It was only a few inches from my feet; did I tell you that yet? Yeah. Two, three inches. Making the coffee, I was. In the list of all the stuff I eat and drink all day, it's the only thing I really care about. The first cup – mug. Good, strong coffee. I picked up the habit in America, in Florida, on the holliers. Orlando. Before the baby. He was conceived there, actually, now that I think of it. During a storm. Thunder, lightning, the works. It was something else; you'd never see it here. And good music on the radio at the same time. Good seventies stuff, you know.

He sings.

'On a dark desert highway, cool wind in my hair.' It all seemed to fit. The music and the weather. Even though it was pissing outside and he was singing about the desert. But it was American. And we were *there*. Myself and herself, after all those years. And that kind of explains why we've one child that's eight years younger than the others. He's a souvenir, God love him. Him and the coffee. I drink tea on the job, unless I go over to Bewley's. I could bring in the coffee in a flask, I suppose, but I was never what you'd call a great man for the flasks. As a matter of fact, if I was doing one of those word association games and someone said 'man', I'd never say 'flask'. I'd go right through the dictionary before I'd say 'flask'.

Anyway, I'm making the coffee. I've done the plunger bit and I've gone to the fridge for the milk. I must have walked past it; I could have stepped on it.

I drop the spoon, taking it out of the drawer.
He points.

There, right beside the pull-out. I drop the spoon and I'm halfway to picking it up when I see it. Jesus. Inches. The fuckin' spoon was right beside it. It's probably the first time I ever dropped a spoon in my life. I *don't* drop things.

Anyway, I'm leaning against the kitchen door and I hear the baby chatting to himself in the sitting room. And that's when I get really upset. I'm nearly crying, I don't mind admitting it. But I'm also thinking for the first time. And I'm straight back in there, back into the kitchen. And I'm thinking, deciding. 'Terry,' I'm saying – out loud, for all I know – 'action stations. Let's get rid of the cunt. Gloves and bag. Gloves and bag.' And I shut the door behind me, to make sure little himself doesn't come in and see it on the floor or me with it in my hand. And I go over to the press where she puts the plastic bags. She's mad into the environment, dead keen. We've a whole house full of plastic bags.

Anyway, so far, so good. I'm doing something. I'm in control, kind of. And the press is over there –
He points.

The one under the sink. Well away from your man on the floor.

There's no need for me to go too near him yet. I'm assuming he was a male. It's hard to imagine that there'd be such a thing as a female rat. But that's just me being stupid. Let's just say it was a male; it's easier for me. I had to go past him, whatever sex he was. But I didn't have to see him, to get to the sink, and I didn't look. I go straight over and I have the door open before it dawns on me that he might have friends in the vicinity. Fuckin' hell, I nearly shat myself, I nearly fell into the press. But it was empty; it was grand. There was nothing in there that shouldn't have been there. No sign of disorder, claws, droppings – it was grand. I take out four of the bags. There's hundreds of them in there. Supervalu. Irish-owned. We're keen on that, too, in this house. Four of them. And one of the big black bin ones. Killeens. Irish company. And I shake out the bags and put them on the counter, one, and one, and one, and the last one. Really fast now; I wasn't fluting around. No procrastinating. No way. Not with the baby in the room next door.

That's the problem, to an extent. He's not a baby, really. Not any more. He used to be, obviously. But he stood up about a year ago, without bothering to crawl first. Up he gets, using the couch and my leg to hoist himself, and he's been flying around the place ever since, except when he falls over asleep. We just call him the baby. He'll probably be the last, so he'll be the baby for a while yet. Even though he's built like a shit-house and he'll probably be shaving before the end of the year, the speed he's growing at. He'll be the last, I'd say. She swings a bit but I'm fairly certain.

So, on with the gloves. Yellow marigolds, way too small for me. I have to force them on but the only alternative is picking him up with my bare hands and that possibility doesn't even occur to me. So, I'm all set. I turn to face him. Gloves, bag, the works. But, God, I feel very exposed. I'm only in my dressing gown – this one here is a new one, from herself for the anniversary. Eighteen years. I got her a brooch. Doesn't sound like much but it's very nice.

Anyway, the old one was a bit threadbare. To put it mildly. I was virtually naked. That wasn't so bad, though. It was the feet. I was in my bare feet.

He holds up a foot, to reveal a slipper.

I hadn't bought these yokes yet. Anyway, look it, I know the rat was dead and not particularly interested in biting my toe or having a goo at what was under my dressing gown. But, still and all, I didn't feel ready for battle. Even if the enemy was dead and stiff. I hated myself then – that was the lowest, really. It's the thing now that really stands out. I couldn't move. I couldn't do what I was supposed to do. I stared down at your man on the floor. In under the pull-out. He was lying on his side. No teeth showing, no grimace, you know, nothing like agony or anger. He was just quietly dead. But I couldn't bend down and pick him up. I just couldn't do it.

I let myself down. My home, my pull-out, my family, my little son next door in the sitting room, this bastard had come into my home – *how* is another story – and I couldn't just bend down, pick the cunt up and throw him in a bag.

I really let myself down.

Then I did it.

Just like that. I bent down. I put my hand around him. He was stiff, solid, like wood or metal with a bit of weight in it. Or one of those transformer toys, but heavier. And he was big. And I could feel him, even with the gloves on. Cold. Cold and hard. I couldn't feel the hair, thank God. I dropped him into the first plastic bag. And I tied it at the top. Into the next bag, and the next one, and the next one, and then into the black bag. Then out the back door. The temptation was there, just to throw him out. But I didn't. I took him to the shed. It was cold out there, and still a bit dark, like now. But I still did it, in my bare feet. Just to have him properly out of the way. Then I shut the shed door and came back in here.

And then – and I'm a bit proud of this – I decided to go ahead with my coffee. 'Why not?' I said. I even rubbed my hands together.

He rubs his hands.

Like this, you know; mission accomplished, the worst was over.
I'd just carried a dead rat from here to there. I'd sorted out the
problem, done what I was supposed to do. I deserved a reward.
So, I opened the kitchen door again, so I could keep an eye and an
ear out for little himself in at the telly. I could hear *The Rugrats*,
and I realized that I was still wearing the rubber gloves. And I was
taking them off and deciding what was the best thing to do with
them when he came in looking for his breakfast.

And that, I suppose, is what got me really thinking. Really
thinking. Not just reacting to the crisis, getting rid of the rat. It
went beyond the rat. The rat isn't really involved.

That's my arse, of course. Of course the rat's involved. The rat's
to blame. But, it's hard to explain. Look.

He lifts a foot and shows us his brown leather slipper.

I never owned a pair of slippers in my life. Until, you know.
Now, I won't get out of the bed if I'm not certain they're right
beside me. I fuckin' need them. I got these ones in Clery's. They're
all right. I didn't mind, as long as they weren't tartan. They're
grand. Warm if I wake up before the heat comes on, and I usually
do. So, they're fine.

But I never wanted them; d'you get me? I never fuckin' wanted
them. I never wanted to be a man who wore slippers. I always
liked the feel of the house under my feet. I could have told you
which room I was in, just by reading the floor with my feet. No
bother. I just never wanted to wear slippers. Get into a pair of
slippers and you're fucked; your life is over. That's what I've
always felt about them, since I was a teenager and my father got a
pair from our granny and he put them on, sat down in his chair in
the corner and never got up again. I mean, he did get up – he went
to work, he went into the kitchen and up to the jacks – but that
was it: he was old. Tartan – I don't blame my granny, by the way.
It's just, I always saw them as a trap. Put them on and that's it,
finished. It got to the point where he wouldn't say hello until he
had them on, after he came home from work. He wouldn't

acknowledge the family, my mother, the works, until after his feet were safe inside the slippers. We weren't getting on at the time. A bit like me and my eldest now, actually. And everything I hated about him, about myself, about everything, I aimed at those slippers. And now here's me, after buying my own slippers. I've no one to blame but myself. And the rat.

Funnily enough – but it's not really funny at all – he's given up on the slippers. He's getting wild in his old age. He says things now he'd never have said when I was a kid. Last Sunday there – I go most Sundays, bring the kids – he waited till my mother went into the kitchen and then he told me he was thinking of getting the Internet. It turns out, he's been spending hours in a pal's house, the pair of them looking at pornography on the net when the pal's daughter is at work. Downloading, or whatever the fuck it's called. Whether there's a link between slippers and porn I don't know; I probably doubt it. All I do know is: I'm wearing them now and there's nothing I can do about it. I need something on my feet and socks just aren't enough.

Anyway, your man, my da's friend. His daughter got her phone bill a few weeks ago and she freaked out. So they have to go easy on the wanking – there's a disgusting thought; a few months ago I'd have laughed. So he's thinking of moving headquarters to our house. My old bedroom, actually. But fair play to him. I see nothing wrong in it, as long as it's just *Playboy* birds or Page 3s he's looking at. Even if he is seventy-four. I just hope he doesn't start making my mother dress up in rubber or something. I'm a bit jealous, I suppose. He knows what downloading means, and I don't. He's taken off his slippers and discovered that he can still have an erection. He has a life. We get on well these days. We're never lost for something to talk about.

So can I, by the way. Have an erection.

He clicks his fingers.

Not a problem.

But getting back to the rat. It's not the slippers. Not really. Look it, I'm forty-two. I don't mind. I was forty-one last year, I'll be forty-three next year. I'm not the worst-looking man in the world. There are lads that work with me ten years younger than I am, more, and they're in bits. I'm Leonardo DiCaprio standing beside some of those cunts.

He points at the book.

And I read. I'm interested in the world. I like some of the kids' music. I never call it noise. I've never given out about it, except now and again when it's too loud, but that's nothing to do with the music itself. I like Fat Boy Slim. I genuinely do. I don't think he's a chancer. And I like Macy Gray. We've her CD here at home. Because *I* bought it. Because I like it. I still get excited about things. I still love watching herself brushing her teeth, for example. I still want to go over there and clean her mouth out with my tongue, just like I wanted to, and did, from day one. And she still knows it. And the other things too.

But I'm forty-two. I'm middle aged. That's a mathematical fact. In fact, more than half my life is over. So my eldest told me, which was fuckin' charming. The last time she said anything to me. Something about statistics they were doing in school. But, really, it was because I won't let her watch *Trainspotting*. It's a good film but she's still too young. In a few years' time, grand; that was what I told her. Just not now. Next year, probably. Which I thought was reasonably fuckin' reasonable. It's a very good film, like I said. But there's too much in it that's not – OK, suitable. Unfortunately, that was the word I used. 'Suitable.' Her face, Jesus. It hurt, I'll tell you that for nothing. Maybe I'm just being stupid; I don't know. She's nearly seventeen. Anyway, that was when she informed me that my life was more than halfway over.

But that's not the point. Middle age. The midlife crisis. Whatever you want to call it. That's not it at all, really. I was forty-two when I saw the rat. And I'd still be forty-two if I'd never seen it. OK, I'm after getting myself a pair of slippers because I'm afraid of being in my bare feet, but I don't believe that they have evil powers, that they've made me grow old all of a sudden. It's not the slippers.

No.

What has really rattled me, what has changed my life, to the extent that it'll probably never be the same again, is the question that came into my head when the little lad came into the kitchen wanting his breakfast.

'Cry-babies,' he says. That's what he calls Rice Krispies. It'd break your heart. As bright as a button. 'Cry-babies, dada.'

And me there trying to take off the rubber gloves.

'What if?'

That was it.

What if. What if he'd been the first one to come into the kitchen? What if he'd picked it up? What if it hadn't been dead? And it goes on and on, backwards and forwards, right through everything. And there's no end to it. What if? What if? And it won't go away and it's not going to go away, and I don't know if I can cope.

Fade to black.

Come up on Terry, again in the kitchen, sitting at the counter, but dressed this time. It is night. He has a mug of tea in front of him, and the same book.

I've never been what you'd call a great sleeper. I don't know about when I was a kid, I don't remember. I suppose I was normal. But since then, especially in the last few years, I've got by on very little. I'll often go up with herself and come back down after she falls asleep, and I'm always first up. Even in the days when I drank a bit, I still got up early, even when my head was hopping. I never liked lying in bed. I'd go down to the kitchen and stick my mouth in under the cold tap until I could feel the water negotiating with the hangover. That was as much of a cure as I ever needed, until a few years ago and I began to feel it a bit more. I've always managed on four or five hours' sleep. And I rarely feel the lack.

And that hasn't changed.

I don't drink at all now. I gave up a couple of years back. I just gave up; nothing dramatic. I'd no real taste for it any more. Not that I was a big drinker. Just the three or four pints. That was what I settled down to after I got married and the kids started arriving. Not every night either; a couple of times a week. Then, gradually, once a week. And then I stopped going altogether. I got lazy, I think, and more and more often I'd go down to the local and the lads I knew, the ones I really liked, wouldn't be there. They'd gotten lazy like me, I suppose, and there was one of them died. And I was never a great man for drinking at home. Some of the lads on the job talk about getting the few cans in for the football, but I'm not that fussed about football either. So, I just gave up. If we go out for a meal, when we do now and again, I'll have a glass of wine but I'm just as happy with a 7up. The hangovers, with the kids and that, they just weren't worth it any more. Especially when there was no more crack to be had in exchange, when the lads stopped coming down – after Frankie died, really. I'd be standing there, looking around for someone to talk to. So, enough was enough.

But, to get back to the sleep thing. Even the night after I found the rat, even after all that, I slept as much and as well as I usually do. I just slept. I didn't dream about rats, as far as I know, and I didn't wake up screaming. I just woke up. As usual. I felt a bit robbed, as usual, with the feeling that I could have done with an extra half-hour. I grabbed the book from beside the bed and got up. Everything as per usual. I went through the whole routine, exactly as I'd done the morning before and every morning before that, going back years.

But it was different, of course. There was the world of difference. I turned on the lights as I came down – landing, hall, in here – which I usually wouldn't have done. But you'd expect that, after the shock I'd had the day before. I gave the door over there an almighty clatter before I came in. Again, that's only to be expected. Even though, in my heart of hearts, I knew there were no more rats. The pest control lads had given the place a right going over the day before. I'd had to go to work but she told me all about it when I got home and, before that, when I'd phoned her during the day.

'They're up in the attic, looking for droppings,' she says when I phoned her the first time. 'Nice enough fellas.' As calm as anything. It annoyed me a bit. The thing didn't get to her the same way it got to me. Mind you, to be fair to her, she never even saw the fuckin' thing. And, to be fair to me, I did. Anyway, by the time I got home she was an expert on rats and mice. The world's foremost fuckin' expert. No, that's not fair. Anyway. 'They're neophobic,' she says when I said I'd go up to the attic to see if the poison had been touched yet. 'They're scared of anything new,' she says, even though I could have worked it out myself. 'So there's no point going up. They won't touch it for a few days, until they're used to it being there.' All I'd wanted to do was prove that I wasn't too scared to go up; I just wanted to do something useful, after running off to work earlier and leaving her flicking through the Golden Pages.

'Did they take the rat with them?' I said.

'What rat?' she says.

'The rat,' I said. 'The fuckin' rat I found this morning.' And I pointed at the floor, at her feet, not exactly where I'd found it. I just wanted to point out, to hammer home the point, the difference in our situations. The reality of it. The fact that I'd been the one who'd had to pick it up.

'Oh,' she says. 'No.'

So that's what I did. I got rid of the rat. I put my coat on and went for a walk. With the black bag. No bother. As casual as you like. I went looking for a skip. And I didn't have far to look. There are skips on every street around here. This area is on the up, apparently. We're always getting cards from estate agents in the door, inviting us to sell. There's even one crowd who drop in a little letter every week, every Thursday with a different story each week. 'Colm and Deirdre have returned to Ireland after fifteen years in Seattle. They have fallen in love with this part of Dublin. Can you help them?' Something different every week. We enjoy it.

She makes up her own versions. 'Julius has been forced to leave his country after imprisonment and torture. He has fallen in love with this part of the city.' 'Packie and Mary's caravan has fallen off its bricks. Can you help them?' Anyway, into the skip with your man in the black bag. I even shoved the bag down under some of the rubble, to make sure no kids pulled it out and started messing with it. No bother to me. I could feel it under the layers of plastic and I didn't mind a bit.

But that's not the point. The point is – I don't know, exactly. What I used to take for granted, the feel of the floor on my feet, that kind of thing, I can't take for granted any more. The rat's gone, on a dump somewhere, eaten by other rats, and I've been up to the attic a few times since – the poison's still there, untouched – and I lifted the manhole outside – the poison's there, too, not touched, and that, now, is unusual. You'd expect them down in the sewer. You're never more than ten feet away from a rat, they say. Grand. Down in the pipes, no problem. Eating our shite. Grand. I'm all for it.

Anyway. I'm straying off the point again. Which is, I don't know what. It's hard to find the words that *fill* the thing.

Right. I used to be able to walk across the floor here without giving it a moment's thought. It was my floor, my kettle, every morning. My quality time. And now I can't. I have to think about it. I have to prepare myself. I have to casually search the floor every step of the way. I have to get down on my knees and check under the presses, knowing full well I'll find nothing, but – every morning. My mornings are ruined. It's as simple as that.

But there's more to it than that. It's the *what if* thing. That's the real point. What if. What if, say, it had been Sunday morning early and *Match of the Day* had been on when I turned on the telly. I'd have sat down to have a goo because I hardly ever watch it on Saturday nights any more. It's hard to get worked up about millionaires half your age; d'you know what I mean? Not that I begrudge them the money. Anyway, I'd have sat down and the little lad would have strolled on into the kitchen. It doesn't bear thinking about. But I've thought about nothing else. And it goes way beyond that. Way, way beyond. Everything. Fuckin' everything is, is *polluted* by it.

I wait up now every night when the eldest goes out, till she comes home, and I was just getting used to it before, you know. I was well capable of falling asleep before she came home. I'd wake when I'd hear her key in the latch, but I was tucked up in bed, not an embarrassment to her, and asleep again before I'd hear her feet on the stairs. Now, Jesus. Now – this is true – last Saturday I sat on the stairs in the dark, in my dressing gown, so I could dash into the bedroom when I heard her outside. It sounds funny, I know, just like any normal father, but it isn't. It's desperate. I had to nearly nail myself to the stairs to stop myself from going out to the street, or driving to the disco – or whatever they're called these days – the club – she said she was going to. It's not that I don't trust her – I don't. But I do, if that makes sense. It makes perfect sense. I trust her – I'm happy, *was* happy to let her out, to have her own key and the rest of it. And I'm absolutely positive she abuses that trust – she drinks the Red Bull and the fizzy vodkas. I know it. And she might be even doing the ecstasy or whatever, and, yeah, yeah, sex, I suppose – and I don't really mind because that's part of the package as well. It's part of the contract, giving her a longer leash. And as long as she doesn't stroll into the house with a smell of drink on her and say, 'Sorry I'm late, I was riding a chap with a car and a ponytail', I don't mind. What isn't said didn't happen. She knows; we know. She's finding her feet. We're here if she needs us.

But *now*, fuck. I'm on the verge of giving out to her because she looks good. As if she's to blame for being an attractive young one, as if it's anything to blame anyone for. And I was never like that. I was always proud of her, always, all the way. And I've always liked the way she dressed. But now I'm terrified. Anything could happen out there. And it's not just the predictable stuff. She could be hit by a car crossing the road, no matter what she's wearing. I remember the first time we let her go down the shops by herself. It was a real event, that day. She was so proud of herself, you know. And so was I. She was just eight. I've always loved that, giving them the opportunity to be proud of themselves. If it was now though, if tomorrow was the day she was going to go the shops by herself, I wouldn't let it happen. Not the way I feel these days.

He drinks the last of the tea.

Coffee in the morning, tea at night. Her idea. She's worried about me. Which is about the only thing going right for me at the moment. Her worrying. It proves something – I don't know what. Love, I suppose. Maybe not, though. But she *likes* me; I'm pretty sure of that. I see her looking at me and I want to shout at her to leave me alone but I'm grateful for it as well.

I don't know anything any more. I don't seem to. And I'm getting pains in my chest. And my arms are stiff when I wake up. Numb, like I've been lying on them. And, let's face it, I can't have been lying on both of them. I remember in a film I saw when I was a kid, *The Bird Man of Alcatraz*, with Burt Lancaster in it. The warden, your man from *The Streets of San Francisco* – not Michael Douglas, the other one. Your man with the nose. Karl something. Anyway, he had a pain in his arm – Malden, Karl Malden – and Burt Lancaster, the birdman, knew that he was going to have a heart attack. And I remember being fascinated by that, that a pain in your arm was a sign that there was something wrong with your heart. It was great. And my father, of course – this was before he got the slippers – he wanted to know if a pain in your arse meant you were going to have a brain haemorrhage. That was always the sign of a good film in our house. It got us talking. But anyway. What do two numb arms mean? Two heart attacks?

And it's not just the body. I don't give a fuck about anything any more. I really don't.

He nods at the book on the counter.

I was reading it ten minutes ago, I'm two-thirds of the way through it, but –

He reads the title.

Cold Mountain by Charles Frazier. It's good, you know. It's very, very good. And I couldn't care less. I'm reading it because it's what I do. Given the choice between the telly and a book, I'll usually go for the book. But now. I'm just doing it. I don't care. She used to like that about me, the opposite, you know. She always said it. My enthusiasm. I was like a big kid, and she wasn't slagging. She loved the way I listened to music. I leaned into it. I really listened. I never noticed, but she did. She said that she'd never really listened to music until she started to watch me listening, after we got married and moved into the house, and she saw how much I loved it. And it was the same with books, and everything really. There was once she made me read in bed, out loud, while she got on top of me, and I read right up to the second before I came – and it wasn't easy, I'll tell you, hanging on to the right page. It wasn't a hardback, thank Jesus. *The Slave*, by Isaac Bashevis Singer. What a book that was. I'd never read anything like it before. Or since. It made me really regret that I wasn't a Jew, because of the way the main lad, Jacob, struggled to hold on to his Jewishness all the way through the book. He was the slave in the title. The peasants were trying to get him to eat pork, to do everything that was against his beliefs, for years. And she noticed how excited I was getting, sitting up in the bed, and she asked me what was so good about it. So I read her a bit. About a party up in the mountains. Poland this was, four hundred years ago. I haven't read the book since but I'll never forget it. Jacob was sent up there in the summer months to look after the cattle, find them grass among the rocks, and the only other people up there with him were the village freaks, the products of brothers riding the sisters and the rest of it. Granted, the writer expressed it a good bit better than I can, but you get my drift. So I read her a bit. I can't quote it exactly but they were all rolling around in the muck, grunting like pigs, barking like dogs, howling, pissing on the fire, hugging the trees, stretched out on rocks, vomiting, screaming, roaring. 'It's just like our wedding,' she said. 'What's it about besides that bit?' 'Well, it's a love story, so far,' I said. 'It's fantastic.' 'Find us a different bit,' she said. So I did. Where he describes Wanda, this peasant girl that Jacob loves. And that's when it happened. I got through about a page and a half, which wasn't too bad because it was very small print and long paragraphs. Anyway, I came and she collapsed on me. 'Ah look it,' I said. 'I've lost me page.' She laughed and cried, you know that way, and kissed me. 'That's the one,' she said, into my ear. Meaning, she'd be pregnant. She took the book out from between us and looked at the cover, at the writer's name. 'We'll call him Isaac if it's a boy,' she said. It wasn't anything, actually. Not that time. But that's how important it was to me, reading, music, even the job. I *loved* tiles. Holding them, lining them up. The word 'grout'. Everything.

She gave me the job of naming the kids. She knew I'd give them names that were important, that meant something. That had a bit of magic in them. So the eldest is Sarah. That's the name Wanda changed her name to after she ran off with Jacob, in *The Slave*. She read the book, last year, the eldest did, and I think she was pleased, even though it's very sad in places and Sarah has a hard time of it. She said nothing, but I think she liked it, the link there, you know. Then there's Oskar, from *The Tin Drum*. She wasn't too keen on him being named after a dwarf but I persuaded her that if our lad got up to half the things that Oskar does in the book then we'd never be bored. Then there's Mary, from *Strumpet City* and *Famine*. They've a lot in common, the two Marys; they're great fighters. And we thought we'd go for something a bit more Irish, even though it's not strictly an Irish name. So, anyway, she's Mary. And the little lad is Chili, after Chili Palmer in *Get Shorty*. He's actually named after me, Terence, because we knew he'd more than likely be the last and she said we should name him after me and my father, and I didn't mind. I quite liked it, actually, especially when it was her idea. Even though I've been reading books all my life and I've never come across a hero or even a baddie called Terence. So, anyway, we usually call him Chili. And that's Chili in the book, not John Travolta in the film, good and all as he was.

Anyway, the point is, I haven't always been the miserable poor shite you're looking at. And, really, it wasn't too bad until recently. And I don't know if it's just the rat. I'm just so tired, you know. And then this thing. How it happened was, we got up together one Saturday morning and found the kitchen flooded. An inch of water all over the shop.

He stands up and goes to the sink.

We couldn't figure out how it was happening. We couldn't see where the water was coming from. Anyway, I turned it off at the mains and then we found it, the source of the leak.

He opens the press under the sink.

There's a rubber pipe back there that runs from the cold tap to a tap outside on the wall, for the gardening and that. And a mouse had eaten into it. The plumber, a pal of mine, showed it to us when he was replacing it. The teeth marks. 'These things are supposed to be rodent-proof,' he says. 'Tell that to the fuckin' mouse,' she says. And that was that, really. No real damage done. I got some poison, the blue stuff – I can't remember its name – and I put it up in the attic and I got a couple of new traps for in here. No problem. We always get a couple of mice in the house, every November or thereabouts, when they come in for the winter. And who can blame them? So anyway, they didn't go near the traps but the poison was gone a few days later, and it drives them out of the house when they go mad for water. So, end of story. And then I found your man and we realized that it was rat all the time, not mice, and he'd had the run of the house for God knows how long. So.

So, I suppose, on top of everything else, my tiredness, the rows with the eldest – I suppose I'm just getting old, really – so the rat was the icing on the cake, so to speak. Not the first time I've seen a rat, by any means. I'd see them all the time on the job, and when I was a kid we used to hunt them. But before, when I saw a rat, they were always doing the decent thing, running off in the opposite direction. This guy, though. Granted, he was dead. But, how long had he been in the house? Through the open door, that's how most of them get in, according to the pest control lads. Or up the drainpipe, and in under the roof. How long, though? Mice stick to one little patch of the house, but not rats. They have the run of the place. He came into the kitchen through a hole in the plaster, where it was drenched by the flooding and fell away from the wall. Grand, that's that explained. He died two feet from the hole. But what about before that, how did he get in before the plaster fell away? Down the stairs? Why not? It's shattering, thinking about it.

But.

Here it is. Here's why I'm here now. Leaving aside the fact that I'm nearly always here at this time of night.

He sits again at the counter.

I'm taking the house back. I'm repossessing it. I'm staying here like this, now and in the mornings, and I'm doing it until it becomes natural again. Until I'm actually reading, and not listening out for noise or remembering our dead friend on the floor every time I go over there to the kettle. Until I look forward to my cup of coffee again in the morning.

I'm not guarding the house. I don't think that there are more rats inside. I don't. Or even mice. And, to be honest with you, after what's happened, the mice are fuckin' welcome. I'll get in some extra cheese for the occasion. No, I'm getting over that bit. That's only a matter of time. The rat's gone. We're more careful about keeping the back door shut. I balled up some chicken wire and stuffed it up the drainpipes, so the chances of another one getting into the house are very fuckin' slim. I believe that. And very soon I'll actually *feel* it. To the extent that I won't feel anything, if that makes sense.

But – and here's where the right words are really hard to come by. In a way, I *am* guarding the house. Not against a rat or rats or mice or anything else that shouldn't be in the house. What I'm doing is guarding it against nature. All of it. The whole shebang.

The only reason that life can go on in this house is because we manage to keep nature out. And it's the same with every house.

And nature, now, isn't lambs and bunnies and David Attenborough – that's only a tiny part of it. And isn't bird watching and saving the whale. Fair enough, but that's not what it is. It's a lot rougher than that. Life is a fight between us – the humans, like – and nature. We've been winning but we haven't won. And we never will. Nature will never, ever surrender. The rats, for instance.

He points at the floor.

They're under us.

He indicates a three-foot distance between his two palms.

A bit more, a bit less. They're down there. Fine. But give them a chance. And they'll be back. They haven't lost and they never will. There's more of them than there is of us. We need the walls and the foundations to keep them out, to let them know – because they're not thick – that we're brighter than them and we're stronger than them. We have to mark off our space, the same as the other animals do. And it's not just the animals. It's everything. It's ourselves. We used to be cannibals. It's only natural, when you think about it. We're only meat. What could be more natural, for fuck sake? We probably taste quite good as well, the fitter, younger ones. But we sorted out the cannibalism years ago. It's not an issue any more, it's not a choice. Take the house away, though, take the farms and the roads and all the organization that goes into human life and it will be a question of choice again. If nature gets the upper hand again, we'll soon be eating each other again. Or, at the very least, we'll be deciding whether or not to. And then there's sex. We're only a couple of generations away from the poor freaks in *The Slave*. Brothers with sisters, fathers with daughters. It goes on anyway, sometimes. We all know that. It's disgusting, but we have to admit it. And it's walls and doors that stop it.

It's nothing new. I've always known it. Only, I've never had to think about it. And that's what the rat did when it decided to die on the floor over there. It was probably trying to find a way out when it seized up. And I wish to fuck it had. We'd never have known. Or even, if it had died in the attic or behind the plaster. I mean, the smell would have caught up with us eventually, but it wouldn't have been as bad. Rat in the attic? Shocking. Rat in the kitchen? Un-fuckin'-believable.

I mean, I recognize what's going on in my head, what's been going on for a while, actually, on and off. It's middle age. I know that. It's getting older, slower, tired, bored, fat, useless. It's death becoming something real. It's the old neighbours from my childhood dying. And even people my own age. Cancer, mostly. Car crashes.

But you can still hang on. And I was doing all right. There's little Chili. He's been like a new battery. Just picking him up strips the years off me. I feel as young and as happy as I did when Sarah was born. And there's music. And books.
He nods at Cold Mountain.

I'm going to start this one again. It's not fair on the writer, claiming I've read it when I have no real idea what it's about. And there's herself. Jackie. We get on great. We have sex, although it always seems to be on Fridays. Which I don't like, that kind of routine. Because I'm a bastard for them, routines. The slightest excuse, everything becomes a routine, and I've always tried to fight it. But anyway, we get on like – two houses on fire, really. I love her. Yeah, I do. She makes me laugh. And she knows I'm struggling, and she's sympathetic. She gets a bit impatient with me now and again, but who wouldn't. Anyway, what I'm trying to say is, up until – you know – I'd been coping okay. Enjoying life. My very educated mother just showed us nine planets. The world was a straightforward, decent place that could be simplified into a line of words running down a blackboard.

And so it is. Only, it has to be protected. If you find a rat in your kitchen the world stops being a straightforward, decent place for a while. You have to take it back. And that's what I'm doing. Taking it back.

And I'm getting there. I don't know how long it's going to take, and I don't care. This is for Chili, and the older ones. I'm no good to them the way I am. I have to be able to say My very educated mother, and believe it.

It's a matter of time.

I bought a CD today. I went down to Virgin during the break. I was going to get one of the old ones, something I loved but didn't have on CD. Dylan or Bob Seger or The Eagles or Bob Marley or Joni Mitchell – I could go on for ever. But I didn't. I had *Blue* and *Blood on the Tracks* in my hand – I was going to get the both of them. But I didn't. I went for something completely new. I bought an album by Leftfield, this band that isn't really a band. They're a pair of young lads who do this sampling and mixing, you know. Robbing other people's ideas and making their own thing out of it. Dance music. Not Barry White dancing, more *Trainspotting* dancing – I'll let her watch it; she's well able for it. Anyway, the music. There's a touch of reggae, a bit of Kraftwerk. At a knackering pace. It's mad stuff. I put it on loud when were having the tea tonight, when I got home. And I love it. I got little Chili to dance with me, and Mary and Oskar joined in – he's five foot ten, by the way. Even Sarah was smiling. There'll be no stopping me now. Ecstasy, cocaine, heroin, Red Bull. No fuckin' stopping me. But I'll tell you one thing – the chips and the egg put in one almighty protest when I was bopping. You'd want to be fit to be a raver. Seriously though, I'm not trying to be cool. I wanted the music to be an announcement. To the kids, and to Jackie. That I'm fine. Because they can't have helped noticing that I've been a bit low, and restless. We never told them about the rat, by the way. None of them has a clue. But the music, especially me dancing to a thing called 'Afro-Left', sweating like a bastard, that was an announcement. I'm grand. And I think they got the point. It was nice.

So.

An album a week from now on. Not necessarily new stuff but back to listening. Listening properly. And sharing it. And not on the same day. I'm not going to go into Virgin every Wednesday just because I did it today. And not Virgin either because, frankly, it's shite. If you don't like Phil Collins or Celine Dion don't bother your hole going into that kip. But, music every week. If I have the money.

And I'm going to go into training to do the Dublin City Marathon. I've always said I'd do it. So I'm going to. I decided today, on the Dart home. I'm not deluding myself. I won't be winning it; it'll probably take me all day. I'll probably hit the wall, you know, and shit myself in front of thousands of people, live on telly as well, knowing my luck. And on *The News* later on. But I'm going to do it anyway.

And I'm starting *Cold Mountain* again. In the morning.

So.

I'm getting there. I believe that. I really do. Fuck the rat. And fuck nature.

It's just a matter of time.

CATHOLIC GUILT
(YOU KNOW YOU LOVE IT)

IRVINE WELSH

t was a steaming, muggy day. The heat baked you slowly. My eyes were fuckin' streaming from the pollutants in the air, carried around on the pollen. Nippy tears for souvenirs. Fuckin' London. I used to like the sun and the heat. Now it was taking everything, sucking out my vital juices. Just as well something was. The lassies in this weather, the way they dress. Fuckin' torture man, pure fuckin' torture.

I'd been helping my mate Andy Barrow knock two rooms into one at his place over in Hackney and my throat was dry from graft and plaster dust. I'd come over a bit faint, probably because I'd hammered it a bit on the piss the last couple of nights. I decided to call it a day early. By the time I'd got back to Tufnell Park and up to my second-floor flat I felt better and in the mood to go out again. Nobody was home though; Selina and Yvette, they were both out. No note, and in this case no note is really a note which SAYS: GIRL'S NIGHT OUT. FUCK OFF.

But Charlie had left me a message on the machine. He was as high as a kite. – *Joe, she's had it. A girl. I'm down at the Ship in Wardour Street. Be there till about six. Come down if you get this in time. And get a fucking mobile, you tight Jock cunt.*

Mobile my hole. I fuckin' hate mobile phones. And the cunts that use them. The ugly intrusiveness of the strange voice: everywhere pushing their business in your face. The last time I was in Soho on a brutal come-down all those fuckin' tossers were standing in the street talking to themselves. The yuppies are now emulating the jakeys; drinking outside in the street and blethering shite to themselves, or rather, into those small, nearly-invisible microphones connected to their mobiles.

But I didnae need too much persuasion tae head down there, no with this fuckin' thirst on me. I nip out sharpish, breathless in the heat after a few yards, feeling the grime and fumes of the city insinuating itself intae me. By the time I get down to the Tube station I'm sweating like the cheese on yesterday's pizza. Thankfully it's cooler doon here, at least it is until you get on that fuckin' train. There's a couple of queers sitting opposite me; the camp, lisping type, their voices burrowing into my skull. I clock two sets of those dead, inhuman, Boy Scout eyes; a lot of poofters seem to have them. Bet ye these cunts have got mobile phones.

Makes me think back to a couple of months ago when Charlie and I were over at the Brewers in Clapham, in that fairy pub by the park. We went in, only because we were in the area and it was open late. It was a mistake. The poncing and flouncing around, the shrill, shrieking queer voices disgusted me. I felt a sickness build in my gut and slowly force its way into my throat, constricting it, making it hard for me to breathe normally. I grimaced at Charlie and we finished our drinks and left.

We walked over the Common in silent shame and embarrassment, the weakness of our curiosity and laziness oppressing us. Then I saw one of *them* coming towards us. I clocked a twist of that diseased mouth, fuck knows what that's had in it, and it was pouting at *me*. Those sick, semi-apologetic queer eyes seemed to look right into my soul and interfere with my essence.

That cunt, looking at me.

At me!

I just fuckin' well lashed out. The pressure of my body behind the shot told me it was a good one. My knuckle ripped against queer teeth as the fag staggered back, holding his mouth. As I inspected the damage on my hand, relieved that the skin hadn't drawn blood and merged with plague-ridden essence of pansy, Charlie flew in, no questions asked, smacking the cunt a beauty on the side of his face and knocking him over. The poof fell heavily on to the concrete path.

Charlie's a good mate, you can always rely on that cunt tae

provide back-up, no that I needed it here, but I suppose that what ah'm sayin' is that he likes to get involved. Takes an interest. Ye appreciate that in a cunt. We stuck the boot into the decked pansy. Groaning, gurgling noises escaped from his burst faggot mouth. I wanted to obliterate the twisted puppet features of the fairy, and all I could do was boot and boot at his face until Charlie pulled me away.

Charlie's eyes were wide and wired, and his mouth was turned down. – Enough Joe, where's yer fucking head at? he reprimanded me.

I glanced down at the battered, moaning beast on the deck. He was well done. So aye, fair enough, I'd lost it awright, but I didnae like poofs. I told Charlie that, as we headed off across the park, swiftly into the dusky night, leaving that thing lying whining back there.

– Nah, I don't see it that way, he telt us, buzzing with adrenaline, – If every other geezer was a queer, it'd be an ideal world for me. No competition: I'd 'ave me pick orf all the skirt, wouldn't I?

Glancing furtively, I felt we'd got away undetected. Darkness was falling and the Common seemed still deserted. My heartbeat was settling down. – Look at the fairy on the groond back thaire, I thumbed behind me as the night air cooled and soothed me. – Your bird's expecting a kid. Ye want some pervert like that teaching your kid in the classroom? Ye want that faggot brainwashing him that what *he* does is fucking normal?

– Come on, mate, you belted the geezer so I was in with ya, but I'm a live-and-let-live type of cunt myself.

What Charlie didnae understand was the politics ay the situation; how those cunts were taking over everything. – Naw, but listen tae this, I tried to explain tae him, – Up in Scotland they want tae get rid of that Section 28 law, the only thing that stops fuckin' queers like that interfering with kids.

– That's a load of old bollocks, Charlie said, shaking his head. – They didn't have no Section fucking nothing when I was at school, nor me old man, nor his old man. We didn't need it. Nobody can teach you who you want to fucking well shag. It's there or it ain't.

– What d'ye mean? I asked him.

– Well, you know you don't want to shag blokes, not unless you're a bit like that in the first place, he said, looking at me for a second or two, then grinning.

– What's that meant tae mean?

– Well, you Jocks might be different cause you wear fucking skirts, he laughed. He saw ah wisnae joking so he punched me lightly on the shoulder. – C'mon Joe, I'm only pulling your leg, you uptight, narky cunt, he said. – We was out of order but we got a fucking result. Let's move on.

I mind that I wisnae that chuffed about this. There's certain things that ye dinnae joke about, even if ye are mates. I decided it was nothing though, and that I was just being a bit paranoid in case somebody might have seen us stomp the queer. Charlie was a great mate, a good old boy; we wound each other up a bit for a laugh, but that was as far as it went. Charlie was a fuckin' sound cunt. So we did move on; to a late nightspot that he knew, and we thought no more about it.

It all came back to me during this Tube ride though. Just looking over at the nauseating pansies across fae me. Ughhh. My guts flip over as one of them gives me what seems to be a sly smile. I look away and try to control my breathing. My fingers dig into the upholstery of the seat. The two fairies get off at Covent Garden, which is ma fuckin' stop. I let them go ahead and into the lift, which will take us up to street level. It's mobbed, and just being in such close vicinity of those arse-bandits would make my skin crawl, so I elect to hold on for the next lift. As it is, I'm feeling sick enough when I get out and head for Wardour Street and the Ship.

I move up to the bar and Charlie's talking into his mobile phone. Twat. Seems to be with this lassie, who looks a bit familiar. He hasn't seen me come in. – A little girl. Four-twenty this morning. Five pounds eleven. Both fine. Lily . . . he clocks me and breaks into a broad grin. I squeeze his shoulder and he nods over at the bird, who I instantly take to be his sister. – This is Lucy.

Lucy smiles at me, cocking her head to the side, presenting her cheek for a greeting kiss, which I'm happy to deliver. My first impression is that she's fuckin' fit. Her hair is long and dark brown, and she has a pair of shades pushed on top of her head. She wears blue jeans and a light-blue top. My second impression (which should be contradictory) is that she looks like Charlie.

I knew Charlie had a twin sister, but I'd never met her before. Now she was standing with us at the bar and it was disconcerting. The thing was that she really *did* look like him. I could never, ever imagine a woman looking like Charlie. But she looked like him. A much slimmer, female, infinitely prettier version, but otherwise just like Charlie.

She smiles at me and gives me a sizing-up look. I suck in my beer gut. – You're the famous Joe, I take it? Her voice is high, a wee bit nasal, but a softer version of Charlie's South London twang. Charlie's South London accent is so South London that when I first met him I thought that he just had to be a posh cunt trying it on.

– Aye. So you're Lucy then, I state in obvious approval, looking over towards Charlie, who's still blabbering into the mobby, then back to his sister.

– Is everything okay?

– Yeah, a little girl. Four-twenty this morning. Five pounds eleven.

– Is Mellissa okay?

– Yeah, she had to work pretty hard, but at least Charlie was there. He went away during the contractions and . . .

Charlie's off the wobbly and we're hugging and he's gesturing for drinks as he takes up the tale. He looks happy, exhausted and a bit bewildered. – I was there Joe! I just went out for a coffee, then I came back up and I heard them say 'the head's coming' so I thought I'd better get in there sharpish. Next thing I knew it was in me arms!

Lucy looks at him disapprovingly; her thick, black eyebrows are just like his. – *It* is a *she*. Lily, remember?

– Yeah, we're calling her Lily . . . Charlie's mobile rings again. He raises his eyebrows and shrugs. – Hi, Dave . . . yeah, a little girl . . . four twenty this morning . . . five pounds eleven Lily . . . Probably the Roses . . . I'll call yer in an hour . . . Cheers.

Just as he went to draw breath, the phone rang again.

– It's funny how we've never met, Lucy says, – because Charlie's always talking about you.

I think about this. – Yeah, he'd asked me to be best man at the wedding but my old man was pretty ill at the time and ah had tae go back up the road. Ah think it was better though, one of eh's mates fae the Manor daein it, somebody that knew the family 'n' that.

The old man pulled through okay. No that he was keen to see me in any case. He never forgave me for no going to our Angela's communion. Couldnae tell him but, couldnae tell him it was because of that Priest cunt. No now. Too much water under the bridge. But that cunt'll get his one day.

– I dunno, might have been nice to have seen you in a kilt, she giggles. Laughter makes her face dance. I realize that she's a little drunk and emotional but she's actively flirting with me. Her resemblance to Charlie, they really are Yin and Yang, makes this unnerving, but strangely exciting. The thing is, I mind that cunt casting aspersions, just after we'd battered that poof on the Common. I'm now wondering how he'd feel if his sister and me got it on.

As Lucy and I chat to each other, I can sense Charlie picking up the vibe. He's still talking on the phone, but it's charged with urgency now; he's trying to end the conversation ASAP so he can work out what's going with us. I'll show that cunt. Casting aspersions. English bastard.

– Nigel . . . you heard. Good news travels fast. Four-thirty this morning . . . A little girl . . . Five eleven . . . Both doing well . . . Lily . . . The Roses . . . Probably nine but I'll phone you in an hour. Bye Nige.

I catch the barman's attention and signal for three Beck's and three Smirnoff Mules. Charlie raises a brow. – Steady on, Joe, it's going to be a long night. We're going down the Roses tonight, to wet the baby's head.

– Sound by me.

Lucy pulls on my arm and says, – Me 'n' Joe's started already.

I'm thinking that Charlie's done a good PR job on me 'cause I've as good as pulled his sister without saying a fuckin' word. By the look on the poor cunt's face he thinks so as well; thinks he's done *too* good a job. – Yeah, well, I got to get back, he whines, get some things sorted out for Mel and the baby coming home tomorrow. I'll see you two later on down the Roses. Try not to get too sozzled.

– Awright, dad, I say in a deadpan manner, and Lucy laughs, maybe a bit too loudly. Charlie smiles and says, – Tell ya wot, Joe, I could tell she was Millwall. She came out kicking!

I think about this for a second. – Call her Milly instead of Lily.

Charlie pushes down his bottom lip, raises his brow and rubs his jaw as if he's actively considering this. Lucy pushes him in his chest, – Don't you dare! Then she turns to me and says, – You're as bad as he is, you are, encouraging him! She's quite loud for a quiet pub and a few people turn around, but nobody's bothered, they know we're just enjoying a harmless high. I'm right into her now. I fancy her. I like the way she moved that one extra wee step forward into my space. I like the way she leans into you when she talks, the way her eyes dart about, how her hands move when she gets excited. OK, it is an emotional time, but she's a banger, game as fuck, you can tell. I'm liking her more and more, and seeing less and less of Charlie in her as the drink takes effect. I like that mole on her chin; it's no a mole, it's a fuckin' beauty spot, and her long, luxuriant dark-brown hair. Aye, she'll dae awright.

– See ya, Charlie goes. He gives me a bear hug, then breaks it and kisses and hugs Lucy. As he departs, the mobile goes off. – Mark! Hello! . . . A little girl . . . Four twenty . . . Sorry Mark, you're breaking up a bit, mate, wait till I get outside . . .

Lucy and I leisurely finish our drinks before deciding to move on. We're off down Old Compton Street and, as usual, the place is teeming with arse-bandits. Everywhere you look. I'm disgusted, but I say nowt to her. It's almost obligatory for a bird in London to have a fag mate these days. A loyal accessory for when the real man in her life fucks off. Cheaper than a dog and you don't have to feed it or take it for walks. Mind you, you don't have to listen to an Alsatian lisping and bleating doon the phone that its border collie partner sucked off a strange Rottweiler in the local park.

Dirty fuckin' . . .

I get up off the stool and have to sit down again for a bit 'cause I feel faint. My heartbeat's racing and there's a pain in my chest. I'll have to take things easier, drinking heavily in this heat always fucks me.

– You okay, Joe? Lucy asks.

– Never better, I smile, composing myself. But I'm thinking about how I had to sit down for a bit earlier today, over at Andy's. I picked up the sledgehammer and was itching to let fly at his wall. Then I felt this kind of spasm in my chest and I honestly thought I was going to pass out. I sat down for a bit and I was fine. Just been caning it a bit lately. That's what being single again does for you.

I get up and I'm a bit edgy in the next pub, but I concentrate on Lucy, blacking out all the queer goings-on around us. We have another couple of beers, then decide to go for a pizza at Pizza Express to soak up some of the booze. – It's weird that we haven't met before, you being one of Charlie's closest mates . . . Lucy considers.

– . . . and you being his twin, I interject. – Tell ye what though, you're a lot better looking than him.

– So are you, she says, with a cool evaluating stare. We look at each other across the table for a couple of seconds. Lucy's quite a skinny lassie, but she's got a bust on her. That never fails to impress, that one: substantial tits on a skinny bird. Never ceases to cause me to take a deep breath of admiration. She takes her shades from her head and sweeps her hair back out of her eyes in that Sloaney gesture which, for all its camp, let's face it, never fails to get the hormones racing. No that she's a posh bird or nowt like that, she's just a salt-of-the-earth type, like her brother.

Charlie's sister.

– I think that's what's called an awkward silence, I smile.

– I don't want to go to Lewisham, Lucy says to me with a toothy grin, as she stoops forward in the chair. She's sitting on her hands, to stop them flying about, I think. She's quite expressive that way, they were fairly swooping around in that last pub.

But aye, fuck South London the now. – Nah, I'm no that bothered either. I'm enjoying it with just the pair of us, to be honest.

Then she says to me, – You don't say very much but when you do it's really sweet.

I think of the smashed poof in the park and clench my teeth in a smile. Sweet talk. – You're sweet, I tell her.

Sweet talk.

– Where do you stay? She quizzes, raising her eyebrows.

– Tufnell Park, I tell her. I should say more, but there isnae any point. She's doing fine for the both of us, and I sense that I can only talk myself out of a shag right now, and I'm no about tae dae that. Not with the way my sex life's been lately.

It's a bummer sharing a gaff with two fit birds and no going oot wi anybody. Everybody says, lucky bastard, but it's sheer torture. But I find that the more you say that you're not shagging either of them, the less inclined people are to believe you. I feel like that *Man About the House* cunt.

Aye, ah could dae wi a ride.

So could she, by the sound ay things. – Let's get a cab, Lucy urges.

In the taxi I kiss her on the lips. In my celibate paranoia I'm expecting them to be cold and tight, like I've misread the signs, but they're open, warm and lush and before I know it we're eating each other's faces. The snatches of conversation when we come up for air reveal that we're both in the process of getting over other people. We urgently rap out those monologues, both knowing that if we weren't so close to Charlie we wouldn't have bothered, but in the circumstances it seems only mannered to be up to speed with each other's recent history. But whether we're really over our exes or not, it's nae bother: rebound rides are better than okay if celibacy is the only alternative.

I remember with satisfaction and relief that I recently visited the launderette and washed a new duvet, which I've got on my bed. So when we get back to mines I'm delighted that Selina and Yvette are both still out and I don't have to go through tiresome introductions. We shoot straight through to the bedroom and I'm fucking one of my best mates' twin sister. I'm on top of her and she's chewing her bottom lip, like . . . like Charlie when we were in Ibiza last years. We'd pulled these two lassies from York and we were riding them back in the room, and I looked over and saw Charlie biting his lower lip in concentration. Her eyes, her brows, so like his.

It was putting me off, I could feel myself going a bit soft.

I pulled out and gasped, – From behind now.

She turned over, but she didn't get on her knees, just lying flat and smiling wickedly. I wondered for a second whether or not she wanted it up her arse. I wasn't into that. She looked good though, and I was rock hard again, the troubling Charlie associations all gone from my nut. All I could see was that long hair, that slender body and that peach of an arse, spread out before me. I struggled to push in to her fanny, trying to keep some of my weight on my arms as I thrust into her.

It was going in though and soon we were fucking away again for all we worth. Lucy gave the odd appreciative groan, without making a big fuss. I liked that. I was looking at a spot on the headboard to avoid getting too turned on and blowing early, it had been a while and I . . .

. . . I was feeling . . .

WHOOSH . . .

PHOAH . . .

OH . . .

OOOOHHH . . .

No . . .

I thought I'd blown it there for a bit, the room seemed to darken and spin, but I came to my senses and we were still at it.

The strange thing was that I was suddenly aware that her dimensions seemed to have changed. Her body was like it was rounder and fuller. And she was quiet now, it was as if she had passed out.

And . . . there was somebody in the bed next to us!

It was Mellissa! Charlie's wife, and she was asleep. I looked at Lucy, but it *wasn't* Lucy. It was Charlie: I was . . . I was . . . I was fucking Charlie up his arse . . .

I WAS FUCK . . .

A spasm of horror shot through me, the rigidness going from my erection to my body. My cock instantly went limp, as God's my witness, and I pulled out, sweating and trembling.

I realized to my further shock, that I wasn't home any more. I was in Charlie's flat.

WHAT THE FUCK WAS THIS . . .

I slid out off the bed. I looked around. Charlie and Mellissa seemed to be in a deep sleep. There was no sign of Lucy. I couldn't find my clothes, all my gear had gone. Where the fuck was this? How the fuck did I get here?

I grabbed a smelly old Millwall top with South London Press on it and a pair of jogging trousers that lay in a heap on a laundry basket. Charlie liked to run, he was a fitness fanatic. I looked at him back there, still dozing, out for the count.

I pulled on the clothes and went through to the front room. This was Charlie and Mellissa's place all right. I couldn't think straight, but I knew I had to get out of there fast. I promptly left the flat and I ran like fuck through the streets of Bermondsey until I got to London Bridge. I headed to the Tube station but I realized that I had no money. So I trotted over London Bridge towards the city.

My head was buzzing with the obvious questions. What the fuck had happened? How did I get to South London? To Charlie's bed? To Char . . . it was obvious that my drink had been spiked in some way, but who the fuck had set me up? I can't remember!

I CANNAE FUCKIN' REMEMBER!

I'M NO AN ARSE-BANDIT!

That fuckin' Lucy. She was weirdo. But no her brother, surely no. Me and Charlie . . . I couldn't believe it.

I couldn't . . .

But the strangest thing was that just when I ought to have been fuckin' suicidal, I was, in spite of myself, settling into this weird calmness. I felt tranquil, but strangely ethereal; somehow disassociated from the rest of the city. Although I was still at a loss to work out what had happened, it all seemed secondary, because I was cocooned in this floaty bubble of bliss. I must have been daydreaming, as I crossed the road at the Bishopsgate, because I didn't see a cyclist come careering into me . . .

FUCKIN' . . .

WHOOSH . . .

Then there was a flash and a ringing in my ears and miraculously I was standing at Camden Lock. There was absolutely no sense of any impact having taken place with the boy on the bike. Something was up here, but I wasn't bothered. That was the thing. I felt fine, I didn't care. I headed up Kentish Town Road, towards Tufnell Park.

The door of my flat was locked and I had no keys. The girls might be in. I went to rap at the door, and bang . . . a whoosh of air in my ears and I was standing inside the living room. Yvette was ironing, while watching the television. Selina was sitting on the couch, skinning up a joint.

– I could handle some of that, I said. – You're no gaunny believe the night I've had . . .

They ignored me. I spoke again. No reaction. I walked in front of them. No recognition.

They couldn't see or hear me!

I went to touch Selina, to see if I could elicit some response, but then I pulled my hand away. It might break the spell. There was something exciting, something empowering, about this invisibility.

But there was something wrong with the pair of them. They seemed in as much shock as I was. It must have been some night they had as well. Aye, girls: we pay for our fun.

– I still can't believe it, Yvette said. – A bad heart. Nobody knew he had a bad heart. How can something like that not be picked up?

– Nobody knew he had *any* heart, Selina snorted. Then she shrugged, as if in guilt, – That's not fair . . . but . . .

Yvette looked sharply at her. – You fucking cold cow, she hissed in anger.

– Sorry, I . . . Selina started, before slapping her forehead in confusion, – oh fuck, I'm going to take a shower, she suddenly decided and left the room.

I opted to follow her into the bathroom, to watch her take her clothes off. Yes. I'm going to enjoy this invisibility lark. Just as she started to undress . . .

WHOOSH . . .

I wasn't in the bathroom any more. I was pumping away . . . yes . . . ye-es . . . I'm fucking somebody . . . they're starting to come into focus . . .

It must be Lucy, it was all some fuckin' daft hallucination, some acid flashback or the like, it was all . . .

. . . but no . . .

NO!

I was on top of my mate Ian Calder, shagging him up his arse. He was unconscious, and I was giving him one. I could see we were on the couch in his house back in Leith. I was back up in

Scotland, shagging one of my oldest pals up his fuckin' hole, like I was some kind of queer rapist!

OH NO, MY GOD . . . NO IN FUCKIN' SCOTLAND . . .

I felt as if I was going to throw up all over him. I withdrew, as Ian started to make those delirious sounds, like he was having a bad dream. There was blood on my cock. I pulled up the bottoms on my tracksuit and ran out the house into the street.

I was in Edinburgh, but nobody could see me. I was going mad as I ran screaming, up Leith Walk, down Princes Street, trying to avoid people. But as I picked up speed on the corner of Castle Street I collided with this old woman and a Zimmer frame.

Then . . .

WHOOSH . . .

I was in a prison cell, but I was fuckin' well shagging this guy up his arse. He lay unconscious on the bed underneath me.

OH, FOR FUCK SAKE . . .

It was my old buddy Murdo. He was inside for dealing coke.

YUK . . .

I pulled out and jumped down from the top bunk. I was sick, but in dry, racking coughs, holding myself upright against the cell wall. Nothing would come up. I looked around as Murdo came to, his face twisted in pain and confusion. He turned round, touched his arse, saw the blood on his fingers and started screaming. He jumped down, and I started to shout, crippled with fear, – I can explain mate . . . it's no what it seems . . .

But Murdo ignored me and moved over to his sleeping cell-mate in the lower bunk, launching into a savage attack on the poor cunt. His fist thrashed into the startled jailbird's face. – You. Ah ken you! You did something tae me! Ah ken you! Ya dirty fuckin' sick buftie bastard! Ya fuckin' beast!

– Aagghh! It's hoosebrekin' ah'm in fir . . . the boy protests through his shock.

WHOOSHHH . . . the guy's screams faded as I was . . .

I was standing in a chapel of rest, at the back of the hall. The crematorium – Warriston, or Monktonhall, or the Eastern. I

didnae ken, but they were all there; my Ma 'n' Dad, my brother
Alan and my wee sister Angela. In front of the coffin. And I knew,
straight away, just who was inside that coffin.

I was at my ain fuckin' funeral.

I'm screaming at them; what is this, what's happening to me?

But again, nobody can hear me. No, that's no quite right.
There's one fucker who seems to be able to; this fat old boy with
white hair, who's wearing a dark-blue suit. He gives me the
thumbs-up. The old cunt seems to have a glow about him, with
shards of incandescent light emanating from him.

I move across to him, completely invisible to the rest of the
congregation, just as he seems to be. – You . . . you can hear me.
You ken the Hampden Roar here. What the fuck is this?

The old guy just smiles and points at the coffin at the front of
the mourners. – Nearly late for yir ain fuckin' funeral thaire, mate,
he laughs.

– But how? What happened tae me?

– Aye, ye died when you were on the job with your mate's
sister. Congenital heart problem you didn't even know about.

Fuck me. I wis mair ill than I thought. – But . . . who are you?

– Well, the old boy grins, – I'm what you'd call an angel. I'm
here to assist you in your passage over to the other side, he coughs,
raising his hand to his face, stifling a laugh. – Pardon the pun, he
chuckles. – I've had all sorts of names in different cultures. It
might help you tae think of me as one of the ones I'm least fond
of: St Peter.

The confirmation ay my death induced in me a bizarre elation,
and no small relief. – So I'm deid! Thank fuck for that! It means I
never shagged my mates up the arse. Ye hud me worried for a bit
there!

The old angel cunt shakes his heid slowly and grimly. – No,
because you're not over to the other side yet.

– What d'ye mean?

– You're a restless spirit, wandering the earth.

– How come?

– Punishment. This is your penance.

I wasnae having this. – Punishment? Me? What the fuck have ah done wrong? I ask the bastard.

The auld guy smiles like a double-glazing salesman who's about tae tell me there's nowt they can dae aboot their crappy installation. – Well, Joe, the truth is that you're not a bad guy, but you have been a bit misogynistic and homophobic. So your punishment is to make you walk the earth as a homosexual ghost buggering your old mates and acquaintances.

– No way! No way ah'm ah gaunny dae that! You cannae fuckin' well make me . . . I said, lamely tailing off as I realized that the sick old bastard had been doing exactly just that.

– Aye, this is your punishment for being a queer-basher, the angel gadge smiles again. – I'm going to watch and laugh at you being crippled with guilt. Not only am I going to make you do it, Joe, I'm going to make you *keep* doing it until you enjoy it.

– No way. You must be fuckin' joking. I'll never enjoy that, I point at myself. – Never! You cunt . . . I sprang at the bastard, ready to throttle him, but in another swish of sound and flash of light he was gone.

I sat at a vacant seat at the back of the chapel, my head in my hands. I looked around at the congregation. Lucy had come up for it, she was sitting quite close to me. That was nice of her. Must've been a fuckin' shock for her. One minute you've a stiffer inside ye, the next it's just a stiff. Charlie was there too, he was with Ian and Murdo at the back of the hall.

They were all standing up.

Then I saw him. That dirty old cunt of a Priest.

Father Brannigan. Him, putting me to rest! That filthy, evil auld cunt!

I'm looking over at my parents, screaming silently at them for this appalling betrayal. I mind of me saying to them, I dinnae want tae be an altar boy any mair, Ma, and my mother being so disappointed. My old man never gave a fuck. Let the laddie dae what eh wants, he said. But when I didnae come tae our Angela's

communion and I couldnae tell them why . . .   Aw fuck . . . that
dirty old cunt touching me, and worse, making me do things to
him . . .

I never would, never *could* say. Never. Never even thought
about it. I always vowed he'd fuckin' well get it one day. Now he's
here, he's sending me off, his pious lies ringing throughout this
chapel.

– Joseph Hutchinson was a kind, sensitive, young Christian
man, taken untimely from us. But through our grief and loss, we
should not fail to remember that God has a plan, no matter how
obscure this may seem to we mortals. Joseph, who once served at
the altar of this very house of the Lord, would have understood
this divine truth more than most of us . . .

I want to roar the truth at them all, to tell them what that dirty
old cunt did tae me . . .

WHOOSHHHH . . .

Then I'm on auld Brannigan and he's screaming under my
weight; his old, skinny, smelly bones, crushed under my bulk. I'm
giving it to the dirty old cunt; pummelling him right up his arse
and he's screaming. I'm snarling in demented rage: . . . You cannae
tell anybody, or God will punish you for being a sinner, and I'm
fucking him and fucking him harder and harder. He's screeching
beyond agony and bang . . . his heart stops, I feel it stop as his last
breath escapes him. Brannigan's body judders underneath me and
his eyes roll towards heaven. I feel his essence rise up through his
body and through mine, planting a thought into my psyche that
says *you cunt* as he floats away, a soundless cry coming from his
spirit like a balloon farts out air as it flies into space.

I'm sobbing and crying to myself, saying over and over again in
my self-disgust, – When will it be over? When will this nightmare
end?

WHOOSH . . .

And then I'm with my best mate Andy Sweeney. We grew up
together, did almost everything together. He was always more
popular than me; better looking, brighter, good job, but he was

my best mate. As I said, we did everything together, well, almost everything. But now I'm on top of him and I'm shagging the arse off him . . . and it's horrible. – WHEN? I'm screaming, – WHEN WILL THIS FUCKIN' NIGHTMARE END?

And he's in the room with us, the auld St Peter boy from the funeral. He's just sitting in the armchair watching us in a studied, detached manner. – When you start to enjoy it, when you cease to feel the guilt, he tells me coldly.

So there I was shagging my best mate up his arse. God, was I feeling disgusted and crippled with revulsion, loathing and guilt . . .

. . . feeling sick and ugly, in constant torture as I was compelled to pump away like a rancid fuck machine from hell, feeling like my soul was being ripped apart . . . going to a place beyond fear, humiliation and torture, and hating it, loathing it, detesting it so fuckin' much . . . a pain so great and pervasive that I'd never, ever grow to feel anything other than this sheer horror . . .

. . . or so I kept telling that daft cunt of an angel.

WALKING INTO THE WIND

JOHN O'FARRELL

There's a moment when you're up on stage when you suddenly become aware that everyone is looking at you; that the entire room is totally focused upon what *you* are doing. In that terrifying split-second your performance can crash to the ground or it can soar to great new heights; but the fact that you have the power to throw it all away is partly what's so thrilling about being in the spotlight. It happens to every performer – I bet you that in the middle of the Nuremberg rallies Adolf Hitler was tempted just to spoil it all by blowing a raspberry and saying: 'Actually I'm gay and I'm proud.' But of course you never do shatter the magic because for that precious hour or so the audience completely loves you and that is why being on stage is the greatest job in the world.

'You have got to be the luckiest bloke I know,' said Richard the first time he saw me perform at the Edinburgh Festival. 'Twenty-three years old; doing exactly what you want to do, everyone thinks you're great; no office, no boss, no suit and you get paid a bloody fortune to boot. How cool is that!'

'It's cool,' agreed Neal.

It was quite cool I have to admit. In fact it was very, very cool, but the thing about being cool is you can't really let on how delighted you are about it. You never see James Bond ringing his mum to tell her how well he's doing.

Fifteen minutes earlier I'd been bowing and wearing my modest 'no-you're-embarrassing-me' smile, as two hundred people cheered me and clapped and shouted for more. I'd glanced down and seen Richard and Neal in the front row clapping proudly and then as the rest of the audience got up to leave they rushed up to me slightly too quickly. 'Guy, that was brilliant, Guy!' they said, and then everyone else knew that they weren't just ordinary members of the audience, they were friends of Guy's.

Now we sat in the pub opposite the theatre and I counted out the two hundred pounds cash that I'd just been paid. I knew it took Richard and Neal a couple of weeks to earn that much money, so I thought I'd better just check it again. A beautiful girl approached our table and asked for my autograph. She blushed and told me that she'd really enjoyed my show and thought I was brilliant. 'Well, I can't take all the credit myself,' I said, which probably sounded a little insincere after a one-man show that I'd written and produced on my own. My friends looked on open-mouthed as I scribbled my name in her programme. It was the first time this had ever happened to me. 'You sort of get used to it,' I told them.

I think that day was the first time they understood why I'd refused to follow them into the slavery of a normal job. Now that they'd glimpsed this world of fringe festivals and beer tents and circus arts, they couldn't believe that this was my everyday life. Richard watched the girl disappear and then continued his eulogy to my existence.

'You know how people become bone-marrow donors or kidney donors?' he said. 'Well, how about if you just donate your entire life to me? How about if we have a life transplant?'

And he took another gulp of beer but tipped the glass back too much so that it spilled all over his shirt and his offer looked even less attractive.

'Last week . . .' I confided, 'I had a fling with a Marilyn Monroe lookalike.'

'And did she kill herself afterwards?' said Neal.

'Funny you should say that, because she does top herself in this play she's in. It alleges that the policeman who found her proceeded to have sex with her dead body. It's called "Some Like it Cold".'

They quizzed me about other actresses I'd met, and I told them about the life on the road, the festivals I'd played and the

European capitals I'd visited and after a while they just stared silently into their pints. I hadn't meant to depress them. Maybe the sentence 'So what's happening in Dorking?' is always followed by a long silence. But they were impressed, amazed and jealous and I realized why I'd got them up there. I was engineering envy.

And yet they'd thought I was completely mad when I'd first told them what I was going to do when I left school.

'Mime?' they'd said. 'That's not a job.'

'Mime?' they kept repeating in sardonic disbelief. It was amazing how it was possible to pack so much contempt into one syllable. Everyone's reaction had been the same. I'd grown up in Surrey, not famous for its theatrical traditions, although I did once take my nephew to see *Adventures in Smurfland* at the Epsom Playhouse. My home town of Dorking was, however, home to the national headquarters of Friends Provident Insurance. The job of my school careers adviser seemed to consist of getting sixth formers into his office, establishing in which particular department of Friends Provident they imagined themselves spending the rest of their lives and then setting up the job interview. I don't know why he was called a '*careers* adviser' because there was only ever the one option. In Manchester in the 1850s you went into the cotton mills. In Dorking in the 1970s you got a job at Friends Provident.

'Well Guy . . .' he said to me, 'you're in luck . . . we could be looking at quite a decent starting salary. For an eighteen-year-old trainee claims assessor at Friends Provident.'

It wasn't until about halfway through the interview that I finally summoned up the courage to tell him: 'I don't want to work at Friends Provident . . .' I said, 'I want to be a mime artist.'

He paused and looked over his glasses at me. I got the feeling he was not inundated with eighteen-year-olds who wanted to go into the expressive arts. 'Mime artist?' he said, flicking though his index box. Management consultant . . . Marketing executive . . . there was no card for mime artist. So a conversation then ensued during which he suggested that a foothold in the world of pensions and life insurance might be the most sensible first step for an aspiring performer. I think he was trying to rack his brains for a department of Friends Provident where an interest in mime might be a bonus. 'Sales and marketing? No . . . Personnel? No . . . The Pretending to be Stuck in a Glass Box Department maybe?' If they'd had one of those I'm sure he would have mentioned it.

'I know!' he said, as if he'd just hit upon the perfect solution. 'How about if you just do a couple of years at Friends Provident and then once you've got the basic qualifications under your belt you could keep up your interest in performing by specializing in *theatrical* insurance?'

'Theatrical insurance?' I said. 'Is there any actual mime involved in that?'

'Well . . .' he said. 'I'm sure one or two of the theatres that Friends Provident insure put on mime shows from time to time . . . But most of the time it would be more office work than actually miming things.'

I spent a couple of years living at home and signing on the dole wondering about how one broke into the closed world of corporeal theatre. There was nothing in the local paper. My parents worried about me and I was sullen and withdrawn. 'The amount he talks . . .' my dad said, 'bloody mime's the only thing he'd be any good for.' Dad was not the intellectual type. I told him about the famous Jacques Lecoq school in Paris but he thought this through and then explained why this might not be the theatre school for me. 'Jacques Lecoq?' he said. 'Well, he's obviously a poof with a name like that.' In the end it was my mother who secretly encouraged me to apply. 'You get your interest in the theatre from me,' she said. 'I've seen everything Andrew Lloyd Webber's ever done.'

I thought my audition piece was fantastic, though looking back there was probably quite a low risk of them thinking 'There's nothing left we can teach this young man'. It was copied directly from a Charlie Chaplin set-piece, and I suppose I was rather hoping that the French might not be aware of the world's greatest ever film star. They said they liked my 'interpretation of the

Chaplin' and to my astonished delight I was in. I bought the make-up and tights and Dad blamed himself for not having taken me to watch rugby more often. Paris was a revelation. They have a different attitude to artistic pursuits on the Continent. They don't say: 'Mime artist eh? Well, I suppose it saves having to learn all those lines!' I studied pantomime, though not the sort that stars Frank Bruno as Widow Twanky. I learned how to use my posture to suggest different facial expressions while wearing a wooden mask.

'Wouldn't it be easier just to take off the mask?' suggested Neal.

'The art of mime . . .' I told my friends '. . . is like learning to play your body as if it were a musical instrument.'

'Well, I think I'd be a wind instrument,' said Richard, 'then I could just go on stage and fart for an hour.'

The three of us carried on drinking in this scruffy Edinburgh pub until we were told that if we wanted to stay there we'd have to pay to watch the comedy that was being put on at eight o'clock. Apparently the saloon bar had been converted into a comedy venue for the duration of the festival, by means of putting a piece of paper on the door saying Comedy Club – Entry £2. Richard and Neal were excited about seeing some stand-up; alternative comedy was quite a new concept back then, so we paid up and the bar gradually filled up around us. There was no PA, no stage, no lighting, just a space by the dartboard where the comic was supposed to perform. It was so intimate that all you could do was adopt a benign smile and hope for the best.

The comedian shuffled out in front of us. He was a bloke about our age who had taken it upon himself to adopt the stage name 'Mussolini's Mother-in-law'. It has to be said that as a stand-up comic he was only partially successful. The 'standing up' bit, he did excellently. He didn't fall over once during his entire set, his balance was impeccable. But as for the description 'comic', well I hadn't been so embarrassed since my parents danced to 'Anarchy in the UK' at my eighteenth birthday party.

He stood there for a moment clutching a hand-rolled cigarette which turned out to be far too small to hide behind. Then he hit us with the opening line of his comedy act.

'Have you ever noticed how there are too many words for small oranges?' he said. An awkward silence fell across the room, which was filled slightly too quickly with the next line. 'I mean, there's tangerines, mandarins, clementines, satsumas – why can't we just call them all *small oranges*?' Neal, Richard and I were right at the front, only five feet away from him, we had to give some sort of reaction. A strangled noise came out of my throat which wasn't so much a laugh, as a nervous grunt to punctuate the awkward silence. It was an attempt to communicate to him that although I wasn't laughing, I was at least aware of the point at which the laughter was supposed to come. I noticed that, like me, everyone had their legs and arms crossed as a sort of improvised 'crap-comic barrier'.

'Er, because I mean, the Eskimos have forty words for snow, right . . .' he went on. 'Because like snow is really important to Eskimos. So clearly Anglo-Saxon society totally revolved around small oranges.' There was a pre-planned pause for laughter and I gave a brave smile because it was easier to fake than convulsive giggles. Even though I am a trained performer, I don't think I could ever again recreate that combination of horror and pity in my eyes with the compassionate smile that was locked upon my mouth. In the Middle Ages when a heretic was being publicly disembowelled, at least the onlookers could acknowledge that the victim was not having a very nice time. They weren't expected to sit there with an artificial cheerful grin that said 'Well, this is all going very well for you!' A chair scraped and a couple of people at the back slipped away. Comedy clubs are like plane crashes, you're always safer sitting at the back.

'He was rubbish,' said Richard afterwards, 'I can't believe it cost the same to him as it did you.' I can't deny I felt a smug sort of personal triumph. Our two genres were at completely opposite ends of the theatrical spectrum. I used no words and so had to work much harder to communicate with my audience. I had to be an actor, a dancer and a gymnast – every second of my performance was carefully choreographed. Whereas 'Mussolini's Mother-in-law' communicated in the easiest manner possible and thus the content became as lazy as the form. I explained this to Richard and he said 'Well that, and the fact he was just a crap comic.'

The next day I was just waving them off at the station when the Marilyn Monroe lookalike came up and threw her arms around me. I can still see their faces pressed against the window as the train pulled away. I was a free man, while they were being transported back to the forced labour camps in Surrey. On the Monday I travelled to Prague and they returned to work at Friends Provident.

*　　*　　*

The following year, Richard and Neal came and saw me at the Glastonbury Festival and were really positive about the new show. I gave them a fantastic time. We'd never smoked dope at school – there were no drug dealers in Dorking as the careers adviser had not had a card for that job either. Cannabis was a sudden revelation to them and we got out of our heads lying in a field listening to Van Morrison, giggling and singing along to 'And It Stoned Me'. It was one of those perfect moments that stay with you for ever after. I said to them as they left the next day that I think I'd put that sunny afternoon into my lifetime highlights video. This was an imaginary compilation that I was assembling in my head; all my happiest and proudest moments, cut together into a five-minute edited greatest hits of my life.

'What would you have in your lifetime highlights video Neal?' I asked him.

He thought for a while and said nervously, 'Getting a B in my geography O'level.'

He looked hurt when I burst out laughing.

'Oh come on . . .' I said, 'you've got to do better than that. You can't have that on your tombstone – "*Here lies Neal Evans. He got a B in his geography O'level.*" What have you done that you really loved and will always remember? What are you really proud of?'

He shrugged. 'Getting off with Abigail Parsons?'

'That was when you were fourteen,' I laughed. 'What about recently?'

Richard came to Neal's defence. 'Look, it's all right for you,' he said. 'You're a mime artist. You have lifetime highlights every week. We're in an office all day and we go to night school in the evenings. We've got exams to get, promotion to work towards. We can't all be bloody mime artists.'

We walked in silence up to the fields where all the cars were parked. They both had company cars by now, Neal had a Ford Sierra and Richard had a Vauxhall Cavalier, and they were neatly parked in between all the beaten-up VW vans and 2CVs. I watched them pull away and then I saw Richard stop at the top of the lane to get his suit out of the boot and hang it up in the back of the car.

I saw them both intermittently throughout the winter and persuaded them to come to Glastonbury the following year. I found the same spot in the field where we could lie and get stoned again, but Neal got cow dung on his trousers and then the end of the spliff fell out and burned Richard on his chest. They said they liked my show though. In fact I think it really bowled them over because it was like they were lost for words. I had that experience in Paris once – when I saw a really moving piece of mime – I just didn't want to talk about it, I simply had to talk about something else. So they talked about their jobs. Richard had got a pay rise so he insisted on buying all the drinks. Neal wasn't working at Friends Provident any more, he said he needed a new challenge. He'd got a job at Commercial Union.

I continued to tour around the country, although it became a little frustrating when one or two of the venues in which I had done really well still didn't want me back the following year. 'You're the mime bloke aren't you?' said the man from North West Arts. 'Are you still doing the same sort of thing?'

'No, it's a completely new show,' I announced proudly.

'But is it still no words and white make-up and all that?' he said.

'I'm still doing mime if that's what you mean, yes,' I said.

'Well, we can't have mime every year, can we? We've got acrobats this year. There's lots of them but they're Chinese so they actually work out cheaper.'

Then I secured a booking at the Pontefract Arts and Leisure Centre, but two days before the show the manager phoned me to cancel my performance.

'Listen, we've not sold enough tickets,' he said in his gruff Yorkshire accent. 'There's folk who want to use sports hall to play badminton. And if no one's coming to see you, then how can I justify cancelling Sunday night badminton?'

I told him that he couldn't pull the show now; that it had taken me ages to persuade my two best friends to come up and see it. And that he had a duty to put on pieces of original theatre – that it was an Arts *and* Leisure centre; that people could play badminton any day of the week, but they only had this one chance to see my performance.

'My, you've got a lot to say for yourself – for a mime artist,' he said. Then he proposed a compromise that would involve me reducing the stage size so that half the hall could still be used for badminton. Call me a precious old luvvie, but I did not feel that my powerful mimodrama about the genocide taking place in the Amazon rainforests would be made all the more poignant by having middle-aged couples lumbering around playing badminton on either side of me.

'Don't be ridiculous!' I said. 'You can't put on a piece of theatre with people playing badminton all around you.'

'Why not?' said the Yorkshireman.

It was hard to know where to start. 'Well, what if a shuttlecock is mis-hit and lands on the stage?'

'Well, a shuttlecock's not going to hurt you is it?' he said. 'It's not like a cricket ball.'

'But they'll grunt and talk and their plimsolls will squeak.'

'Yes, but you do mime. They don't have to listen to any words, do they?'

Did Shakespeare ever have to go through this I wondered? Negotiating with the manager of the Globe Theatre who wanted to cancel *Hamlet* because Thursday night was the Southwark Over-Sixties Music and Movement class? I was forced to agree to having three courts at the far end of the sports hall kept open for badminton and then he came out with it: 'Now what about the rock climbers? Our concrete recreation of Scafell Pike is on the wall overhanging your stage and it's very popular on Sunday nights.'

It was still a great show though. My most challenging to date in fact. A two-hour narrative mime tackling issues like the environment and the annihilation of the indigenous people of the Amazon basin by the multinational mining corporations.

'Was it about Jack and the Beanstalk,' said Richard afterwards.

'Jack and the Beanstalk?' I said. 'What on earth are you talking about?'

'Well, when you were doing all that chopping – I thought that might be Jack chopping down the beanstalk.'

'That was the destruction of the rainforest,' I said.

'Oh. Yeah, well I thought it was probably something like that,' he said.

Honestly! It did make we wonder if I was being over-ambitious dealing with serious social issues in my work. But I think I really conveyed the terrible suffering that was happening in Brazil. Because the audience looked quite depressed by the end of the evening.

The following Christmas Eve we went on a pub crawl through Dorking as we'd always done when Richard let slip that he and Neal had already booked to go to Club Mark Warner with their girlfriends at the end of June.

'What about Glastonbury?' I said, 'I've got this new army surplus tent which I thought could sleep all five of us.'

'It's a bit of a clash actually,' said Richard.

'Well bring the girls up to Edinburgh instead. Or there's the East Midlands mime festival in Leicester in September.'

'Erm, to be honest Guy . . .' he said, 'I'm just a bit bored with all that farting about with white make-up on.'

What a strange thing to say, I thought. Richard was trying to tell me something and I was determined to find out what it was.

'But you love my stuff,' I said. 'You said "Return to Hiroshima" was a very brave piece of theatre.'

'Did I?' he said. 'Er, yeah, well it's quite interesting to see someone do it once or twice. But you don't sit down with your missus every night, turn on the telly and flick through the channels till you get to *UK Mime* do you?'

'Is there really a mime channel?' I said excitedly.

'Of course there bloody isn't. That's the whole point,' he said.

'So you're not going to see the new show at all?' I asked him, straight out.

'Probably not,' he confessed. 'Sally doesn't like mime. She likes musicals.'

Aha! That was the give-away, wasn't it, mentioning Sally. Of course, they didn't want to appear all boring and square in front of their other halves did they? They didn't want their girlfriends to see what they were missing, the magic of corporeal mime, the life on the road, sleeping in the van, the excitement of setting out the chairs in some far-flung arts centre. No don't let your world be challenged by ground-breaking art, just write out a cheque and fly off to the sunshine for a fortnight's windsurfing. It's just so easy isn't it? I sent them details of the Barcelona Mime Workshop which was only five hours drive from their resort, but if they went, they never mentioned it to me.

A couple of years went by and before I knew it their girlfriends had become their wives. Neal was the best man at Richard's wedding and Richard was the best man at Neal's. Obviously they'd seen a lot more of each other down the years and besides I don't think either of them felt they could trust me with a best man's speech! I think they were worried I might have mimed it the whole way through. Honestly, I'm not that obsessed. I would have done some talking as well.

But it was at Neal's wedding that I met Carol and the triangle was finally complete. She had that petite elfin quality that reminded me of Mia Farrow, though fortunately she didn't have a house full of adopted Vietnamese kids that I'd have to be father to. We had a modest little wedding at the registry office and then round to the pub for a couple of pints and some miniature vol-au-vents. At closing time her dad took me aside and went all serious on me. He told me that before he was married he'd been in a jazz band; played all the clubs and dreamed of making it big. But he said that when he started a family he realized his priorities had to change. And then he looked at me meaningfully as he struggled to keep his balance.

'Message received loud and clear,' I said to him.

'Good man,' he replied, looking reassured as he patted me on the back. But really; as if I'd ever be even remotely interested in playing in a jazz band.

Carol worked in the health service, dealing with psychologically disturbed children, which was tough for her because it wasn't always easy to get time off to come to the shows. But in the evening we'd talk about all the problems we'd had at work – trying to hang on to my Arts Council grant, having to find rehearsal space, trying to discover why I'd not been invited to perform at the London Mime festival. 'I'm glad to be out of that one actually,' I said to her, 'because the whole British mime scene is far too London based already . . .'

'Guy . . .' she said.

'It's all stitched up at the Montreal Festival anyway,' I told her. 'If you can't afford to fly over to Canada then you can forget London.'

'Guy,' she said, 'I think I'm pregnant.'

Carol had planned to go back to work after she'd had the baby, but then we had another one and she couldn't bear to leave them. 'We can live on what I earn,' I said, confident that this suggestion would be contradicted. When she agreed with me I wanted to say 'Are you mad?' The flat was only one bedroom so they had to sleep in our room, but it wasn't too cramped because I was away a lot of the time performing around the country. My pieces worked best in more intimate settings, so I tended to get bookings from smaller venues. But the trouble with these little halls is that a lot of them put out those awful plastic chairs which are very uncomfortable if you're sitting through a two-hour show. It means that some people with bad backs or whatever can't come back for the second half, which is a shame because they miss the real message of the piece. But, in a way, I almost prefer a small audience, the exchange is all the more personal. Of course if you're on a door split you don't take so much home, but I never became a mime artist to make my million. I hate the way that everything has become so commercial in our society – the way that money is held up as being more important than mime.

Even Carol isn't immune to this I regret to say. Things were obviously a bit tight after she gave up work to look after the boys, but sometimes I worried that she was turning into a breadhead like everyone else. I wasn't so insensitive that I didn't get the hint when she started talking about the different types of children's car seat one could buy. She wanted us to get a car. But if all this sudden materialism wasn't bad enough, she started going on about life insurance and a pension and all that other square stuff that keeps Friends Provident in business and pays for Richard's big house in Leatherhead. Like he needs any more money. I told her we couldn't afford to go mad at the moment – things were always tighter in the winter – 'mime work is seasonal,' I said, 'you knew that when you married me. Anyway there's a recession on and mime artists are always the first to feel the pinch.' Oh yes, if you're a teacher or a fireman, your job's fine; you're safe enough, but mime artists – well, we're suddenly surplus to requirements aren't we? But then mime has never been a pursuit that is particularly overvalued in British society – it's not like being a doctor or something. You don't get a sudden crisis where a member of the public shouts 'Help! Help! It's got very windy outside – is anyone here a mime artist who can show us how to walk against a really strong wind?'

So Carol and I had our ups and downs like any couple. She did threaten to leave me once, said she'd find a man who might talk to her about things more. She thought it was because of what I did for a living. But her mother said to her, 'No dear, all men are like that, it's not just the mime artists.' But she worried about us being in debt and the boys seemed to be costing more and more and they were getting too big to be sharing a room with their parents and then one day she just suddenly came out with it. 'Guy, you're forty-one years old,' she said, 'I don't think you should be a mime artist any more.'

*　　*　　*

There comes a point in a man's life when he must face up to his responsibilities; when he has to put his family first and sacrifice the dreams he had when he was young and carefree. This was the theme that I explored in my next one-man mime entitled 'Sell out in the Suburbs'. For the first time ever I spoke during a performance, I actually re-enacted that moment with Carol – at the very end of the show I said out loud, 'And my wife told me not to be a mime artist any more!' You should have heard the applause. Something in that piece really connected with people.

I know why she'd said it. All her friends in Dorking had money and husbands with flashy cars and thought that Carol was strange because she didn't have a nanny or a black labrador. They were always going on at her about me, they just couldn't handle that I did what I did, like I was some sort of threat to their comfy suburban existence. That was the trouble with living in Surrey; it was full of people who lived in Surrey. When the pubs shut in Dorking the landlord shouts, 'Come on; haven't you all got second homes to go to?'

Why did people always imply I ought to be spending my life

doing something else? Teaching mime was the usual suggestion, but that's not being a mime artist is it, that's being a teacher. People didn't look at the Sistine chapel and say to Michelangelo, 'Hmm, nice ceiling, Mike, why don't you teach interior decor.'

I'd go to pick the boys up from school and the mothers would go quiet as I approached as if I was some sort of social leper. I may not have been the richest father at the school gates, but my kids loved the fact that their dad did something a bit more interesting and exciting than all the others. Marcel is nearly six now so he's seen some of my more recent pieces. He's so funny, I was talking to him about my work when he was sitting in the bath a few months back when he said, 'Dad, it would be much less boring if you talked at the same time.' The things that kids come out with! So I told him about the sublimated tragedy of the comic performer who's lost the power of speech. About how silent mime evolved out of performing restrictions imposed on the early French theatre and that I used no spoken words because mime is a poem written in the air. And when I finished this explanation I looked down at him in the bath to see if he had taken it in. He was stretching his foreskin into different shapes and he said, 'Look, I can make Pokémon faces with my willy.'

I'm taking the boys to see their first-ever kabuki theatre on Saturday. They're very excited, bless them; I hope I haven't built it up too much. It's hard to explain to kids that so much of the material stuff that they want won't really make them happy. That they're being tricked by big businesses and advertisers and that it's a never-ending spiral. Someone has to say this to them because the talking Buzz Lightyear (£34.99 from Toys 'Я' Us) didn't seem like he wasn't going to mention it. I'm sure Carol knows I'm right but she can't seem to help herself from buying them bits of plastic junk that have been made in some sweatshop in China. Eventually we got so far into debt that I had to take some drastic action. So I swallowed a few principles and joined the other commuters squashed on to the 9.07 from Dorking to Waterloo. I had heard what Carol had said to me. That something had to change, that I needed to take some serious action. So I started doing a bit of street theatre up at Covent Garden.

You may have seen me there in my cyberman get-up; silver make-up on my face, the bacofoil suit; Kraftwerk blaring out of the tinny beat box. I had a private chuckle about the irony of it all, because there was me dressed as a robot when of course the real robots were all those poor office workers who came out to watch me during their permitted one-hour lunch-break. My act involved standing completely still for a few minutes and then suddenly coming to life. My head would swivel and my arms would mechanically relocate; each joint and muscle was activated with precision control as if individually powered by its own electric motor. This would cause great delight; I could feel the buzz of excitement in the circle of tourists around me but I could not even acknowledge that I knew they were there. I was a machine you see; a piece of mechanical hardware, and when you're giving a public performance convention demands that you remain in character whatever might be happening around you. However, this long established principle does not take into account the possibility of being kicked up the arse by a drunken teenager.

It had started with just a bit of heckling. There were three of them, lurching dangerously between the tourists, clutching cans of cheap lager.

'Oi, CP-30! Where's Obi Wan Kenobi?' shouted the tall one.

I didn't understand how this was supposed to constitute an actual joke, but his friends fell about in hysterics anyway. Professional pride meant that I could not allow myself to even blink as they continued to harangue me.

'Oi, Robot! When you have a piss, how do stop your knob going all rusty?' he said. Now the crowd were laughing as well and I wondered if he was the theatre critic from the *Sun*. I tried to cling on to some professional dignity but it's hard to conjure up witty put-downs with mime. The best I could do was to swivel round slowly and just stare at him; my face remaining totally dead-pan. This didn't intimidate him in the way that I'd hoped. He surveyed me up and down, swayed dangerously and then with no warning whatsoever just kicked me up the bum.

I think some of the crowd imagined that this was part of the show because they laughed and applauded all the more. A Japanese tourist had failed to capture the moment on video and asked him if he'd do it again and he was more than happy to oblige. Finally I breathed a huge internal sigh of relief; a couple of policemen had seen what was going on and were heading towards us. The performance-artist-baiting section of the show would now be over and the yobs would be sent on their way. But no. Instead of coming to my rescue and ordering the delinquents to leave me alone, the policemen stood on the edge of the crowd, folded their arms and chuckled along at the show with everyone else. They adopted one of those benevolent 'it's all just a bit of good-natured fun' expressions that they learn at Hendon Police College. I wanted to shout out to them – 'No, it's not just a bit of good-natured fun, it's not fun at all; arrest these drunken yobs at once.' Agents of the state condoning the kicking of the mime artist; that just about says it all. Because the next day I lost my Arts Council grant as well.

They said they didn't have to give a reason. I went down to their offices and no one was available to talk to me. I'm afraid I lost control a bit actually and I shouted at the bloke on the desk that I couldn't carry on without the grant any more, that the philistines upstairs had just killed off the only one-man performer in the whole country who was trying to deal with serious social and political issues through the medium of mime. 'Is that what you want?' I shouted. 'To live in a country where there is not one socially aware mime artist touring the regions?'

'I think I could live with it,' he said.

I walked back through the West End and as I was walking down Shaftesbury Avenue I saw a face on a poster that I recognized. 'Johnny Lee – live one-man show!' the theatre boasted. I stared and stared at that familiar face and eventually it came to me. It was 'Mussolini's Mother-in-law', the comic from the Edinburgh

Festival all those years ago. He'd lost the stupid name but gained a successful career, judging by the queue at the box office. 'Single tickets only' said a note on the window, so I bought one and took my place in the audience. A solitary microphone stood in a circular pool of light in the middle of the stage, like some sort of statement about the minimalism of one man and his jokes. There was a warm-up act who played seventies glam-rock tunes on different sized Marmite jars, and then finally a booming deep voice came over the PA and announced 'Ladies and Gentlemen – Johnny Lee!'

Johnny rushed up the centre aisle, leapt up on stage and confidently grabbed the microphone out of its stand. He waited for the applause and cheering to die down, until he shouted into the mic with amazed and outraged incomprehension, 'Have you ever noticed how there are too many words for small oranges?' A huge laugh washed across the room. I looked round at the rest of the audience in disbelief but they genuinely seemed to think that this was hilarious. 'I mean, there's tangerines, mandarins, clementines, satsumas – why can't we just call them all *small oranges*?' he went on, as the people on either side of me doubled up with laughter. He hit them with the next line – 'Because I mean, the Eskimos have forty words for snow, right; because, like, snow is really important to Eskimos. So clearly Anglo-Saxon society totally revolved around small fucking oranges.' By now the audience were red-faced and weeping with laughter and it was inexplicable. He'd just, well – got better.

Johnny Lee went from strength to strength after that. He got the lager ad, which made him a household name, and soon the networks were falling over each other to give him his own series. He must be a multi-millionaire by now. He presents a show on Carlton called *Celebri-TV*, linking clips taken from closed-circuit TV cameras in which celebrities have been spotted shopping or putting petrol in their cars. There's a picture of him in *OK!* magazine this week. He's at a charity drinks party, chatting with TV gardener Charlie Dimmock and Falklands hero Simon

Weston. Richard and Neal tell people that we saw him right at the beginning of his career at the Edinburgh Festival. 'He was brilliant back then as well,' they say. I suppose it's just the luck of the draw if your particular talent is in vogue during your lifetime. Comedy was the new rock 'n' roll. Then cookery was the new rock 'n' roll. And mime; well, mime was the new mime.

I've reapplied for Arts Council funding every year since, but with no success so far. They're probably frightened that putting on white make-up is racist or something. I'm investigating getting funding from the National Lottery and I've just written to Channel 4 using Neal's name suggesting that it's about time that their remit for minority interests included a season of mime and then I mentioned this very good performer called Guy Jessop who I saw doing a wonderful show at the Harry Secombe theatre in Sutton. I was spending so much of my time writing letters and submissions that I had a rather good idea. Instead of doing all my office work from the kitchen table with the kids getting under my feet, I've got myself a part-time job, which allows me to do all my admin and get paid at the same time.

So that's why I'm sitting here now. I haven't told them it's only a temporary arrangement, but I'm just doing it to clear a few debts till I get some funding. I work on my own and I don't talk to anyone so that's a bit like what I was doing before. I sit in this little booth from 7 a.m. till 3 p.m. and when the cars come into the car park I press the button and the gate goes up. And then I press another button and the gate goes down. So now I'm stuck inside a real glass box! I said to them, 'You don't have to provide me with a glass box, I can do glass boxes you know, that was day one at mime school.' I reckon I could have done a passable electric gate with my arm as well; right arm goes up – a little judder when it stops at the top, hold it up there for a second or two and then like a piece of well-oiled machinery the arm goes slowly down again. 'I'll be the gate if you want,' I joked to the head of security. He looked at me as if I was a nutcase.

I wanted to talk to Richard about corporate sponsorship for my next show, but it never seemed the right moment, so this morning I wouldn't let him into the car park until he gave me a straight answer! He said that Friends Provident did put some money into the local community but they'd already spent this year's budget paying for a flower bed to be put in the middle of that new roundabout on the A24. 'Anyway,' he said, 'it might look odd spending the community sponsorship allocation on an employee.' I said 'I'm not an employee, I've just got a part-time job here to subsidize my theatre work, that's all.'

Because I am a mime artist, that's what I do. Oh, here comes another car! Press the green button, gate goes up, a little nod and a smile, press the red button; gate goes down. 'You're the luckiest bloke I know,' Richard said to me once. Well, he didn't say that as he drove past this morning – he didn't say anything – he was too busy talking on his mobile. Neal and Richard are renting a converted farmhouse out in the Dordogne this summer, swimming pool for the kids and everything. I think they knew we wouldn't be able to afford it, so they didn't embarrass me by inviting us along. Anyway I can't commit to dates in the summer, I'm going to be touring the new show by then, probably. It's just a question of plugging away for a bit until enough people get what you're on about. But sitting in this box all day, you do sometimes wonder if anybody really cares. Richard and Neal stopped coming years ago. Even Carol didn't come to my last production. Talk about walking into the wind. It seems that more people want to go and see the latest Julia Roberts movie than my mime about the African AIDS crisis – what does that say about our society? Oh they've got money if it's for the pub or the curry house. But ask them to pay £7.50 for an evening of thought-provoking mime and they've already spent it on a chicken tikka masala. Actually, I could murder a chicken tikka masala right now. A couple of onion bhajis, pilau rice, lovely. Except I can't really afford it. Bloody mime. It's freezing inside this little box. I wonder if Richard could get me a job inside the main building.

EDITOR'S NOTES

Nick Hornby is the author of three books, most recently *About A Boy*.

Giles Smith is the author of *Lost in Music*. A collection of his journalism, entitled *Midnight in the Garden of Evel Knievel*, will be published by Picador in 2001.

Roddy Doyle's most recent novel is *A Star Called Henry*.

Melissa Bank is the author of *The Girl's Guide to Hunting and Fishing*.

Irvine Welsh's most recent novel is entitled *Filth*.

Zadie Smith's *White Teeth* will be out in paperback soon.

Dave Eggers is the author of *A Heartbreaking Work of Staggering Genius*, and the editor of *McSweeneys*.

Colin Firth was Mr Darcy in *Pride and Prejudice*, and a character loosely based on the editor in *Fever Pitch*. He will also star as Mark Darcy in the upcoming film version of *Bridget Jones's Diary*.

Helen Fielding is the author of *Bridget Jones's Diary*. She is obsessed with Mr Darcy.

John O'Farrell is the author of *Things Can Only Get Better*, a memoir, and *The Best a Man Can Get*, a novel. He went to the editor's school, funnily enough.

Robert Harris is the editor's brother-in-law. His most recent book is *Archangel*.

Patrick Marber wrote the plays *Dealer's Choice* and *Closer*.

Boringly, everyone lives in London except Robert Harris, who lives with the editor's sister in Berkshire; Roddy Doyle, who lives in Dublin; Dave Eggers and Melissa Bank, who are American and live in New York; and Helen Fielding, who is not American but lives in Los Angeles.

TreeHouse

In his introduction Nick Hornby explains what TreeHouse means to parents of children with autism. It is everything. Thank you for the support you have already provided by buying this book.

TreeHouse is a unique new school, which was set up in 1997. It offers a pioneering approach to the education of children with autism and related communication disorders and is the first school in the UK to adopt a highly effective educational method known as Applied Behaviour Analysis, which has substantial research proving its effectiveness. TreeHouse is a centre of excellence offering a model to others wishing to establish similar schools.

From an initial pupil body of 4 the school has grown to 20 pupils. A planned intake of 5 pupils each academic year will take pupil numbers to 80 in the next 10 years. Further, TreeHouse needs to extend its help to the tens of thousands of other children with autism in the UK. Other plans for the future therefore include supporting parent-led schools in different areas of the country, and a major capital appeal to fund a permanent building for our school and establish TreeHouse as a resource from which many can benefit.

If you would like more information about our work, or would like to make a donation, please complete and return this form to the address below.

Please return this form to: TreeHouse FREEPOST LON 14496, London WC1N 2BR

Please send me more information about TreeHouse ☐
and/or
Yes, I would like to support the work of TreeHouse ☐

Name _____

Address _____

_____ Post Code _____

Telephone Number _____

- I enclose a cheque for £ _____ payable to The TreeHouse Trust OR

- Please debit my Access/Visa card
  Card number ☐☐☐☐☐☐☐☐☐☐☐☐☐☐☐☐☐
  Full name of cardholder _____
  Expiry date _____ Signature _____

☐ Please treat the enclosed donation as a Gift Aid donation. This will enable TreeHouse to reclaim an extra 28 pence for every £1 donated at no cost to you. (You must pay an amount of income tax or capital gains tax equal to the tax we reclaim on your donations) Signature:_____ Date: _____

Every penny counts so thank you for your help in completing this form

If you are unsure whether your donations qualify for Gift Aid tax relief, please do not hesitate to contact The TreeHouse Trust on 020 7792 2517, or ask your local tax office for leaflet IR113 *Gift Aid*.

Autism has a huge impact on family life – home was a living nightmare for Donna and Paul after their son Daniel was diagnosed. Donna tells how TreeHouse helped bring laughter back into their family:

Daniel is six, an oldest child (his sisters are Jamey, three, and Billie-Jade, two). We were delighted by Daniel's early progress. At twenty months he was affectionate, sociable and bright with a good understanding of language, constructing simple sentences, and mixing well with other children.

The first problems started soon after Daniel's second birthday. He went to bed fine, and when he woke all his speech and understanding had gone. Our life became a living nightmare. Daniel would cry most of the day, was hyperactive, and threw things around the room. He lost all eye contact and didn't recognize his family. When I tried to cuddle Daniel he would bite, kick and scream. It would take both of us to restrain him for the simplest tasks like dressing.

I now know that on that night in August 1996, Daniel had a severe convulsion. In January 1997 they told me that he had autism, and to go home and take one day at a time. No cure. No behaviour programme. No future. But most of all, no hope.

At the time Daniel was in a mainstream nursery, happy living in his own world and mostly left alone in repetitive play. He certainly wasn't progressing. Life at home just got worse and worse. We had no social life, very little sleep and our daughter Jamey started to copy Daniel's behaviour. I met some mums who were running ABA home programmes. I knew Daniel would benefit from 1:1 therapy, and felt very sad because we lacked the finances and space – we live in a two-bedroom council flat. I did make some progress with Daniel by copying the techniques used on videos lent to me. I managed about ten hours a week but knew he needed much more. Then I read an article about an ABA school, TreeHouse. It had one adult for every child, and Daniel would be sitting at a table learning for most of the day. He desperately needed that to regain his lost skills.

Daniel started at TreeHouse in January 1999, and very quickly we felt we had our little boy back. Once again he was calm, happy, affectionate. He has his own unique sense of humour. He can colour, shape, and match twenty words to pictures, do simple drawings, play independently on the computer and make simple sentences using pictures. He points and does actions to all his favourite nursery rhymes. He can follow complex instructions such as 'pour your juice and drink it'. He now has about forty spoken words, and very good understanding and has been toilet-trained. He just loves going to school every day.

Family life is so much easier for us. I have the energy to give fun time to my daughters, and there's laughter in the home again. The biggest reward by far is seeing Daniel and Jamey play together. When they kiss and cuddle I cry tears of joy; even watching them fight makes me happy. There was a time when he wouldn't even be in the same room as her.

Life is really great now. We still have good and bad days, but we have a method – ABA – that really works; encouraging and praising the behaviour that's good, and ignoring the behaviour we don't want. Life is really great now.